GABOS

Game Ain't Based On Sympathy

GABOS

Game Ain't Based On Sympathy

A Novel By

KeyKey

PUBLISHER'S NOTE

This book is a work of fiction. It is not meant to depict, portray or represent any particular real person. All the characters, incidents, and dialogues are the products of the author's imagination and are not to be construed as real. Any references or similarities to actual events, entities, real people, living or dead, or to real locales are intended to give the novel a sense of reality. Any similarities in other names, characters, entities, places, and incidents, are entirely coincidental.

About The Author

GOD, family, then me is how I like to live my life. GOD first because HE'S the foundation for everything I do. There is nothing possible without HIM.

My family is my back bone and without each and every last one of them I don't know how I would make day by day in this sometimes-crazy world.

Then it's me because I believe more in myself as I get deeper in my faith GOD gives me the strength to be better and do better and gave me the foundation to build on and I have so much more to give. I love and respect everyone who's trying to get it out the mud and provide for their families.

So until next time stay free safe alive and blessed and no matter where you at, what you're doing or how messed up your situation is, just know GOD got you I promise you that.

Table of Contents

Authors Note

Putting yourself first is the only way to make it to the top because don't nobody love you like you love yourself if you have to rob kill or backstab the ones around you to elevate and make things better for yourself then do it because I'm one hundred percent sure they would do it to you if it was the other way around.

M.D.R Jr

Chapter 1

It was after 12, and Rilo could see the club was jam-packed as he maneuvered his new Mercedes through the VIP parking so he could park right in front of the club, "Right their bae," Toya said from the passenger seat, pointing at an empty spot upfront. After parking, they both got out and headed to the VIP line, which they skipped and walked past. Her natural ass and breast hugged the all-white Versace dress she had on. Rilo was matching in his all-white Versace dress shirt and jeans, "What up nigga," Bezo said as they walked into the booth, "You already know, getting money, looking good like always," Rilo said, as he sat down. Toya started dancing in front of him, club (Legit) was lit, he thought as he looked around, Bezo was throwin' money and letting all the baddest bitches in the club inside the booth. Rilo was well known around the city, supplying the whole county with the best dope and fucking all the baddest bitches.

Toya was the only woman who stole his heart, for the time being, they only been together for six months, but it felt like a lifetime, she was all he was missing in his life. He sat back watching as she moved her ass side to side to the music, she glimpsed back every so often to make sure he was watching her. "Ayee Rilo," Bezo said, sitting down next to him, "Yeah, I wanted to holla at you about something. I ran into this nigga in St. Pete through the nigga Jacob I been fucking with over there, you know the nigga with the X5 BMW truck?" "Yeah, I know who you talking about." "Well, the nigga name Kenney and Jacob told me the nigga is 100, moves a lot of work through the city but, his plug got killed in some type of robbery, so he's been out of work. The nigga grabbing 10 at a time, I told him the best we could do is 30-grand apiece, he acted like he wasn't down, then, he hit me back up and agreed to it. I wanted to run this by you first before I fucked with him. I know there's another shipment comin' in a few days, this will be good for business, expanding our brand." "Yeah, if you feel good about it, handle up and make sure dude ain't on no funny business." "You know I got you bra," Bezo said as he held his hand out for Rilo to lock it in. After the club was over, Rilo waited until most of the crowd flooded out, then he and his team left out. "Damn my nigga, this you?"

Draco, one of his goons, said as he hit the unlock button on the Benz, and it lit up, "Yeah, I just got it today, this motha fucka tight ain't it?" Rilo said as he watched the bitch's jock and the niggas hate. He was used to this, being on the top for the last couple of years, hate and love came in together, but the hate outweighed the love, that's why he always had his goons present wherever he went. They lingered around for a while, then he told Toya, "Let's head out." Bezo followed him until he got on the interstate, then they parted ways. "I am so hungry," Toya said as she scrolled through her phone, "I'm going to order something from Denny's so we can just pick it up before we head home," "Yeah that's cool," Rilo said as he hit the blinker and got off the interstate. He continued driving until he was sure nobody was following him, then, he got back on the interstate miles down the road, "Your ass is so paranoid," "I got to be. If I'm not, I'll become food to the sharks that's lurking baby girl," Rilo replied, reaching and putting his hand on her head. She already knew what that meant as she leaned over and unzipped his zipper, pulling his dick through the hole. She wasted no time putting it inside her wet and warm mouth, Rilo took his foot off the pedal and put the car on cruise control as Toya bobbed up and down making sex noises like she always does when she got his dick in her mouth. He felt himself about to cum, so he began pushing her head further down on his dick, and she complied as she sucked harder and got louder, "Oh shit," Rilo said as he exploded in her mouth and she kept sucking and pulling on his dick until every drip was gone. She wiped his dick off with a napkin and put it back in his pants. Rilo was still breathing hard as she straightened her hair back up in the mirror. Twenty minutes later, they pulled up at Denny's, he watched as she got out of the car then ran inside the restaurant to grab their orders. Moments later, she came out with the food and drinks in her hands. Pulling out of the parking lot, Rilo got back on the interstate. Pulling up to the gated community 15 minutes later, he put the code into the Box then waited for the gate to open. As soon as it did, he sped through, headed around all the curves in the community where he recently purchased a four-bedroom home, he pulled directly into the garage then waited for it to shut before he got out the car, "I got to pee," Toya said, getting out the car putting her key in the lock then running in the house. Rilo laughed, then grabbed the food and drinks then headed in the house. As soon as he got through the door, his heart stopped because he didn't even hear the alarm making its beep sound waiting for him to put the code in, then he looked over to see a masked man holding his hand over Toya's mouth with a gun to her head. There was liquid spilling down her leg. Before he could say anything, he felt a hard object come across the back of his head, and then everything went pitch black.

Chapter 2

"I think you killed this nigga bra," "I didn't even hit him that hard," 'Well this nigga ain't breathing, and I don't feel no pulse," "You got to be kidding me, why the fuck you even hit him across the head with a bat for anyways, that was stupid, six months of work gone down the drain just like that, leave it up to Leo, and he'll fuck shit up every time," Toya said, as she paced around the living room. Leo was her lil' cousin, and the other robber was her ex-boyfriend Doe. After Toya moved down to Tampa, she began stripping and ran into Rilo, who fell right into her lap, he didn't know about her wild past because she wasn't from around here. Every time he started asking her questions about her past, she began to cry and tell him she didn't want to talk about it. She did everything he told her to do, plus she fucked and sucked him good, and cooked. Once he moved her in, she called her ex, Doe, and her cousin, Leo, to town to rob and kidnap him, but now he was lying on the floor dead.

"Y'all lucky I know how to work my mouth and pussy because I got the code to the safe, but it would have been way better if we could have found out where he kept the real money," Toya said as she walked directly into the walk-in closet were the waist-high safe was at. She bent down and began pressing the 7-digit code in then waited for the beep sound confirming it was correct. As soon as it was confirmed, she held her breath then turned the knob. Her mouth fell open, and her eyes were bulging out her head because the last time she took a peep in this same safe, there wasn't that much cash in it, but now, it was filled to the top with money. This had to be over a million dollars! "Oh shit," Leo said, pushing her out of the way and pulling the money out the safe. Doe followed suit, stuffing money into the black duffle they brought in with them, they were so caught into all the cash that was in front of them they didn't see the black Box she was holding in her hand. It was on top of the cash when she opened the safe, she stepped back and opened the Box, and her heart stopped, she couldn't believe what she was looking at; this nigga was going to ask me to marry him, she thought as she looked down at the massive diamond ring. Damn this was fucked up, out of all the fucked-up shit I did, this was the worst, Toya thought, as she backed out of the room, and reached under the pillow where Rilo kept the 9mm with the silencer. She walked back into the closet without hesitation and shot Leo right in the back of the head-blowing his brains inside the now empty safe.

"What the fuck are you doing?" Doe said, turning around with his hands in the air, she mouthed, "I'm sorry," with tears coming down her face, then shot him in the forehead. The impact knocked him back; now, he was lying on the floor sideways. She walked over both of them and grabbed as many clothes and shoes she could carry. She headed back downstairs. Rilo was still laying in the same spot; she leaned down and kissed his now cold face. Then she headed into the garage where the Mercedes was, threw everything in the back seat, started the car, and then backed up out the garage. Not knowing where she was going, but she promised herself she would never cross anybody again the way she crossed Rilo. As she drove and stared down at the diamond ring that was now on her ring finger, she said a quick prayer, turned up the music, then put her foot hard on the pedal.

Chapter 3

I've been calling this nigga all day, Bezo thought to himself as he paced the hotel room. He tried calling Rilo's phone again, it was 3:30 in the afternoon and not one word from this nigga. What the fuck was going on? Bezo checked out the hotel and headed across town to Rilo's sister's house to know if she heard from him. She told him she ain't heard from him in a few days then asked if everything was ok, he told her he didn't know. After calling him again with no answer, he decided to head out to his house, the one he recently purchased, it was an hour north of where he was. Rilo gave him strict instructions - when he showed him where he lived, to never come to his house without permission unless it's life or death, and right now, deep down in his gut, he felt as though something wasn't right. He called Draco and told him he would meet up with him later. After getting off the exit, he drove for another 20 minutes, then drove up to the gate and put in the code Rilo gave him, the gate opened slowly, and he drove through it. It took him 5 minutes to remember where the house was. Once he found it, he parked in the driveway, then got out and walked up to the front door and began knocking. There was no answer; he fumbled with his keychain and found the extra key that was given to him by Rilo. He placed it in the lock then unlocked the door. He slowly opened the door with his gun in the ready position; he didn't have to go far to see why Rilo wasn't picking up the phone because he was lying on the floor with a huge gash on the back of his head, it was clear he was dead. Bezo had to grab the edge of the wall to keep himself from passing out. He gathered himself back together then, walked over to Rilo, kneeling beside him, he touched his face, and it was cold. What the fuck happened? He thought to himself as he stood back up and began running up the stairs, where the fuck was Toya, he thought as he reached the top of the stairs, preparing himself for a gruesome scene, he knew she had to be dead too. When he walked in the room, he led with his gun, he looked immediately to his left inside the walk-in closet, what the fuck was this, he was confused as he saw the two dead bodies sprawled over the closet. Who the fuck was these niggas, he thought as he moved closer looking down at the two of them, he didn't recognize them, but somebody smoked their ass and emptied the safe?

He searched the whole house looking for Toya, but she was nowhere to be found. The car wasn't in the garage either; damn, they must have taken her and smoked these niggas that came with them. Somebody must have got greedy and crossed everybody unless Toya was the one who set all this shit up. Naw, couldn't be, he erased that thought out his mind as soon as it appeared. They must've kidnapped her and killed her somewhere else. But who the fuck was these niggas? Bezo thought as he looked back down at the bodies still no clue? Bezo walked back downstairs and put his gun back in the stash spot in the car and dialed 911.

Chapter 4

After leaving Rilo's house, where he answered a million questions and watched the medics carry all three bodies out in body bags, Bezo stopped by Rilo's family house and gave them the bad news. Staying there for over an hour, letting the sister and mother cry on his shoulder and trying to figure out who was behind this shit, Bezo got back in the car and headed across town where the stash house was. He knew there was over a million dollars cash there, and another 20 bricks stashed at another house. Making sure no one was following him, he got off then back on the interstate then made his way to the stash spot. Pulling right into the garage, he got out and made his way in the house, gun out as he put the alarm code in, Rilo and Bezo were friends since kids. Only three years younger than Rilo, Bezo proved he was loyal to him more than enough times; that's why Rilo made sure he knew where everything was and who everybody was even the plug out in Cali, who he met only once on a trip out to Cali with him. After searching the house and making sure there wasn't any hidden danger, Bezo walked in the main bedroom then reached under the bed where there were supposed to be 2 duffle bags, but there were 4. He unzipped all of them, and they were all filled to the top with cash. He walked into the walk-in closet, reached on the top shelf, and pulled down the money machine. After 2 hours of counting money, there were 3.5 million dollars there! Bezo stood back looking at all the cash on the bed, then for the first time in a long time, he fell down to his knees and began to cry like a baby.

After getting himself back together, Bezo put all the money back in the duffle then headed out. As soon as he made it out of the neighborhood, he dialed a # that he knew he had to call. After three rings, a deep voice came over the line, "Yeah," "this Ricardo?" Bezo asked, there was a pause on the phone for a few seconds, "Yeah, but who this?," "You might not remember me, but I'm Rilo's lil' homie, I came out there one time about a year ago, and I met you," "Yeah, I remember you, Bezo right?," "Yeah, that's my name," "Ok, so why you calling me, what's up with Rilo, he good?" Ricardo asked. "That's why I'm calling you, last night, Rilo was robbed and killed," before he could continue, the phone hung up. Bezo looked down at the phone thinking he lost service then it began to ring, "Hello," he said, "Now what the fuck were you saying?" it was Ricardo calling from a different line, "I was telling you that bra got robbed and killed last night and don't nobody know Shit, there were two other niggas dead in the house that I never seen, I guess they were part of the hit crew but somebody out the crew got greedy and killed them after they emptied the safe, plus they kidnapped his girl too, she hasn't popped up yet, this shit is all crazy, plus I know bra was 2 in the hole with you, I wanted to let you know that was all good, I know this is a lot to take in, I don't really know how close y'all two were but Rilo was my mother fuckin brother' and he built an empire down here and I'm gonna find out who did this shit, but for now the show have to continue to go on, and we continue to do business," Bezo waited to hear what Ricardo had to say, the phone was silent for a while then he said, "Text me your name and catch the first flight out to LA I wanna talk to you face to face," then the phone hung up.

Chapter 5

Toya rolled over in the king-size bed and looked at the clock that was on the dresser; it was after 5 pm. She didn't have anything to do, so she laid in the bed for another hour, flipping through the channels on the TV. She checked in at the Western Inn as soon as she made it to Tallahassee. Her plans were to drive all the way to GA, but Tallahassee was as far as she could go, she was tired. After getting out of the bed, she walked to the bathroom naked and ran herself a warm bubble bath. She needed to relax her mind and clear all her thoughts from her past, and last night was her past. Rilo was her past, her ex-boyfriend, and her cousin was her past, there was 1.5 million dollars cash in the room, and she could start a whole new life and be whoever she wanted to be. Only 27 years old and still in her prime, beautiful as hell phat ass and all, she thought to herself as her body soaked in the warm water. Maybe I'll start a business or some shit like that in the A, this was the most money I ever had and I damn sure wasn't going broke again, ah bitch had to get really nasty and dirty for that bag. Them niggas probably was going to kill me anyways how they were acting when they saw all the money in the safe. The only thing I felt bad about was Rilo; he was going to ask me to marry him, she thought to herself as she twirled the ring on her finger. She shook the thought from her mind then got out the shower. After drying off and putting on the white robe that was hanging on the door, she ordered food and red wine. An hour later, there was a knock on the door. She peeped thru the hole to see an older Hispanic woman with a cart in front of her along with the food and wine. She opened the door and let her in, after giving her a $20 tip, the women left out, and she locked the door. Damn, this shit smells so good, she thought after she removed the lid; there was steak, potatoes, mac and cheese, and broccoli. She opened the wine and poured a glass, sat down, and ate enough for two people. After gathering all her stuff and the duffle with the cash, Toya checked out the hotel and headed down to valet parking and waited to receive the Benz. She was glad Rilo put the car in her name, but she would ditch it or sell it as soon as possible. The next few hours, she drove just thinking to herself as she made her way to Atlanta. After getting there, she checked into the Ritz downtown, under one of her fake names, with a stolen credit card. For the next couple of hours, she searched around the internet looking for rental condos or townhouses; she needed her own place to stay asap. She didn't feel comfortable riding around with all that money in the car. She had three appointments in the morning with the relators of the condos she liked the most. After taking another shower, she got back in the bed naked and began flipping through the TV.

Chapter 6

It was after 8 o'clock when the plane landed at LAX. Bezo made his way through the terminal, when he made it outside, there was a black town car out front and an older black guy holding a sign up with Bezo written across it. He walked up to him, and the guy shook his hand and opened the back door. Bezo got in, and they pulled off. They drove for at least an hour as he stared out the window, taking the beautiful city in; it was amazing, people and foreign cars everywhere. The city was alive, maybe I'll move cut here one day when my cash is way up, he thought to himself as the car slowed down so the gate could open. They drove down a long driveway then stopped in front of a massive house. The chauffeur got out, then opened the back door for him, and then led him in the house past two security guards that were standing post outside the front door. They walked right through the house to the back yard, where Ricardo was sitting alongside the massive swimming pool where there were two women swimming naked. Ricardo dressed in an all-white Gucci suite and shoes puffing on a Cuban cigar. He was a big black guy in his late forties. The gold presidential Rolex on his wrist will let you know he was paid, "Take a seat," he said, pointing at a chair that was next to a glass table. Bezo complied and sat down, there was a bottle of XO Hennessy on the table, "Pour yourself a drink and relax, take in the beautiful scenery," he said, spreading his arms out wide, "All the beautiful things to live for and die for," he said looking back at him. Bezo took a huge gulp of the liquor; it burned going down his throat. He watched as Ricardo came over and sat down in the chair next to him, then poured himself a drink. After taking a sip, he set the drink back down on the table. "So, let's get something straight, my good friend for the past few years gets robbed and killed last night, his safe gets emptied out, two people you never saw before is found dead in Rilo's closet and Rilo was down stairs dead," Bezo nodded his head, "Then his girl comes up missing, the brand new car he bought is gone too," "That's right," "Hold up now, then you being a good friend, call me way out here in California and tell me the bad news and also tell me you got the money Rilo owes me and you want to continue doing business but you're going to find out who killed Rilo, while you continue to run the empire Rilo built?," "Yeah that's what I said," "I think that's bullshit and you killed Rilo because you're greedy and didn't want to play second any longer," "What you say my nigga?," Bezo said standing up, but Ricardo got up quicker whipping a gun from his back and placing it right on Bezo's forehead, "Sit the fuck down! Before I push your shit back nigga," Bezo sat back down. "Listen man, I don't know what you are thinking, but it ain't like that. Rilo was my brother, and I never cross bro, never, not one time, I know it sounds crazy, but that's what it is. He trusted me, and I knew where everything was, and I'm ready to hold shit down like I always did. I could of just ran off with the cash and not tell you shit but I'm 100, and I need you man to keep supplyin' me, and I'm going to make sure shit straight but don't think for one minute I crossed my brother out," "You think the bitch did it?," "I don't know, I know he was gonna ask her to marry him next week on his birthday," "Damn, that's fucked up," Ricardo said placing the gun back on his waist and sat back down. "So, you got all the cash?" "Yeah, it's 2 million right," "Yeah, that right," he said, looking at the women in the pool sipping his drink. "You think you could handle 100 blocks by yourself?" "I got a team," "You know with Rilo out the way niggas gon want the throne and they won't stop at nothing until they get it," "I know that, I'm the one that made sure Rilo held the throne," "Yeah, but someone took it from him," he said with a sideways glance. "I'll die before I let whoever did what they did to him live, and I stand on that," "Well, make yourself comfortable; enjoy the females, there here for you. Let me get things situated, and I'll have you out of here, and the package sent down. You'll get it in a few days, I'll send someone to pick up the cash also," Ricardo said, getting up from the table and heading towards the house. Bezo took another sip of his liquor, damn that was crazy he thought to himself then headed for the pool.

Chapter 7

After landing back at T.I.A., Bezo got his car back from short term parking then headed to the hood where he told Draco and a few others in his crew to meet up with him. Ricardo promised the shipment would be here today after tomorrow. He still had 20 kilos of Raw leftover, and the nigga, Kenney, been ranging his line since he landed. "Yo, what's good?" Draco said, hopping off of the couch when Bezo walked in, "shit all crazy bra," he already informed them about Rilo's murder. They were ready to shut the whole city down, but he told them to just chill and let's figure things out. "Man, I think that bitch had something to do with this shit, bra was head over heels for that bitch. Now look what happened, she ain't nowhere to be found," Draco said lightin' a cigarette, "And how bout that bitch azz nigga D-Rock done set up shop right on 12th, not even 72hrs after bra gets instilled," "The nigga did what!" Bezo stopped in his tracks. "Yeah, that nigga open up a trap on 12th when he known that's a no-fly zone for him, that's our area, I was just waitin' to holler at you, and I'm gone dead that shit asap bra," "Yeah, do that asap, matter of fact, let's go pull up on them niggas now," Bezo said walking back out the door and loaded up in the SUV Draco had parked out front. "This some real disrespectful shit,"

"Yeah, I know bra, and you got to make an example out of this nigga, ain't none of this shit going down," Draco said as he navigated through the city. The other two goons were sitting in the back quietly with their guns in their laps. When they got on 12th, they could see a crowd of people in front of a duplex. "There go the nigga D-Rock right there pulling off!" Draco pointed at a dark green LS460 Lexus, "Follow that nigga," Bezo said, leaning up in his seat. They followed behind him for two blocks until they come to a red light. They pulled right alongside the Lexus, "Bra open up on that nigga. What you waiting for?" Draco said as Bezo let down the window and began emptying the 40 inside the driver's window. The Lexus sped off, but Draco kept up with him until Bezo emptied the 30 rounds into the car, and it wrecked into the back of a minivan. Draco sped off swerving through traffic then jumped on the interstate until he was far enough from the scene. "That's what the fuck I'm talkin' bout," Draco said, jumping up n' down in the driver's seat. "I want you to round back through there and burn that duplex to the ground," Bezo said. That was his first order after taking the throne. He switched cars then headed to the stash house, where he picked up 15 blocks. Then hit Kenney up and agreed to meet him somewhere in the city. He said he already had a hotel room and was waiting for him. When he arrived, he let Kenney know he was outside then headed into the room. "What up my nigga?" Kenney said, holding out his hand, Bezo shook it and walked over to the bed where there was a book bag laying at. Kenney grabbed it and dumped all the cash on the bed. "It's all there, but we can count it, I brought the money machine," "Yeah let's do that," Bezo said without trusting anything. After they ran all the cash through the machine, then they put it back in the bag. Bezo handed over the duffle, "Man you a blessing, I needed this, if it's as Jacob claim, you gon have a lot of business coming from me, I can promise you that," "Yeah, that shit A-l bra," "Well then, we locked in bra," Kenney said, dapping Bezo up again before he walked out the door. He got back in the car; he had 5 more blocks to break down and put in the spots he owned around the city. It was crunch time, no games, all business, if anyone got in the way of that, they get smoked like D-Rock.

Chapter 8

The condo came furnished, and it was downtown. It looked right over downtown. Toya paid an extra two thousand dollars to move in immediately. She was now cleaning and wiping down the house with Clorox and pine sol. With the surround sound blasting, she was walking around in a tank top and a pair of boy shorts. Every time she got by the mirror, she admired her perfect features, her yellow complexion was perfect, and her green eyes were to die for. That's why every man she ran into fell directly in her arms. After cleaning up, Toya took a shower then got dressed; she had to go shopping before it was too late. She put on a pair of ripped jeans, a white t-shirt, and a pair of crisp Jordan's. After finding the local grocery stores off the internet, she got into the car and drove for a short distance then pulled into the grocery store parking lot. Grabbing a cart, she began scanning the aisle and throwing everything in the cart she thought she wanted and needed. The cart was halfway filled when she turned on the aisle that held all the cleaning supplies, she added a mop and a broom to the cart, and extra bleach and pine sol, when she heard a male's voice from behind her, "Excuse me" he said. Her heart dropped, and she turned around, there was a tall, dark skin handsome gentleman standing there with his hand extended. She took it, "Hello, my names Ryan, Ryan Reynolds, but my friends call me Double R. No disrespect, but I couldn't help to notice how beautiful you were, I mean, you're amazingly stunning, and I was wondering, were you working with an agency?" "An agency?" Toya said, now realizing she was still holding his hand. "Like a modeling agency," "Oh," she said, smiling, "No. I don't model, but thank you for the compliment," she said, turning around to finish her shopping. "Hold up, wait, one more thing," he said digging into his pocket pulling out a card, "If you're ever interested in trying modeling out, I have a new company that I'm just getting off the ground, I believe that your beauty could help the business go far, plus the pay is good, you should try it out, I promise it won't hurt," he said looking down at her with a boyish smile. His teeth were so white and perfect, she thought to herself as she took the card, "I'll think about it," she said, stuffing the card in her back pocket. "Can I at least know your name just in case you don't call and I accidentally run into you again?" There, that boyish smile go again, she thought as she paused and thought what name to give to him, "It's Queen, my names Queen and you're Ryan, right?" "Yeah, Ryan's ok, but you could call me Double R," "I thought your friends call you Double R?" "Yeah, they do, but it'll be nice to have someone as fine as you be my friend too if that's cool, no disrespect intended," "I'm going to finish shopping Ryan, and maybe I'll call you one day that's your cell on the card, right?" "Yeah, that's my cell," Double R said, as she waved good-bye then continued shopping. After getting everything, she needed to the register were cashier rang everything up. It came up to $500 and some change, which she paid with a stolen credit card. After all her bags were in the cart, she made her way outside. Just as Ryan closed the trunk on a brand-new Maybach, got damn this nigga was ballin', she thought to herself as she pretended like she didn't see him and rolled the cart up to the AMTG 63 Mercedes she was driving and hit the alarm and popped the trunk. "You need help with them bags?" Ryan said as he jogged over, "Yeah, that'll be nice," she said as she opens the back door, "Damn this motherfuckah nice," he said as he put the groceries in the trunk and examined the car, "Yeah, I just got it," "Oh, this you?" he said surprisingly. "Yeah, all mine and thanks for the help, I'll call one day," "You promise?" he asked, she laughed then said, "I don't make promises," and the pulled off.

Chapter 9

Just as Ricardo promised, the package arrived, and someone came to pick up the cash that was owed to him. Bezo spent the majority of the day breaking down a couple of the blocks and cooking them up. Rilo's funeral was this weekend, and he made sure he went out in style promising Rilo's mother she would have to worry about nothing as long as he was around and he meant that. Word was already out that he smoked D-Rock for disrespecting the set and opening up shop where he wasn't supposed to. Bezo put everything up then headed out. Draco said it was important and he needed to talk to him. He could not lie, Draco was on top of everything, he got in front of every situation before it could get out of hand. But he wonders what this was about, he didn't know, but he was on his way over to find out. "What up bra?" Bezo asked as Draco got in the car, "Shit you know me trying to stay ahead, wanted to run something by you, I know you gave me the streets to make sure everything's in order, and that's my job, but I been thinking man, these niggas out here pussy we could control the whole city, you got me on your team and my lil' niggas is ruthless, we can break all this shit up what these niggas got going on, everybody should be buying work from us or working for us.

No disrespect but Rilo gone and the way he ran things was smooth but he could of been way bigger, and somebody got underneath him and crossed him out, I wanna put so much fear in these niggas that they gon be scared to even look your way, matter fact, our way because we a team, right?" "Yeah, we a team, why you even ask that," Bezo said, looking at Draco with a funny look, "Why you looking at me like that homie?" "Because you nigga you trippin'. You wanna go around and fuck up the whole city because of what? Man, the balls in our court, you gon eat and get full, but niggas got the right to eat too. Niggas and bitches love swag, so when we start pulling up and hopping out, niggas ain't gon' have no choice but to fuck with us." "You just need to sit back and do your job and your job only because what other niggas eat don't make us shit, the person who wins is the one who last longer, if you go around robbing and killing niggas we go to jail ASAP, you got to think man, you watching to many movies and listening to much music. It ain't going down like that, let's just control what's at hand, you make sure everything is good and eat, get fat bra chill out and quit doing all that damn molly because that shit done burns your brain out," they both began to laugh. Bezo reached in the back seat, "That's 4 blocks, sell that shit how you wanna, just bring me back 100 racks, 25 apiece, that's cheaper than everybody else getting them, so handle up nigga, and Imma get at you later," Bezo said, dapping him up then pulling off. The rest of the day went by smoothly as he dropped the last couple of blocks on Jacob. He looked at the red light that was flashing on the dash, he had to get some gas, or this motha fuckah was going to give out, he thought as he got off the exit and pulled up to the BP gas station. He was driving a 5-year-old Dodge Charger, everybody knew his car, but he was good in the city. Even though the BP was on the other side of town, after running in the gas station and paying for the gas, Bezo walked back to the car just as a newer black Silverado pulled up and parked at the pump next to him. Bezo watched as the driver door opened, and a cat he knew from many different encounters got out. His name was Box, and he just got back out of prison about a year ago, and already his name was ranging around the city for being the neighborhood stick up kid and bodying a few good niggas. "Heard you runnin' shit since your main man Rilo got whacked, word on the streets you did that shit," Box said, "Fuck what the word on the streets is nigga and fuck you too," Bezo said, gritting his teeth and clutching the gun on his waist, "Oh, it's like that my nigga?" "Yeah, just like that," Bezo replied quickly. Box looked around then said, "You're on the wrong side of town to be talking like that," "I talk like I wanna talk anywhere I'm at nigga, if anybody know that, you should," "Naw, I don't know shit," Box said walking towards the store looking over his shoulder, "Consider this a pass nigga and your only pass," he said as he walked inside the store. Bezo screwed the gas cap back on, then got back in the car and drove off. Maybe I should let Draco off the chain; just maybe I should have, Bezo thought to himself.

Chapter 10

3 Days Later

Draco stood over the stove while his youngin' was around him watching him beat the coke in the Pyrex pot, "See this shit fish scale, this shit gon be A-l that's why I ain't put too much water in this shit, I just hit it a few time and lay it down. Imma leave 9 ounces here with you and you single this shit out. Take over the whole block, these niggas ain't gon' have no choice but to fuck with us because all the junkies gon' be eating this shit up and they ain't gon' be able to sell that water whipped ass shit they got, you feel me?" he said looking around the kitchen, and they all nodded their heads. Draco finished cooking up then left the house. He was on the way to his baby mama, Kiesha's house, ever since she found out he was in position, now she was all on his dick.

Gold diggin' ass bitch, he thought as he pulled up to the projects, then got out and walked straight in the house without knocking. "Why you feel like you could just walk in a bitch house without knocking?" Kiesha said, jumpin' up off the couch. She had on a small pair of cotton shorts that were hugging her phat ass and was stuffed in that phat pussy that got Draco's attention immediately. "Why the fuck you trippin', I help pay the rent around this bitch anyways. You need to cook ah nigga something, and were the fuck my son at?" "He with his grandma, maybe if you were really concerned, you'll know that," she said, turning around, walking towards the room. He watched her ass jump from side to side as he grabbed his dick and followed behind her. She was leaning over the bed reaching for something that was on the other side, he walked behind her and pressed his hard dick that was standing up in his basketball shorts on her ass, "What you think you finna do?" Kiesha said, lookin' back at him while she was still bent over, "Man you know what's up," he said as he pulled his shorts down. She didn't have no panties on, "Move boy," she said but didn't put up no resistance, as he pulled his dick out and forced his self-inside her and began to pound on her ass as she began throwin' it back and moaning out loud, "Fuck me Draco, I'm finna cum!" Every time she talked like that, he began pounding her pussy even harder, he felt himself about to cum, he pulled out and ejaculated right on her phat ass, then rubbed his dick across it until it went soft. "Damn that pussy good," he said as she walked to the bathroom and got in the shower. He peeled off a $100 bill and left it on the dress, "You beta not be giving nobody no pussy either," he said as he peeped in the bathroom. "If I do it's mine, the fuck wrong with you, you better tell your other hoes to not be fucking around nigga," she said. "Well, you heard what I said, and I left you some cash on the dresser," "It better be more than a hundred dollars because your son needs some clothes," Keisha said, peeping her head out the shower. Draco peeled off two more $100 bills and put them on the dresser and headed back out the door. Clutching the gun in his pocket as he walked to the car, he wasn't trusting anything; the streets were wicked, and he was planning on getting even wickeder as soon as Bezo let him...

Chapter 11

2 Weeks Later

Toya rolled over in the bed, slamming her hand on the alarm to shut it off. She had to get up this morning because she had a meeting with a car salesman and an appointment at the beauty salon. After bathing then getting dressed, she took the elevator down then retrieved her car from the parking lot. She felt a little more comfortable after putting most of the money in different bank accounts and opening several business accounts. She drove for a while until she came to the BMW dealership that was in East Atlanta. She drove by this place several times and fell in love with the BMW truck; she was planning on paying cash for it. It was brand new, and she had tons of money to blow. After parking, she was met by an older white gentleman with the name Joe on his name tag that was on his shirt. "May I assist you with anything today, mam?" Toya had on a yellow sundress with her long natural hair pulled back in a tight ponytail, so all the beauty her face had to give stood out, and she could tell she had Joe nervous just standing in front of him, "I have a 10o' clock meeting with Mr. Terry Jackson," she said, "oh, right this way mam," he said, holding his arms out, leading her into the building where he took her to a desk where a younger black gentleman was sitting behind it, he looked to be no older than 35. His hair was short, and it was full of waves, and his brown skin was smooth, and you could tell he worked out on the regular, his movement was athletic, she saw as he jumped up with his arm extended, "Ms. Dixon isn't it?" She shook his hand and said," "Yes," "My names Terry, Terry Jackson, I'll be assisting you today, I talked to you yesterday on the phone," "Yes you did, but I don't need to look around. I already know what I want, it's right there," she pointed at the all-white BMW K6 that was on show in the middle of the floor, "Ok let's go take a look at it," he said walking towards the truck as she followed. "This is the fully loaded X6, 0 miles, just got it in last week," he said, opening the driver's door so she could take a better look. When she got in, she could see how he had his eyes on her ass and wasn't paying any attention to the truck at all, "How fast does it run?" Toya asked him as she gripped the steering wheel with both hands, "Oh it's pretty fast, it's a V12 and should have 220 on the dash," "Yeah, this exactly what I need, how much is she?" Toya said, turning to face him, but his attention was on her thighs, "Oh the price?" he said as he looked up, "This baby here is 74 grand flat, but I could pull a few strings and maybe get it down to 70," "I'll take it!" "Are you financing?" he said looking at her seriously, "No I want to pay for it today and I want it now, I'm ready to write a check, is that a problem?" "No, no problem at all, let's head back to my desk and do the paperwork," After all the paperwork was filled out and the check was written he promised that he could have the truck dropped off to her house in a few hours. "Are you some type of model or celebrity?" he said as he opened the door for her to get in the

Mercedes, “No, why do you ask that?” she said, “I don’t know, you just look like one, sorry I mean you look beautiful, and you come in here and spend all that cash like it’s nothing,” “Oh,” she said smiling, looking up at him as he stared down at her, she couldn’t lie, this nigga turn her the fuck on. He was trying to control himself around her but was losing control every second, and she could tell. “Are you from around here, did you move here like everybody else?” he asked. “Yeah, I just moved here from Miami, Imma tourist, I have only been here for a few months, really haven’t explored the city like that,” she said still looking up at him, there was a moment of silence, he smiled then asked could he take her out. “You know maybe go out to eat or catch a movie, I’m new around here too, but I know where the good spots are at, I can show you around if that’s cool?” He sounded nervous, and that turned her on even more. She loved being in control, “Yeah, that’s fine, when would you like to show me around?” “Tonight, if that’s ok with you, let’s say around 8 o’clock. I can pick you up, or you could meet me there,” she thought about it for a while, wondering what kind of car he drove, “You can pick me up,” she said, smiling. They exchanged numbers; Toya drove off, smiling to herself because Terry was fine as hell.

Chapter 12

Toya was running around the condo, putting her last touches together. Terry texted 30 minutes ago, letting her know he'll be downstairs at 8 o'clock on the dot, and it was 7:50 at the time. This was her 5th time checking her makeup in the mirror. The red lipstick she had on her big juicy lips would turn any man instantly on, and that's exactly what she was trying to do to Terry tonight. The blonde Brazil weave she had in her hair hung all the way down her back to the top of her ass. She squeezed in the finest dress she owned, and it was a designer just like her YSL purse and heels. She stood in the mirror and put on her new diamond-studded necklace and bracelet. She decided not to wear no panties or no bra tonight because who does that anymore? Checking herself out again in the 6ft mirror that was on the wall, she agreed with her image like always, Toya looked like money. She took the elevator down just as Terry texted and said he was out front. She walked out of the building to see Terry stand next to a Porsche Panamera, and it was all white. Her favorite color and he was dressed sharp as a nail but not too much to overdo it. White Gucci shoes, a white, green and red Gucci shirt and white jeans. The gold necklace and Rolex stood out just like his muscles. "Look at you, Terry, looking like a celebrity," Toya said, walking up to him and giving him a hug, she could smell the expensive cologne he was wearing. "Oh my God, your drop-dead gorgeous," Terry said as he lifted her hand, and she spun around so he could admire her beauty. "So, where we going?" she asked as he opened the door and let her in, "I got somewhere special, you'll like it, I promise." He ran back around to the driver's side and got in the car.

"This is so nice," she said, looking around the vehicle, "You like it?" "Yes, it's so nice and spacious, is it fast?" she asked, leaning over looking at the dash, "Yeah, it's real fast," he pressed down on the gas, and it zoomed forward. "Wow!" Toya screamed playfully glued back in her seat, and he let off the gas. "Yes, I love this car, you got a good taste," he smiled then continued to sneak peeks at her, "Man you are gorgeous Ms. Dixon, I mean heavenly beautiful, you look so good your making me nervous," Terry said looking over at her, she was just smiling. "You can call me Queen, that's what everyone calls me, I don't like Ms. Dixon, that makes me sound old," "Ok cool Queen, that's nice, you can call me TJ, you know Terry Jackson, TJ is short for my real name," "I know what TJ stands for boy," she said playfully slapping his arm. "Wow, you so strong!" she said, reaching back over, squeezing his arm. "Yeah, I work out a lot, well I used to, Now I just hit the gym every chance I get," "I need to start going to the gym," she said, rubbing her flat stomach. He looked over then said, "The way it looks, I thought you hit the gym all day," that made her blush. A few minutes later, they pulled up to an expensive-looking restaurant. They left the car to the valet and walked arm and arm into the establishment, where they were greeted immediately. "Mr. Jackson this way, please," a small Asian woman said, leading them to a table in the back. "I made a reservation,"

TJ said. The lighting was low, and music whispered out invisible speakers as they set down, and she looked around at the crowd. Everyone looked nice and wealthy. The culture was mixed. "They serve a mixture of really nice food here you'll love it, I promise," he said, looking over at her. "I already love the atmosphere, it's beautiful, the people are beautiful too," she said, still looking around. The waiter came back to the table to take their orders. They both looked through the menu then gave her their orders and ordered wine. An hour later, they were laughing and having a good time. "So, you say you used to play professional football?" "Yep, for the Detroit Lions for two years until I broke my leg and just like that, my career was over, so now, I do a little this and a little of that to make ends meet, just started at the dealership, you were my first big client, so tell me a little about yourself," he said, taking a sip of the wine, looking over the glass at her. "Well, I'm from Miami, I went to Miami University and got my Bachelors, I moved to New York for a while where I tried acting, but it didn't work, then I fell in love with a very rich guy that was charming in the beginning but turned out to be just like every other man," "What's that suppost to mean? if you don't mind me asking," "A liar, a cheater, and a heart breaker, it took me over a year to build myself back together after the divorce, he cheated on me with my only sister and there still together. I took what he owed me and got the hell out of there, and now here I am in Atlanta sitting across from Mr. Terry Jackson, and I hope he's not a liar, a cheater, and a heart breaker because he's so fine and charming," she said, looking at him with suspicious eyes. "Well, I can't speak for every other man, but I'm neither of the three you believe every man are, I'm just a guy out to have a good time with someone as beautiful as yourself, and as of now, the night has been perfect, and I enjoy having you as a company," "Well, that's nice TJ," she said, smiling over at him. The night was still young, and he asked if she wanted to catch a movie or hit a club or something. She said that was cool and they decided to hit the club. He said he knew a spot where it was grown and sexy, and the crowd was mature. They drove for a short distance then pulled in front of a club called Quaver's. She wondered if it was the rapper's establishment as she got out and looked around, she saw nothing but expensive cars and people of all races in designer clothes and expensive jewelry. They walked up to the entrance and was led right in were the bouncer ushered them to a VIP area, "Your well known everywhere TJ," she said, over the music, "I told you, I used to play ball," he said, smiling. As they set down and a bottle girl brought a bucket of ice with two bottles in it, Grey Goose and Hennessy. "White or brown?" he asked as he grabbed the glasses, "White, thank you," she said, looking around the club. This was her first time out, and she had to stay on point because all the fucked-up shit she did in life wasn't no telling who she might run into tonight, hopefully, no one. After drinking a glass of goose, she was beginning to loosen up and began to wine her body while he stood behind her, pressed up against her. She was looking over the balcony when she recognized Double R in a booth across the club. He had on so much jewelry; it looked like the lights were on over there. There was a group of females and young dudes all around them as they popped bottles and flashed money. "Who's that over there, that's a rapper or something?" she asked, pointing in Double R direction, "No, that's just Double R, he's real big in the city, got his hands in everything, use to be a friend of mine, but we no longer communicate," She could sense hate in his voice as she continues to dance on him and act like she wasn't paying any attention to Mr. Ryan no more, but she was locked in on him. The more she drank, the looser she got she was dancing all over him now, and he was loving it, she knew she was the baddest bitch in the club because she was looking around and none of the females compared to her, they were all exotic but nothing like she was. It was around one o'clock, and she told him she was ready to go. They exited the club, and the car was parked right up front, so they didn't have to walk far. As she was getting in the car, she could see Double R a few cars ahead, getting inside an all-black Wraith. This nigga was full; she thought as they pulled off. They got to her building a short while after, he opened the door and offered to walk her up, she declined but gave him a hug, and a kiss on the cheek then walked off slashing her ass. She knew he was watching and that his dick was hard, but tonight he was getting none.

Chapter 13

"That's a hundred grand flat my nigga, just like that, what I tell ya," Draco said as he set the cash on the table in front of Bezo, "I already know my nigga, that's what real niggas do, let's just keep this shit moving like this and the next thing you know the city will be bowing down to us but what's up with Ratchet, they moving shit ok over in the projects?" "Yeah, Twan them cool, is just that bitch ass nigga Box that nigga set up shop around the corner and he's been muscling shit, he ain't moved in on Twan and them yet, and I said yet because you know that bitch nigga would try anything." The name Box got Bezo attention when he looked up from the cash he was counting. "Box, that nigga starting to give me a headache, I want you to make that headache go away, could you do that for me? That'll be nice," Bezo said, sliding 20 thousand dollars over to him. Draco slid it back over, "Not right now my nigga, thank me later." Draco said, giving him an evil smile then turned around walking out the house. Bezo finished counting all the cash then headed out himself. Ever since Rilo died, the city went their own way, everybody that was loyal to Rilo wasn't loyal to him. So Bezo was introducing him to niggas around the city that had a name for their self, and all the people he was still dealing with, the people he was fucking with before. Jacob was a loyal customer, that's who he was on his way to meet. Jacob was older than he was but way smoother than most guys he knew. Rilo always kept Bezo on a leash' and didn't want to expand his empire out of the county, only fuckin with a select few people, but now since he was in charge, Bezo was thinking about expanding. Jacob was from across the bridge where he swore everything was sweeter, and he just needed a team of niggas that didn't mind putting down and stepping on toes until they got what they wanted. All Bezo wanted was money and no problems. He thought to himself as he parked the car and walked inside. The IHOP, where Jacob was sitting at a table in the back, he was dressed casually and looked more like a professor than a drug dealer. "My main man!" Jacob said, getting up to embrace him, then sittin' back down, "You love meeting at these lil' restaurants," Bezo said as he sat down and looked around the room, "Yeah man, I like the peace and quiet, I would tell you to meet me at the library, but that might freak you out, plus I meet a lot of older freaky white women in these type of places, and they pay top-notch for a nigga to dig deep in them if you know what I mean," he said, with a smirk on his face. "But anyways, I wanted to talk to you about something. I hear you and Kenney did some good business, and good business is always good until it's bad, you know?" Bezo nodded his head but didn't know where he was going with this. "I could see that you're confused," he said as he placed a napkin on his lap and grabbed the fork and knife and began slicing through his pancakes. "You want anything?" he asked Bezo, lookin' over from his plate, Bezo shook his head, "Well, Kenney is a good dude, but he's also food," Bezo still didn't understand because he was the one who introduced him to Kenney. "I'm saying fuck that nigga, that nigga ain't apart what you trying to build. I'm saying I'm on your side, and I'm your team, and I've been one of your loyal customers from the beginning. So, when niggas become food, I'm the one you should call to eat them niggas. It's different times, and you and I got to keep up," he pointed at both his-self and Bezo with his fork as he chewed his cakes and looked deadly serious. "The reason I introduced that nigga to you because I knew you'd give me that nigga when he cashed in, I want to be the one to eat that nigga, he's not righteous, and he's not gon be along for the long hall," "So you telling me to set that nigga up so you could rob him?" Bezo asked, Jacob stopped eating then set his fork and knife down then washed his hands off with a napkin, "You not hearing me Bezo, I'm trying to control my city, I'm trying to be the big fish in the sea, but with this nigga in the way, that's not gon happen. You my nigga, I know you even doe your young, I still trust you, your loyal, with the product you got and the team I already got with your backing, I'm untouchable, and I'm going to start moving everybody in my way out the way. Now if you look at it the way I look at it', that's more money for me, and you then you're not dealing with 20 different people, you're dealing with me, and I'm dealing with everybody else, you were your big homies right hand man. You was right hand to his empire, so if you trying to run things like he was running them, you're not gonna be able to do that because niggas that was loyal to him they don't got to be loyal to you, plus you don't know everything he did to build his throne, you don't know all the dirt and all the behind the scene shit that was going on, it's time for you to spread your wings and be your own boss, you that nigga, I been telling you that man. You ever seen that movie American Gangsta them niggas wasn't trying to respect Frank until he went to smokin' niggas and doing shit his way, he built his own kingdom. So, you and your niggas need to start cleaning up everything and everybody that don't want to be down with what you got going on, this your city and that's my city," he said, pointing in the direction of St. Pete. "Now, if you tell me I got your backing, I'm going to start cleaning up today, and you don't get to set Kenney up; I'm go get that nigga myself," he said, picking his fork and knife back up and began eating again. Bezo was nodding his head because this was gon build up what he was doing; he reached over and shook Jacob's hand then said he was in.

After leaving from meeting with Jacob, Bezo, now in traffic, watching through his rear-view mirrors, wasn't because he was paranoid; it was just a part of the game. An hour after leaving from meeting with Jacob, he pulled up to the stash house and hit the remote, the garage came up, and he drove in. He had over 400-thousand-dollars in the back seat. He threw the bags over his shoulders and headed into the house. The other house was left to Rilo's mother. She still didn't move in yet; she claimed she didn't want to stay anywhere her baby was killed, he thought to himself as he set the bag on the bed and pulled the other bag from under the bed. This was a lot of money, there was almost 2 million cash, not counting all the bricks he still had. He pulled money out the other bags, stuffing it into the one duffle bag where the majority of the other cash was. Bezo walked to the back room and lifted the mattress; there were numerous handguns and rifles underneath there. He went inside the living room where he set on the couch and turn on the television and began watching the monitors. There were ten hidden cameras all around the property, even up the street; he could tell if anybody was around the house, in the house, or down the street. He really didn't feel comfortable keeping all the cash in one spot. He promised himself he would get another spot way out of the area and stash some of it there. Walking to the fridge, he peeped inside to see nothing was in there and then thought about ordering a pizza, then canceled that thought and headed back out the door, making sure he set all the alarms and locked all the doors. There was too much to lose, and he wasn't trying to lose shit.

Kenney pulled his Q-50 Infinity into Jordan park and backed in looking around. He texted that he was outside, he then watched a heavy-set younger guy come down the stairs with no shirt on and chains dangling around his neck. Kenney unlocked the doors, and the guy got in, "What up cuz?" he said as he reached over to give Kenney a dap then reached in all his pockets pulling out wads of cash trapped in rubber bands, "That's 15 racks cuz, I was trying to do the same thing, and I'll have the rest of the cash for you later," he said, biting down on his jaws. Kenney could tell he was rolling on E, "Ya I gotcha," he said as he reached back and grabbed the bag, he kept the work in, then gave him what he purchased and the other he fronted he stuffed the coke in the pocket of his cargos then gave Kenney a dap and jogged back upstairs. It was after 9 pm, and that was the last person he was meeting tonight. As he exited JP and headed out, he was going to call it an early night, having over 100 thousand dollars; he did good for the day. The coke he was getting from his new plug was A-l, he could step on it three times if he wanted to, he thought as he backed up in his yard. The Q-50 was new; he purchased it the other day and was already in love with it, glancing back over his shoulder, hitting the alarm. Fumbling with the keys, he found the right one then he walked in the house, he knew something was wrong immediately as he reached for his waist but was too late as the taser hit him directly in his chest. He fell on the floor and passed out, 10 minutes later he woke up naked and hogtied on the floor. There were two masked men standing over him, "Were the rest of the cash at nigga, don't make me fuck you with the end of this broomstick and it's hot!"

He said, "Look man all the cash I got is in the attic and inside the mattress in the second room to the right, just cut the mattress with a knife, I swear that's all the cash I got, it's over 250 thousand dollars, and if you check the back yard, I got 5 more bricks under the dog house, the dog don't even bite man. I ain't lying, that's all I got, I ain't playing no games, I don't know who you are. I'm not gon call the police, I ain't doing no resisting, it ain't no reason to kill me." After he finished talking, all three of them disappeared. Kenney sat on the floor and prayed the whole time, begging God to let him live, and he promised he wouldn't sell another crumb, he would cheat on his baby momma no more, he would marry her and go to church. He didn't want to die like this. He was only 30 years old and had a lot to live for and had a lot of life ahead of him; that's why he told them the truth the first time. He was interrupted from his prayer as all three of them came back up-front, with more bags in their hands, "That's everything man," he said, looking down at the floor not looking up, he didn't want them to have a reason to kill him, "Let's get out of here," he heard a voice say. Then all of them walked to the front door opening it then closing it. He kept his eyes closed for another 5 minutes then opened them when he didn't hear anything else. He thanked God for letting him live, and then he promised he was going to keep his word. Now he just needed to wait til' Pie his baby momma came home to untie him because he couldn't move and he had to shit really really bad.

Chapter 14

After seeing Double R that night in the club, she wondered if he also saw her over in the booth with TJ. She pondered on that for three days, then finally pulled the card out he gave her and dialed his number. She told him she thought about the modeling thing and wanted to take a few pictures to see what she looked like before she really dived into it. He promised her it was going to be 100% business, no bullshit in between. He had a comfortable atmosphere he worked in and had five different photographers on payroll, and if she was uncomfortable shooting with a male photographer, he had females who shoot as well. She agreed and set an appointment for today at 1 pm. She was dressed in a pair of fashion nova jeans and Louis Vuitton sneakers. She straightens her hair then left the condo to head to the address Double R gave her. For the last couple of days, she's been driving the BMW, and she was in love with it. It was everything she hoped it would be. She made her way through traffic with the music turned all the way up, Nikki screamed through the speakers as she got off the interstate and drove a little while longer until she pulled into a plaza on the North-side of Atlanta. She drove around until she found a parking spot then parked, getting out and grabbing her designer bag, she put in her bag the lingerie that she wanted to shoot in. She closed the door and hit the alarm. She walked up to the door, then hit the button that was on the door and then waited. There was a voice that came over the intercom asking if she could help her, she responded with her name and let them know she had an appointment at 1 pm. There was a pause, then the door buzzed open, and she walked in. The furniture was all white, and there was lots of it, there were expensive paintings on the walls, and there was a beautiful receptionist behind the desk with a big beautiful smile. She was white and had long blonde hair. She stood up and extended her hand and said, welcome to Double R Art Center. Her breast set up so nice on her chest Toya wondered if they fake as she shook her hand. She told her to have a seat, and someone would be out to take her to her booth in a moment. She set down in one of the chairs, but before she could get comfortable, the door opened, and a younger black guy with huge eyeglasses came out and told her to follow him to the back. She grabbed her bag and followed him, the space in the back was huge, and there were other beautiful women getting their hair and makeup done and there were carts with designer clothes hanging on them and boxes of underwear. Every corner you turn, Victoria Secret, and Pink, this was a real fuckin company she thought to herself as he led her to the booth, they would work in. There were a lot of lights and white backgrounds, "We wanna get you over here and get your makeup done and your hair," he said, pointing at an area where a model was getting her finishing touches. He looked down at her bag then asked, "Did you bring your own things to wear?" She nodded her head. After dressing in her lingerie, she then headed over to the chair to get done up. She told the women that would be hooking her up just what she wanted. As she started, she could see Ryan coming her way out the corner of her eye, he was dressed in a Gucci sweat suit with 2 Styrofoam cups stacked on one another sipping from it as he approached her, "Hello Queen, you liking the setup?" he asked as he turned around, looking around. "I got a few things to touch upon, and it'll be just right, but for now, it'll do," he said, looking down at her, smiling with his perfect teeth. "Yes, this is really nice, it's a real company, and you got real nice employees, they make me feel welcomed and comfortable," "Yeah, I know, that's why I handpick everyone I hire, they fit all my requirements, but I'll let you finish getting ready then I'll come back around. "Do you mind if I peep in on your shoot?" he asked, she said she didn't mind then he promised he'll be back and walked off talking on his phone, damn she thought as she watched him until she couldn't see him no more, this nigga is a certified boss and act as if he controls the whole world with his sweet-talking and that smile that melts you and the way he looked at you. I'm at that nigga, and he don't even know it yet, Toya thought. As they finished up and she was led back to the booth where the photographer told her to relax and sit on the stool, she complied then he went to snapping pics. "Open up the top a little for me, Queen," she complied, then he kept taking pics. "Just do your thing, switch positions for me and open the rope up all the way and when your real comfortable let's get you in your lingerie because those are the shots to die for, you're so amazing, you're so beautiful, that's it right there," he kept saying as she slowly slid the rope down. Now she was only in her thong and bra as she switched positions on the floor. He kept complimenting her as he kept snapping; she saw the look of surprise on Ryan's face as he walked in. Now she was really ready to put on a show. She was in a different set of lingerie by the time he came in. She was now on her feet, bending all the way over and looking back at the camera with a sexual look on her face. Then she was on her knees, bending all the way over, knowing her phat pussy print was all in the camera. Turning around, squatting down spreading her legs like wings and giving the camera all, she had, coming out of her bra, keeping her nipples covered, she teased the camera and watched as Ryan was little by little losing control. She could see the front of his sweatpants rising up, and she knew he was turned on. She knew she was a dime plus 10 and the green eyes she had were irresistible, as she stared in the camera and continued to buss it open every way she could. Putting' her' bra back on and the robe to cover herself up and walked over to Larry, the photographer, and asked how did she do, he was wiping sweat away from his face with his dingy red t-shirt, "That was amazing, to be honest, that was one of the best shootings I've done in a long time, this was a good session, I'm going to edit these photos and put them together then email them to you and you tell me what you think," he said and then exited the booth. "What did you think? Was I good?" Toya asked Ryan, smiling up at him. "Yeah, that was crazy, you act like this was nothing, like the camera was your best friend, that's what I need, someone as beautiful as you to take this company to the next level," "You think I can do that?" Toya asked. "Yes, I know you can do that, your flawless and just standing in this room with you alone is driving me crazy," he said, playing right into her game, she took the smile off her face, "Well let me put some clothes on because I don't want to give you the wrong idea." Moving towards her bag, grabbing the sundress throwing it over her head, then letting it fall over her body. "No, I'm sorry that came out wrong," he said, holding his hands up in defense, showing he was harmless. "How was it suppose to come out?" she asked, sitting down looking up at him from the chair, she was now sitting down and taking a sip from the bottle of FIJI water she brought with her. "Let's forget about that, let's talk about business, where was I yeah," he said, clapping his hands sitting down. "I want you on the cover of the first magazine I'm putting out. It's going to be huge and even bigger with you," he said with sincerity on his face. "What's in it for me?" she asked, "You'll get your cut plus business is going to be booming for you, videos, walkthrough, more magazines, more people are going to be checking for you. I'm like a god at stuff like this when my heart tells me something, I follow it, and it never led me wrong," he said. "So, you think I could be as big as a real model, like Kiesha Dior?" "I'm thinking bigger," "Yeah but she her own boss and that's what I want to be, I'm not trying to sign no crazy contract and be stuck and controlled by Double R for years, that's what I'm not trying to do because I already got my own cash and I'm already in control of my own life, so I don't mind fucking with you MR. Double R, but you got to be 100 with me all the way," she said, staring at him. "I can do 100 that's all I know, but in the meanwhile, you wanted to grab something to eat, there's a nice spot right up the road, everything's on me, plus they got really good soul food," "Hell yeah I'm hungry as hell." Ten minutes after getting inside his Range Rover, they pulled up to a place called Terresa's, they walked in and ordered at the register then chose a place to sit down and waited for their orders. "I come here at least once a week, they got amazing red velvet cake and pink lemonade, and it's my favorite,"

"Oh yeah," "Yep and the hamburgers are to die for," he said, taking his sunglasses and setting them on the table and pulling his sleeve up to check the time, but with all the diamonds flooding the bezel she knew he was only doing it for show because ain't no way in hell he could tell the time on that thing with all the ice that was flooding it. "So tell me, Ms. Queen, what brings you to Atlanta, I know this the city of dreams but you say you wasn't down here looking for a career, you must a heard all the hype about the city and came to see for yourself. Well, let me tell you myself the hype is real and the come up is real, it's so much to get into here and it's fun, it's really what you make it, plus the people here their great. Have you met anybody here yet, or do you have family down here?" he asked. She shook her head and said, "Nope I'm down here by myself, I met a few people, went on a date or two, but it didn't lead to nothing, so I just shop and stay home, haven't really got into nothing since I've been here, the photoshoot was the most fun I've had in a long time. I had a bad break up, well divorce, and as soon as the ink hit the paper, I packed up all I needed and got the hell out of dodge. It was bad, and the last year and a half, I've just been putting myself back together and staying the hell out dodge because they say sweet talk and a nice smile would get you in a hell of a lot of trouble," she said, looking at him sideways. "Well let me tell you something about me, what you see is what you get, this is me until somebody pisses me off then I'm a different guy," he said, seriously as a big thick beautiful younger girl came with their food and drinks on a tray. "Hello Ryan, how's it going today?" she said, then looked over at Toya with a smile on her face saying hello to her as well. "I'm doing good, and thank you for your service." She told him he was welcome and then walked off. Toya turned around to watch her walk off then turned around and said, "Damn her ass phat, you ever shoot with her?" she asked, he laughed then said, "No, I asked her, but she declined, said she's in the church, different strokes for different folks," "Do you bring a lot of women here?" she asked as she took a bite out of the macaroni which was her favorite dish. "No, I told you, I only come here once a week, and why would I bring a lot of women here?" "I don't know you seem like the player type with all your expensive jewelry and cars and all the beautiful girls you got down there shooting for you half-naked," "Hey, I can't help the way you think, but I can assure you I never slept with any of those women and I love looking nice that's why I buy, drive and wear the finer things. Your cars are expensive too. I see the new BMW truck you're driving, that's yours too?" he asked, sipping his lemonade. "Yes, I just got it, and I love it, but I wouldn't mind having a Maybach, now I'll be the shit in one of them," "That's why I'm telling you to fuck with me and the next thing you know you'll be driving Maybach's, Rolls Royce's and living in mansions and shit like that. I promise I can take you all the way like I tell you, I'm a god when it comes to putting shit together and must I tell you," he said, bowing his head, "Your beauty is Godly, your everything and some more, your drop-dead gorgeous so I want you to think about all we talked about, and you sleep on it, you got my number, hit me up whenever you ready and don't go running off with some other guy talking all this big talk because I can promise you, can't nobody deliver like I can, and my work speaks for itself, look me up, Double R Productions, Double R Entertainment, Double R Real-estate, it goes on and on. Shit hell just put Double R in by itself and watch what pops up. Don't listen to none of the negative shit it says about me, I mean I had a wild past and had to do a lot of nasty shit when I was a part of the game, but this is a whole new time, and I'm a bigger and better person, and I can promise you that." Toya sat there and listened as she dug in her food and chowed down, she couldn't lie, she loved everything about Ryan, his ego was so big, and his personality was like no others. "Are you into music?" she asked, "Well, I was thinking about starting a label and scooping a few of these lil' niggas up like everyone else is but, I got wrapped up in a few one-hit wonders, and sometimes you kick out more money than you make off them niggas. There's more money in beautiful women. Everyone needs beautiful women, rappers, promoters, and everybody else, and it's me Double R who's here to deliver." "You be pimping bitches or some shit like that?" "Naw, I'm not into that, women pimp themselves, all I do is get money and look good and surround myself around people that's full of ambition, that's it, so don't you go to making me out of a bad guy Ms. Queen," he said, smiling as the beautiful big booty waitress came back with the dessert and more drinks taking their empty plates with her. "You didn't lie, this cake is so good," she said, with her eyes rolling behind her head as the cake melted in her mouth. "I told you, that's why I come here once a week and enjoy the taste of it, but I try to keep down on the sweets because I'm trying to keep my weight down," he said, patting his stomach. After they got back, he dropped her off at her BMW, and she promised to give-a call once she got the pictures, and he promised she'll love them because Larry was one of the best photographers he had. After getting back home, she stripped out of her clothes and makeup then took a warm bath. She got on the internet with her phone and did just as he told her, she began looking him up, and there was a lot on the website about him, all his businesses and success. He owns a club called Double R downtown that was shut down last year because there was a double-homicide that happened inside his club, and the family of the victims was suing because of the poor security. More searching showed mug-shots of Ralph from 10 years ago, Rico charges which he beat because everybody that was scheduled to testify on him came up dead or missing. There was another case where his ex-wife was murdered. She and her boyfriend were questioned about it but were never arrested. Damn, this nigga was serious, she thought as she kept scrolling until her phone ping. There was a text message from TJ asking if she wants to hang out tonight, he knew a few other great spots. She texts back to let him know she didn't mind, he texts back letting her know he'll stop by at 8 pm, "Ok," she texts back then set her phone down and slouched lower in the tub and closed her eyes.

Chapter 15

"How come your stupid ass don't never do shit right, man I asked you to set everything out so I could cook the rest of this shit up for y'all before I leave," Box complained and yelled at one of the lil' niggas he had working in his trap on the second shift. "Shit man, I got high and forgot," he said, getting up off the couch and headed to the kitchen to get out the pots and heat up the water. Box didn't really sell drugs; he only did when he robbed niggas, and they have that shit on them. He'll take it and sell it to make more money, but since he been out of prison this time, he only robbed a few niggas. He was starting to like this trap shit because he could make more money trapping and there lil' niggas worked for a little of nothing. He wasn't even from this side of town, but just like everywhere else, he bullied his way through because everybody knew he'd merk something quick, "The water boiling," the lil' nigga yelled from the kitchen. Box got up off the couch and made his way into the kitchen. He began whipping the coke. His uncle taught him how to water whip, and he was stretching his shit out until it wouldn't eat any more water. "Swim bitch swim," he was saying as he beat the coke with the fork. After he whipped a 4-way for them, he grabbed his bag and told them he'd be back in the morning. He walked out the door clutching the pistol that was in his pocket," he hit the alarm on the rental car he was in. He wasted no time hitting the push start, putting the car in drive, then pulled off. He was texting while he was driving, he met this new bitch yesterday, and she promised she was gone give him some pussy tonight. Swerving through traffic, he wasn't paying any attention to his surroundings as he came to a red light, it was after 11 pm, so the traffic was light. The van that followed him from the project was now beside him. The driver pushed a button, and the back door slid all the way open, and Draco jumped out with a fully automatic assault rifle firing shots right through the driver's window. Before Box knew what was going on, he was dead. Draco let the whole clip ride, then jumped back into the van and sped away. At the same time, he had his other goons kickin' in the door at the spot Box just left; he told them to kill everybody that was inside the house. He told them not to shit, leave everything there. After they all completed their missions, they ditch their cars and meet back up at an abandoned house in what they called the shelter, because this is where most of them stayed when they had nowhere else to go. Draco pulled off his mask and then asked them what happened. They told him they did exactly what he told them to do, there were exactly five people in the room, not counting himself, and he knew personally, that all of them had bodies and he knew about them and what they were about that's why he trusted them. All of them were family and were loyal to each other. Draco took a bag of molly out of his pocket and licked the crystals off his palm; he could feel the drugging working immediately, as he passed the bag around then lit a blunt. They all waited for Draco to talk, but he didn't; he set down on the couch then told them to turn on some music. One of them started playing "All Black" by Plies, and the whole house went dancing like they always do at the shelter. Smoke, drink, fuck hoes, and party. Now that Draco was in the position, he promised he was gon make sure all his lil' niggas eat because they deserve it, and he knew they did. He texts Bezo and let him know that was done, then he set the phone back down, then popped some more molly because his mind was going a million miles per hour. Little did Bezo know he just let the dog off the leash, and shit was finna get really dirty and ugly.

Chapter 16

Bezo woke up the next morning in the hotel room he was staying in and turned on the TV. He flipped through the channels until he found the news. It was 10o' clock and the 10o' clock news was on, "This is Shakira's Tutu with Fox 13 News here in Tampa. There was a bloodbath last night, 5 bodies, and no suspects. The first victim is Julius Walker, he was gunned down at the red light with a high-powered rifle. There were over 75 rounds left at the scene. Not even 3 miles away in the Robles Park projects, there were 4 black males in their late teens and early twenties all gunned down with high powered rifles. These murders seem to be connected but there's no one coming forward. If there's any witness out there, we're asking you to come forward and speak to detectives, or call our TIP hotline at 1-800-555-TIPS or 1-800-CRIMESTOPPERS. We need your help and we need it fast, I'm Shakedris Tatum and this is Fox13 News. God bless and good night."

Bezo set up in the bed and was lost for words, he told Draco to kill Box but he killed his whole damn squad. He got himself together then texted Draco and told him to meet him at the shelter. Draco text back and said he was already there. After checking out of the room, Bezo hurried downstairs and flew cross town. On getting to the shelter, he parked the car and hurried inside the house, slamming the door behind him. "What the fuck wrong with you nigga?" he said, storming up to Draco, who was sitting on the couch with everybody around him either sleep or looking in their phones, they looked up at him for a second then closed their eyes or looked back down at their phones. "What you mean bra? I did what you told me to do. I got rid of the nigga and his homies in the process and I made it ugly just in case anybody wanted revenge, they'll think twice, why you trippin'?" He said, sitting up and setting the remote down. "Why I'm trippin' is because you do some stupid shit like that. You move'n how you wanna move, you move like a fuckin idiot without any guidance like you ain't been through shit my nigga. What do you think, you run shit? You go off and do what you wanna do, fuck what I say you run shit ha! You think this lil' niggas go do whatever you say and move however you want them to move, what you trying to build your own team to test me or something?" "Homie what the fuck you talkin' bout, you buggin' now," Draco said, standing up from the couch he was face to face with Bezo now. Bezo moved closer now his nose was touching Draco's. "I said what I said and I stand on that, if you don't want to play your position, you won't have no position at all and you can get the fuck up out of here!" "Nigga you got me all the way fucked up, I'll beat your azz!" Before he could say another word, Bezo sent a right jab to his jaw and knocked him back on the couch. Draco bounced right back scooping him off his feet slamming him against the TV knocking it down on the ground. Bezo fell on top of it with Draco on top of him, he rolled over fast slamming his fist in Draco's rib knocking the breath out of him, he stumbled backwards and Bezo bounced up squaring back off. Draco threw two punched which he weaved and slammed a blow to Draco's chin buckling his knees, he backed up to let him regroup, as soon as he did, he came at him, throwing wild and crazy blow's all over the place never coming within an inch of Bezos's face. They were childhood friends, their mothers were friends and both of them died from drug overdose, that's when they got lost in the streets together. The abandoned house they were in right now, The Shelter, is where they slept many cold nights together. This had to be there 100th time fighting in this same house, Draco never won but he never backed down. One of the wild punched caught Bezo on the side of the head and it stung like hell as Bezo grabbed him and fell back on the couch with him. They were both breathing hard, Bezo pushed off him and walked out the house slamming the door behind him. He got in the car and sped away. 20 minutes later, he pulled up in the driveway of the other house they chilled at and did business. This used to be Rilo's aunts house, she left it to him after she died and it's been the hang out ever since then. The only rule this house had was not to fall asleep here, never sleep were you eat. He dropped the book bag on the floor and went to the restroom where he ran cold water on his face looking at himself in the mirror. He had a small cut on the right side of his face. He set on the couch and rolled a blunt real fast, not caring how it looked. He dried it with the lighter then lit it asap, the Kush relaxed his nerves as soon as it hit his lungs. He held it in for a minute then let out a heavy cloud of thick smoke. He smoked the blunt down until it burnt his fingers, he set in the couch alone for the next few hours, only getting up off the couch when niggas came through to buy work. The 3 bricks he came there with was already gone and he had over 100 racks in the bag and he was ready to go but Draco text him and ask where he was at. He told him and waited for him to show up. When he came through the door, he looked relaxed but his jaw was kind of puffy. He came and set on the couch right next to Bezo. Bezo just looked at him. He watched as he took a deep breath then moved his hands around trying to figure out what to say. "Look man, you wrong in this situation bra, storming in the house talking to me the way you did in front of my lil' niggas then, poppin' off on me. All I did is what I felt like I needed to do, I put in work and you mad at me for that. You think them niggas was gon sit around the projects and don't do shit when they big homie just got wacked like that. So, I killed two birds with one stone, that's it but you can't be disrespecting me like that bra, you got to holla at me. We are better than that, then you talking about taking my position and kicking me out the spot, then what?" he threw up his hands. "Then were I'm ah go, who I'm gon have, you all I got out here, we all we got, don't forget this, I know you think I don't got shit to think with but I know these streets and it's our time and we got to be on top forever if these niggas don't respect us, I'm gon damn sure make show they fear us, man you got to feel me on that bra." he said, looking over at Bezo, who took a deep breath then said, "Fuck it man do what you do, rob who you feel like you need to, rob and kill who you feel like you need to kill, but no kids my nigga, no kids." he said, shaking his head. "And you got to move smart, don't get caught because if you go down I go down and remember this was your idea not mine and my nigga, I apologize about the way I came at you, I don't even know why I was upset, it's just I got a lot on my plate right now and I want you to get rich with me I want you to have something if you goon be a rich goon my nigga. Rich is for recoil my nigga and again I'm sorry and I love you, you my nigga, you my brother." They stood up and embraced each other then set back down on the couch. Draco reached for the blunt and rolled one up, after the smoke was in the air, he began to laugh, laughing really hard. Bezo asked what the hell was funny. He looked at him then said, "I almost beat your azz today nigga!" They both began to laugh, Bezo said, "Alright," and snatched the blunt from him.

Bezo pulled up to Gyro's after leaving the stash house, it was after 8o' clock now and he was hungry. He placed his order and was told to pull up to the window. There were two cars ahead of him, he hated being blocked in like this because the drive-thru was small, there was a fence right next to it; it made it hard to pull out if he needed to escape fast. After the other cars got their orders then pulled off, Bezo pulled up to the window and paid for his order. While he waited to receive his food, he was looking around but his attention was caught by a female that was inside the establishment at the counter. That couldn't be, he thought as he leaned up to get a better look, that was her. "Damn I ain't seen her in years." It had been over 15 years since the last time he saw her, he thought as he got his order out the window and pulled up front still looking through the window, yeah that's Elisha. She was his first girlfriend from the neighborhood but moved away when her grandfather died. Heard she moved to Jacksonville which was four fours away from Tampa. He could see that she had a lil' boy with her; he looked to be about 3 years old standing next to her bouncing up trying to grab the edge of the counter. Damn this was crazy as he parked his car and ran inside the building. "Excuse me mam, can I get some ketchup, y'all forgot to put it in my bag?" he said as he came up to the counter right next to her but not looking in her direction, he wanted to see if she recognized him. The lady apologized then handed him a hand full of ketchup. He could see Elisha looking at him from his **peripheral** view, as he turned around to leave, he could see her turning around watching him. "Hey!" she said, just as he reached the door, he paused then turned around. She was smiling a big smile, then she said, "Don't I know you from somewhere?" "Maybe, I don't know, where you from?" "I'm from right here, but I moved away a long time ago, I just moved back." "What's your name?" Bezo asked. She said, "Elisha, Elisha Gilmore." He acts as if he was shocked, "Elisha Gilmore, Mr. Gilmore's granddaughter from 22nd, quit playing, you playing right?" "No, I'm serious!" "If your Elisha you got to know who I am." "I know, you look so familiar, but I been gone so long and I've been through so much over the last 15 years, I can't figure it out." "Ok, just look at me for a little bit longer and I'll give you a hint." She said, "Ok," "You remember the candy lady that was on the street behind your granddad's house?" "Yeah, I remember," "Well, there use to be a short cut we use to take and one time we were running through their bare footed and you cut your foot really bad on a piece of glass and you were crying and couldn't walk." She was smiling while he told the story; her head was crooked to the side with her eyes squinted trying to bring the thought back to her brain. "I was the one that picked you up and carried you back home and your granddaddy spanked both of us for not having no shoes on." "Oh my God, Bryson, is that you?" He nodded his head and she ran up to him and gave him a big hug. He hugged her back, he could see her lil' man standing back looking confused. He smiled then asked if that's her son. She said yes and told him to come here. "Say what's up Coby." He looked up and said, "What's up man, let me get a dollar." She laughed then said, "Excuse him, I don't know where got that from but he didn't learn it from me." She told him to hold up then went back to retrieve her food then she came back and they walked outside, "So you've been staying here the whole time or did you move away and come back like I did?" she said, pushing a strain of hair behind her ear. She was beautiful, he thought as he snuck glances at her while they talked. She was a thick woman, big breast, big thighs and ass. She had a slight pudge in her stomach from the baby he believed, but he didn't mind, she was gorgeous, her teeth were white, her fingernails and toenails were done, he could see them through the thong sandals she was wearing and her long hair was natural. He made his mind up he wanted to hit that. "Naw, I been right here the whole time just floating through life. So, were you staying at?" "Well, right now I'm living with my cousin, I'm supposed to be looking for a place to stay but things kind of messed up for a girl right now, one of the reasons I moved back." "Whats up with his pops?" he asked nodding at the kid who was playing with a stick, "Oh, that's a whole other story, that nigga is what you call a straight dead beat and he's in jail right now for beating up one of his other baby mothers. I just got tired of the atmosphere of North Florida and figured I'll give Tampa another shot and here I am." "So, you just be sitting around doing nothing, you should hang out with me some time. I could show you around, I know you probably forgot about the city, or is that too much to ask?" "No, that's ok but that's it Bryson, I'm really not trying to get in anything else right not, when I tell you I've been through hell and back, Bryson I've been through hell and back." He could tell she was serious by the look on her face. "Yeah, I fill you, nothing like that, just old friends catching up with each other, if you want to you can bring lil' man, we probably could hit the zoo or Busch Gardens or something like that, I haven't had fun in a while either, I wouldn't mind having fun," Bezo said. She looked back at her son smiling, "That will be nice, but remember I told you, I'm doing kinds of bad, it's tight for me." "Look you don't gotta worry about none of that, why you trippin', I told you I got it matter fact," he said putting the ketchup on his hood, then dug into his pockets he pulled out a wad of cash straight blue hundreds, he pulled off 20 of them and tried handing it to her but she threw up her hand and declined. "No, I'm not doing that bad where I'm looking for handouts, so please no." "It's not like that," he still had the money held out towards her. "It's just I wanna help a friend, if you don't take it, I know who would," he turned and said, "Hey lil' man, check it out," he dropped the stick and came running over, "You still want a dollar?" Bezo asked as he nodded his head, Bezo handed him all the money, without hesitation he snatched it then started stuffing it in his pockets. "See, now he knows what to do, you go make sure your mama gets some to lil' man?" he looked up smiling nodding his head. She was laughing at her son. "Now he needs to quit!" "So, what's your number so I can call?" he asked. She gave it to him and he promised he would call tomorrow to check on her. He got in the car and drove away. That was crazy, he thought to himself but he was glad he ran into her. He hoped that cash would help her out with whatever she was going through, he really did.

Chapter 17

JoJo was from across the town and was well known in the city for getting money and fuckin bitches and he didn't mind flaunting his money or his bitches. That's why he was riding around in his new Range Rover truck with the baddest stripper in the city. The tint was dark and nobody could see him as Reginae had her head in his lap giving him the best head he ever had. "Got damn gurl you gon' make me crash this mother fuckah, keep suckin' this dick like that," he said pushing her head further down on his dick. He made a left not even using the blinker then he turned into the hotel where they always went. He back in then let his seat back so she could finish giving him the head. He came in her mouth, she sucked it all up then rolled down the window and spit it out. He hated when she did that shit but she said she didn't swallow nut; she never did and never would.

They got out and walked into the hotel and rode the elevator up to the third floor and walked to the suite he got earlier. This was the second bitch he would fuck here tonight. "Let me take a shower first," she said as she went to the bathroom and ran the shower. He watched her undress because she left the door open, all she had on was heels and a dress, nothing underneath, damn that bitch fine, he thought as he grabbed his dick through his Robin Jeans. He made a straight line of powder on the table and snorted it up. He got naked and laid flat on his back; his dick was standing straight up rock hard. The combination of goose, coke and molly kept his dick rock hard. She walked out the shower drying off and leaning over to hit a line of coke he left for her, he could see her pussy from the back and he stroke his dick hoping she would hurry up. She took another bump leaning her head back sniffing the drain down her throat then she walked in the room dropping the towel and getting in the bed. She laid next to him opening her legs wide then began playing with her clit in a slow motion, with her eyes closed, she was moaning and making fuck sounds. JoJo moved her hand out the way then began licking and sucking on her clit, placing a finger inside her warm wet pussy. He could tell she been fucking already today because it wasn't as tight as it usually was. He climbed on top of her sliding inside her then began fuckin her hard and fast as she screamed his name and dug her finger nails in his back. He knew his baby mama was gon be trippin' with all the scratched on his back but fuck that shit, this pussy was good as hell, he thought as he dug deeper and deeper then told her to turn around. She did spread her ass, he slid right back inside her fast and hard fuckin her while she threw it back at him. He felt himself about to cum so he stuffed his dick inside her ass and began pumping slow as her asshole gripped tight around his dick. He started pounding faster, he felt he was about to explode, he took 10 more strokes and burst right in her hole, she twerked and bounced her ass the whole time he was cumming. He fucked her one more time then looked at the time on his phone, it was after 12am and he had to be getting home. He left her $200 on the dresser, took a shower then left out the room.

He took the elevator back down and walked outside, getting in the Rover, he got on the interstate, he did 20mph over the speed limit all the way to his neighborhood. As soon as he turns the corner to get to his house a Dodge Ram truck came out of nowhere and slammed into his passenger door, then another car looked to be a Nissan Altima zoomed up. He couldn't tell because he was losing consciousness. He watched as the doors opened and two masked men holding guns ran up to his truck and burst the window, unlocked the door, and snatched him out. The Dodge Ram was already backing up then pulling off. They carried him to the Altima, threw him in the back seat then pulled off. He looked around trying to figure out what was going on but he was hit cross the head and passed out. He awoke tied to a chair naked with tape over his mouth. "Nigga we don't plan on being here all night but if we got to, we will be so, I'm gon ask you one time, where the cash and the work at, if you don't tell us, that's fine, we'll beat it out of you," the masked man said then snatched the tape off his mouth. "Nigga fuck you, I ain't giving you shit, do what you do! Jojo said then spit, Draco put the tape back on his mouth then began beating him across the face with the pistol he had in his hand. There was blood everywhere. "Heat the spoon up bra!" Draco said as his young one grabbed the spoon and put heat to it. Draco snatched it then set it right on the head of Jojo's dick, he instantly jumped and started rocking back and forward in the chair. "Now if I tell you again, I'm going to cut that motha fucka off, now where the fuck the shit at nigga, play with me!" he snatched the tape off his mouth. "Listen man, let me make one phone call and I can have it for you, I promise I got over 500 thousand dollars and 10 bricks left, one phone call it's all yours." "Wrong answer nigga!" Draco said taping his mouth back shut. He pulled the silencer out screwing it on the 9mm. Then shot him in the knees. He pointed the gun at his dick and said, "If you try to play me one more time, it's gone. Just one more time now talk nigga!" he said pulling the tape back off. Five minutes later Draco sent 2 of his goons out to check what he told them. He told him he lied about the 500 thousand and only had 200 and 10 bricks and it was stashed away at his grandmother's house. An hour later, he got the text that everything he said was true and they were leaving the house now. Draco put his phone in his pocket, stood up then shot JoJo in the head. He turned around to leave, "You should have told the truth the first-time nigga now look at you."

Chapter 18

Jacob was crossing the bridge on the same thing. Him and his lil' cousin, P, kicked the door open to Monae's house; she was the only female in the city that controlled most of the traffic on the north side. Rumors where she was working with more than 20 bricks. She was spread out across the floor with another chick that was walking around naked when they kicked in the door. "Do you know who you fuckin with, you fuckin with the wrong bitch!" Monae said as they continue to tear up the house, "Don't you know y'all gon be dead before the nights over, I mean asap you fucked up!" P came over and sent a hard kick right to her mouth splitting her lips and knocking out her teeth, she was fast asleep. "Bitch if you get to talking, I'm gon fuck you up to." The naked lady didn't even lift her head from the floor. They continue searching the house. After another 30 minutes then P yelled out, "In here!" Jacob walked in to see what he was looking at, after moving the huge dresser out the way, all the drywall was busted in the wall and there were piles of money and a few bricks inside. "Jackpot!" P said as they filled the garbage bags then began leaving out the house. "You want me to smoke these hoes?" P asked, Jacob then thought about it for a minute, he looked down at the woman that was laying on her stomach naked. Her ass was phat and he could see her big phat pussy poking out from the back. He held the bag out and told P to hold it, he dug in his pocket and came out with a condom putting it on his already hard dick. He told her to bend over, without hesitation she complied. He got behind her and stuffed his dick in her and began fuckin her hard and fast within a minute he was breathing and cumming hard. He moved out the way then P began fuckin her next after he was finished, they made her get in the shower and they watched her wash off. They tied her back off then left. Hopping into the stolen car they sped away. After getting back to the duck off spot, they counted up what they had. There was over 150 racks and 3 bricks, they were doing good, he promised his self he wouldn't rape a bitch again but that bitch was tempting. He gave up some of the cash then headed home where his wife and 2 little kids were waiting for him.

Chapter 19

The last couple days, Bezo was laid low not showing much face, the city was in an uproar. Liked promised, Draco was robbing a whole heap of niggas and he was behind a couple more bodies after the Box situation, the heat was on. Vice was riding and the nares was out, Niggas were too scared to talk but they were whispering, he knew that, and that's why he was laying low not selling nobody shit. Jacob kept in contact and said he'll be paying him a visit in a few days, he wondered what that meant. The news reporter was claiming it was a drought in the drug supply and that's why the murder and crime rate was sky rocketing. Little did she know she was way off; it wasn't no drought at all and he could promise that, he thought as he flipped through the channels on the TV. When his phone pinged, he looked at it and his face lit up with a smile, it was Elisha asking what he was doing.

The last couple of days they've been communicating on the phone. Sometimes talking for hours, he found out that she was working at a clinic and was trying to go back to college and for the 10th thousand time, she told him she'd been through a lot and didn't want to go through that shit no more and she wasn't looking for anything serious, he wasn't trippin' because he wasn't either. "Nothing just chillin', WYD?" he text back then and waited for a response. "At work going on my break in the next 45 minutes, you want to have lunch with me or nah?" "Yeah, that's cool. Send me the address to your job." She did and he laid back for another 15 minutes then headed out. Because of the heat, he wasn't driving the Charger, he was in a rental car with tinted windows. Having to dodge the police and these hatin' ass niggas and all the enemies Draco and his crew were piling up, he was on the south side of town and the GPS said it was gon take another 20 minutes to get to where her job was located. The traffic was light, so he made it there in 15 minutes. He went back into a parking spot in the parking lot. He was watching the front door. Elisha came out right on time, looking down at her phone pressing digits. His phone ranged but he was already pulling up on her. She didn't know this car so she wasn't paying any attention, he declined her call then rolled down the window, "You looking for me?" she smiled then got into the car. "Oh, I didn't know who the hell you were, I like this car, it's nice." "I like it too but it's a rental, got to take it back in a few days. But were you wanted to eat? I know you only got 30 minutes on break so were you wanna go?" "There's a subway right up the road, I want to grab me a cold cut, there so good." "Oh yeah, I fuck with subway too." he said as he pulled into traffic then pulled up to the establishment 5 minutes later. They both got out and he watched her as they walked to the door, her ass was everywhere, man that shit was phat no bullshitting he thought as he followed behind her and they waited in line. "So, when you gon take me and my son to Busch Gardens like you promised because he was asking about that man with the money, you won over his lil' heart," she said, smiling. "Shit, whenever you got the time off, we could chill, I'm just waiting on y'all. I ain't got shit to do." He said as he kept hitting decline on his phone, it rang every few seconds, niggas were wantin' work but he wasn't fucking with nobody right now. "It looks like you busy to me." She said looking at his phone. "That's your girl or something?" She asked looking up at him "Naw, I told you I don't have a girl, it's just a whole lot of unnecessary people I'm not trying to deal with that's all." He said. They moved up in line and he waited as she told them what she wanted on her sandwich. She asked what he wanted, he said "The same thing but make it a foot long, I'm hungry as hell." They got their meals then headed back outside, still watching her ass. She turned around to catch him staring, she only smiled. "So, were you live at if you ain't got no girl, I know you ain't just bouncing from house to house being a hoe." "Naw, nothing like that but I do bounce around a lot, after me and my ex split up, I just never got nowhere else to stay so I just been living in and out of hotels for the last year I think." They were now back in the same parking spot at the clinic as they ate their sandwiches. "So basically, you're a bachelor, bang out with your thing out." That got both of them laughing really hard. "Man, you crazy that was funny." "I'm for real though, that's why I need a break from men because they are more dogs than dogs themselves." You think every man is like that?" He asked, looking over at her, she was leaned over biting her sandwich nodding her head. "Well, I like to think I'm a different breed. I'm one of a kind and I don't really get off fucking a lot of women. The only thing that turns me on is a woman with ambition and goals in life. If I'm fucking a hundred bitches then I'm spending a lot of money and that could cause me to lose focus on the plan."

"The plan?" She asked, looking confused. "Yeah, the plan, everybody got the same plan or at least they once had the same plan, but lost focus because of negative distractions or they got too old or too far into a dark place that the plan didn't matter anymore." "And what's the plan?" She asked again more in tune now. "You know the plan." "No, I don't, if I did, I wouldn't be asking you." "The plan is to get rich that's everybody plan in life, at least it was until they lost focus or fall into a dark place in life then say fuck the plan. But my plan is still to get rich and I can't lose focus and I don't need no distraction, well, no bad distractions, but if the distraction is good then that distraction could only make the plan easier. You feel me on that, Z minds are better than one and great minds think alike. So I hope you think the way I think and still got the plan." Bezo said, looking over at her. It was 3 minutes past her break but he could tell he touched her somewhere in her heart, in her brains or maybe in between her legs, the way she was looking at him. "Yah, I still got the plan you can bet your ass on that." She said as they pulled up to the front door and she got out. She promised to call later, he said ok then watched her phat ass until she disappeared inside.

***

"Listen, I wanna get 10 if you let me get them for 25 flat, I'm telling you man, this shit gon be beautiful. All you gotta do is sit back and eat like a fat cat and get full my man." Jacob said from across the table. "Damn man 25 kind of low that's gonna hurt me in the pockets, you're the one go be getting fat." Bezo said, "But since it's you I could do 25, but only because you're my man." Bezo said, extending his hand, Jacob took it then shook it. "I'm going to be doing like 10 a week until things speed up. But don't forget when shit get ugly for me, I might need some assistance from you. But for now, I'm just glad to have you as a friend and a plug, but other than that, what's been going on with you?" "Shit, you know I'm just laying back, staying low. It's really hot in the city and a lot of killing is going on right now so the police are out real hard and I heard the feds in town, other than that, everything's good. I hear a lot of people getting robbed in St. Pete and don't nobody know who it is. I got a friend over there who says they seen Kenney the other day and he was on the way to church with his family and was speaking about how good God was." "Yeah man, it's been crazy over there but nothing I can't handle. I'm ready for whatever somebody bring my way." Jacob was dressed in a suit and tie; he was a weird dude but weird in a good way if he was on your side. Bezo met him about 10 years ago in prison when he was 18 and fresh in, Jacob was 28 at the time and was finishing up a 10-year bid for manslaughter and instead of getting off on him and cheating him out of his canteen, he showed him the ropes and all the bull-shit the chain gang was about, they hung out for a year until Jacob was released, Jacob came back six months later for violation and had to do another year. But that time Bezo saved his life and his man hood, after 2 gang members rushed into his room because of a debt he owed. Bezo peeped the play and ran in their behind them and stabbed one of them and fought the other one off until Jacob got back together and they fought back to back, ever since then, they were good friends. When Bezo got out, Rilo was in position and put him on and Jacob was selling work from time to time, he gave them to him for an all right price. But Jacob was always different, talking, walking and dressed differently. And he was a gangsta ass mother fuckah. Sometimes, he made Bezo wonder what his true intentions in the game were. He was so different it sometimes didn't fit him selling dope and robbing and there was always a look in his eyes, a look Bezo wasn't certain of but Jacob was a good dude at least for now, he thought. "You stay safe and hit me up when you ready for them things," "You already know my nigga, probably tomorrow, you know I got you," Jacob said as they got in their cars and pulled off. Bezo got back to the shelter and it looked like a party was going on when he walked in the house. The music was loud, there was smoke everywhere and they were passing bottles around and shoes, Bezo had a smile on his face. Draco came around the corner from down the hall, he was dressed in designer clothes and shoes plus he had on a lot of jewelry. "Damn, my nigga you look like a million dollars nigga, shit all you niggas lookin' like money what ah nigga missing?" Bezo said, "Shit you ain't missing nothing got a lil' something for you to, check it out," he said turning around walking over to the kitchen, reaching into the cabinet. He came back down with a shopping bag, "This your cut," he said, handing Bezo the bag. Bezo looked in it and could tell by experience that this was over 50 thousand dollars. "My cut for what?" Bezo said, still holding the bag, "For letting me loose and plus I wanted to grab a few of them things from you, with these niggas out the way that we moved out the way, the rest of these niggas ain't go have no choice but to grab from us. So, I don't want you to front me nothing else I want to pay. I want 10 of them tomorrow bra, real shit all you gotta do is lay back and eat but I'm all the way out their bra, watch and see how this shit comes together." Bezo just got through hearing this same story, he didn't know if this was a good thing or a bad thing with

Draco branching off and getting his own money and having his own team, he was going to be a problem later down the line, or was he trippin'. But he played it cool and said, "Yeah, now that's what I'm talking about nigga, whenever you ready I got you but you got to be safe because these niggas ain't go be playing fair for too much longer, so just slow down and get money and it's your time, I like the new look all the shine that's you my nigga." Bezo said. "Oh, this ain't nothing. I wanna show you something else." He turned around then began walking towards the backdoor when they got out back. Bezo mouth dropped. There was a brand new i750 BMW sitting right there on the lawn. "Yeah, I grabbed this bitch yesterday, brand new off the lot, can't wait to pull this bitch out tonight my nigga. Them hoes gon go crazy what you think?" "What I think, I think you spending too much money nigga, you need to be stocking that shit, not spending it, is you crazy!" "Naw bra I got plenty of that shit, believe me when I tell you money ain't a thing." "Oh yeah?" "Yep, just like that, I was going to put some rims on her but I said I'll keep it factory." He bent down swiping invisible dust away from the sparkling tires. Damn this nigga was trippin', robbing everybody then flaunting their money, this was gon be bad Bezo thought to his self while they walked back in the house. "I got one more thing to show you, I know you'll be proud of me for this move." He said going back in the cabinet coming out with a couple sheets of paper, he handed them over to Bezo with a smile on his face. Bezo looked down at the papers and studied them for a few seconds; he knew exactly what they were. This nigga went down to the city and paid $9,000 for the shelter. It was considered abandoned and the city sold it to him. Bezo had a smile on his face, at least this nigga did something smart, "And I'm ah get it fixed up so nobody in the hood would never go without some where to stay or starve as long as I'm around, and this house is standing up, I promise bra." Bezo handed the papers back over then let him know that was some real shit and God was going to bless him for that. They sat around and smoked and drank until it was time to go. Bezo grabbed his things and was walking out the house. He stopped to grab the bag of money Draco gave him, as soon as he grabbed the bag, all hell broke loose and bullets started flying through the house. Somebody was out front with some heavy artillery trying to kill everybody in the house. Bezo grabbed the gun off his waist then began firing back. Everybody else started shooting so there was somebody on the floor not moving but he couldn't tell who it was, he knew it wasn't Draco because he was next to him shooting. They heard car tires screeching away and Draco ran outside, he was standing in the middle of the road firing shots at the back of the car but they kept going. Bezo ran out behind him. "Oh, shit it's Steve, he's dead!" One of the young niggas said. Draco said, "Oh shit!" then ran back into the house, Bezo followed behind him, and as soon as he saw him, he knew he was dead. The whole side of his head was gone, they could hear sirens coming from a distance. "Man, I'm out of here, Draco get your shit straight and get out too." Bezo grabbed his things and then a fan outside got in his car and pulled off. As he got down the road, he could see police flying towards the shelters, he was hoping they got out, he slowed down, when he was sure he was far enough away from the scene, he thought about Draco buying that house. He thought it was a smart move where he saw the paper but now thinking about it, that's probably the dumbest shit he could have ever done.

Chapter 20

"This is so nice!" Toya said as she looked around the candle lit room. This was their 3rd date and TJ went all the way this time. He made a reservation at a 5-star restaurant and they were seated in a private section, "You like?" He asked as he pulled her chair out for her. "Yes, I love it; it's so romantic and very thoughtful of you." "Well thank you, you know I try." He said as he set down across from her. The waiter came with the wine then took their orders. "Did I tell you; you look amazing tonight?" "Yes, you have, a hundred times," she answered him blushing. Her long hair fell over her shoulders down her back, the red dress she was wearing came all the way down to her ankles and had a slit that ran all the way up her leg and thighs showing so much skin, it made him tremble, and the cleavage that was bursting out had his heart beating uncontrollably. As he sips his wine and peeped over his glass the way she smiled and looked at him with those green eyes was absolutely the reason. He was already head over heels for her and this was only the third date. He knew this had to be the night that he scored because he had put too much time in and he didn't mind because she was something special. She wasn't like these other girls from Atlanta that he was used to. She was different and he was cool with that, this was the type of girl he could see himself really settling down with and he hasn't been thinking that way since he left his ex-girl and that was 3 years ago. "So, how it's going with you and your lil' record label?" Toya asked from her side of the table, referring to a conversation they had the other day, TJ told her he started a record label and had one artist from east Atlanta who he swore was the next to blow. "We were in the studio all night matter fact; I want you to hear something." He said, reaching in his pocket then coming back out with his iPhone. After hitting a few buttons, he set the phone on the table. A song went to play. "Ok this is nice." Toya said, winding in her chair to the beat. "For real and the hook catchy too, you might be onto something." After the song was over, he put the phone back in his pocket. "I told you, that's why I went head and started this label and made sure this lil' nigga was in the booth and not in the streets because he could make it in the game for real and go far, his name Looney." "How did you meet him?" She asked, he paused for a moment then said, "Through a friend of mine who knows him from the streets. Knowing I'm trying to chase a dream and make a dollar," he said. "Starting a label with this dude would be a good idea, so I thought what the hell arid did it." "Ok, I'm feeling that move, that was a smart one." Toya said as he leaned over and poured her another glass of wine. "Oh, you trying to get me drunk, you think that's go work. Well let me tell you, I can drink all night and still don't give my box up so you got to try something else Mr. Nice Guy." "Oh yeah, that's what you think I'm doing?" "That's exactly what I think you're doing." He only shook his head and smiled. They watched as the waitress brings the first course of their meals to them then disappeared again. "This smells good," she said as he took her hands in his then began saying grace like he did every time they were out, after he was done, they both said Amen. "So, what about you and this modeling thing?" He asked her. She had told him she was thinking about working with a modeling agency, because she was approached by someone in her building, who gave her a card. "Well I took some pictures the other day with them and now I'm waiting on them to email the photos to me. They also said they couldn't use them in their magazine unless I signed a personal appearance release. So, if I don't like them, I ain't letting them put me in shit, they promised I would love the pics though and they really want to work with me." "Oh, they have a magazine too?" "Yeah," "What's the name?" He asked. She prepared for this question already so she lied and said, "Smooth girls," "Oh, I know that magazine, that'll be nice if you're doing your thing in there. That could open a lot of other doors for you." "I know, that's why I hope I like the pictures, if not fuck that, I'm good, I'll figure something else out." Before she knew it, he was ordering another bottle of wine, and filling her glass to the top. "So how come you don't have a girlfriend or a wife, you seem all put together like you know what you want out of life and to me it seems like you're on top of your shit and you're a real cool dude for real, plus your fine as hell." She said blushing and looking at him with a glow in her big green eyes. He knew she was tipsy because she was talking loosely. "Well, I date here and there but haven't fan into anything that I thought I should take seriously. You know, sometimes your energy just doesn't match with certain people so there's nothing there. Then when you run into someone that makes you feel a certain way inside, and your energy's all over the place. Sometimes they don't feel the same way about you. So that's how it's been for me. I just been going with the flow. You're actually the only person in the last 3 years I've been on 3 dates with, I'm glad you're sticking around though." Toya wasn't saying anything, she was just looking at him from across the table. "You think I'm a nice person?" She finally asked, "Yeah you're very nice as a person, one of the nicest girls I met in a long time," "What if you are wrong and I'm this crazy psycho girl that's full of trouble and I'll break your heart." "I got a good sense for people and I think you're a very nice person and you haven't proved me wrong yet, plus I love your company and your energy is good." He said trying to pour her another cup of wine but she pushed his hand away. "That's enough for me tonight, you'll have to carry me up out of here and up to my door." "I wouldn't mind doing that," "I know you wouldn't mind Mr. Nice Guy and could you excuse me for one moment, I need to go to the ladies' room." She got up from the table and walked to the back of the restroom. She held herself together, until she got into the stall, then she broke down crying really hard. She didn't know if it was the wine or was it just reality catching up with her. All the nice things TJ was saying to her and all the good things he thought of her but only if he knew how fucked up, she was. She thought as she opened her clutch wallet and pulled out the ring Rilo bought for her. She began crying again but got herself together when she heard the toilet flush two stalls down. She put the ring back, used the restroom, dried her face as much as she could then walked over to where the sink was, she looked in the mirror then used the water to rinse her face, she fixed her make-up, then walked back out. "You miss me?" she asked as she sat back down. "Like crazy, I almost came in there and got you, you ready to go?"

He asked, she nodded her head. He waved the waiter over and paid with his credit card, leaving a hundred dollar on the table. They walked out and waited for valet to come around with his newly purchased Escalade. They got in and drove away. "You ok? You've been quiet since you came out the rest-room, I didn't say nothing to throw you off, did I?" "No, nothing at all, why would you say that." "I don't know, you just acting weird." "OH," was all she said. He waited for her to say something else but she didn't. "See that's what I'm talking about, you all quiet and turned down." "I'm just chillin' TJ, it's nothing you did or said, I just get like this some time, matter fact do you have some weed?" She asked looking at him seriously. "Do I have weed?" "Yeah, don't play crazy, TJ I smell the smoke when I got in the truck, you tried to spray air freshener but it didn't work and you got Visine right there and I really need to smoke right now." He shrugged his shoulders then reached over in the glove compartment and pulled out a blunt and a bag of granddaddy purp. "You know how to roll?" "Ya," she said, but wiggled her long fingernails, "I'll mess it up," "I got it." After putting the truck on cruise control, he controlled the wheel with his knee. He rolled the blunt while he drove and used the ashtray lighter to fire the blunt up. After puffing it a few times he handed it to her and told her to be careful because that was really exotic. "Boy I know how to smoke," she said taking a huge drag on the blunt then inhaling all the smoke she held in seconds later she was bent over in the seat coughing really hard. "I told you," he said, reaching over patting and rubbing her back until she stopped coughing, she handed him the blunt back now. "That's some good shit!" She said as she hit the button to let her seat back. Minutes later, they were parked in the lot of her building;

she was taking smaller drags from the blunt and keeping it in rotation. "I needed that, my nerves were all over the place, I needed to relax." She was laid back with her feet on the dash. Her feet were perfect; she had the French tips going, he thought as he watched her. "When I drink, that shit had me thinking and you talking all that sweet talk and telling me how nice of a person I am and our energy colliding, I can't lie, I'm feeling you but I didn't come down here for that. You're such a nice guy. My last situation was really nice until that shit went all bad. I just left a really messed up situation and I'm not looking for anything serious and I don't want to lead you on. I don't want to hold you up either. If you're looking for love and a woman that's ready to settle down, I'm not the one. I'm not ready for that. I'm just chillin' you have a cool vibe and all but it's too good to be true and maybe I'm too good to be true. So let's just keep vibing and let's stay away from that serious shit, you ok with that?" She asked, passing the blunt back to him then he took it and said, "Yeah, I'm cool with that, I'm cool with all that. Just a moment ago, I thought you was finna bug out on me and this was going to be the last night I saw you, that would have been fucked up." "How come," she asked, still laid back. "I don't know, it just would have been." "Why because you wasted all that time with me going out your way being all romantic and shit and I didn't let you get none?" She asked laughing now leaning up looking at him. "Yeah, something like that but I'm still cool with the friend thing." He put the roach in the ashtray. "So you cool, you don't want none of this?" She said with her back against the door, she had her legs wide open facing him, she watched his mouth fall open as she pulled her thong to the side to let him see her phat bald pussy. "You don't want non?" She asked again. "I didn't say that." He responded almost sounding like a child reaching over, but she slapped his hands away then pulled her thong all the way off dropping it onto the floor. She began rubbing her clit slow, moaning softly looking at him the entire time as he bit down on his lip gripping his dick through his pants, "Damn ma," he whispered as she kept playing with her clit in the circular motion, moaning even louder, she spread her lips with two fingers and let him see how wet and pink she was inside, she started playing with her clit again. Sticking her finger in and out her tight hole. "You wanna taste it?" She asked as she leaned up putting her fingers to his mouth, he took it without hesitation and began sucking on it, she moaned and wined her body while he did, she leaned back again opening her leg backup telling him to come over but stopped him short and reached for the back of his head leaning up shoving her tongue in to his mouth kissing him long and hard. He played with her clit then stuck his fingers inside of her. She grabbed his head then laid back pushing it between her thighs. He started licking and sucking on her clit driving her crazy. Her hands shot up to the roof. "Oh my god TJ. Just like that," she said through moans. "I'm about to cum," she screamed out, he kept sucking and licking sticking his fingers in and out of her, her body began shaking uncontrollably as she began to climax and squirt all in his mouth he never let up, he kept sucking and moving his fingers in and out of her. After he was done, she was slumped over in the passenger seat breathing heavily with eyes shut. "Toya," he said shaking her leg, she woke up and smiled. "Oh, I fell asleep." She said leaning up she reached down and picked up her panties and all the rest of her things. She reached over and gripped his hard dick that was poking up through his pants then gave him a kiss on the cheek. She would have kissed him on the mouth but it was still wet with her pussy juices, she got out the truck then disappeared into the building. He was still sitting up in his seat with his dick hard. Now ain't that about a bitch, he thought as he put the Escalade in drive and sped out of the parking lot.

Chapter 21

"Is this shit clean, my nigga?" Jacob asked, looking down at one of the ten bricks he just purchased from Bezo. "Why wouldn't they be, the same shit you've been buying, you can step on that shit as much as you want. I usually take a nine out when I'm fucking with these other niggas, but I know you just like me, so I don't touch yours at all." "Yeah, I know these shits do be doing flips, ain't nobody got no coke like this. It's still good even after I take what I take out. I only take out a four-way. You say you're talking out a nine," Jacob asked, looking at Bezo. "Yeah, a whole nine my nigga" Bezo said. "Dam, you putting a dent in the sack and that shit still A-1 coke." "Yeah, it's fish scale, what you expect," "Yeah, you right about that, but I got to be getting up out of here." He said then embraced Bezo. "I got a lot of business I got to handle, so be easy and be safe my nigga." "The same to you," Bezo said. After Jacob left, he finished putting the cash up then he headed out. Making over $500,000 this week just fucking with Draco and Jacob, he felt good and ask Draco if they wanted to hit the club. After losing one his lil' homies, Draco agreed and thought they should ride with each other in his new Beamer, Bezo said, "Hell yeah!" Then he told him he'd meet him after he finished handling some business. He stashed the cash then hit the mall. Afterward, Draco picked him up. "Damn my nigga you shining like a mother fucka," Bezo said to him when he got into the car. "Oh, this ain't nothing but Louis Vuitton you know it ain't nothing major," he said, feeling himself. "That's a lot of ice to my nigga. You spending a lot of cash." "Because I ain't scared to. We can't die with the shit nigga." "I'm with you when you right," Bezo said. "Plus, I got to get a new whip my nigga, I can't lie, this bitch nice." Bezo said, looking around and loving everything the 750 had to offer. They swerve through traffic with a truck full of goons behind them, "I don't go nowhere without my lil' niggas," Draco said, "Them lil' niggas ready to die for me, for real, that's why I make sure I feed them too. My nigga, you feel me?" Bezo shook his head, "Like Ross said, you can't forget about lil' bra them, that's why when you got in position without even me asking, you put them blocks in my life then let me spread my wings like a real nigga should and I've been having the time of my life ever since. I appreciate that to bra, and I love you for it." Bezo knew when Draco was high, he always got in his feelings then started telling him how much he loved him. "I love ya too my nigga and we gon have a good time tonight. Fuck with bitches, throw a lil' money and get up out that bitch safe. But what's up with the spot on 12th, y'all still holding that shit down over there? I heard it's three new spots on Brocks street now." "Yeah, that's how I'm doing it, and I'm trying to squeeze my way cross Busch but them niggas ain't budging right now but soon as nigga go to disappearing and dying then niggas ah start complying, you know how that goes sooner or later, I'll be moving 50 of them things and don't think I ain't out here trying to figure out who killed Rilo either because I am but don't know body know shit my nigga. I swear I be torturing these niggas trying to figure it out. I'm telling you that bitch Toya did it bro, she ain't popped up yet. You know I really don't know her. Because I wasn't that close in the circle. You know her better than me. But if you ask me, I think that hoe behind all that shit, she loved bra then skipped town how she some were living large. That bitch cut-throat you know how them out of town bitches do, bra probably ain't really know that bitch anyways, you know how tender dick he was." "Yeah but if that hoe ever pops back up and you see her before I do, snatch that bitch and bring her to me don't touch a hair on her head. If she had anything to do with it, I'm go torture that bitch for weeks!" Bezo said, and Draco believed him. They parked across from the club in the big parking lot where the food trucks were. Twan, the one that was driving the Tahoe behind them came up to the driver's side. Draco let down the window, "You want all us to come in, or you want me to keep at least two heads out here by the truck with choppers on standby?" "Yeah do that, keep them niggas on standby, and you and two more come in with us; that'll be good." He nodded his head, then walked off. They got out of the car and headed across the street to the VIP line. This was Bezo's first time coming out since Rilo died. When they got to the booth, Bezo ordered five bottles off top and watched as they came; it was as if the whole club was watching them. This is what fame felt like, or was it hate, or was it love he didn't know and didn't care about because he came to have a good time, and that was all. "Yo, let me try some of that molly shit, you got some?" Bezo asked Draco, "Yeah, I got some, you wanna turn up with the kid." "Yeah, I'm ah fuck with you boys tonight." He said as Draco passed the bag full of the crystals, he poured a decent amount in his hand then threw it back in his mouth. After a few minutes, he could feel the drug working as he bounced up and down inside the booth. Draco had a pile of $1 bills in front of him. Bezo reached down, grabbing two hands full and started making it rain, Draco was dancing with a stripper bitch, she was throwing her ass everywhere, he put the bottle of rose to his mouth. He watched the crowd as he took gulps from the bottle, he was sure it was going to be a problem tonight, he just wasn't sure who it was going to with, everybody was a potential enemy. Draco didn't give ah fuck, his lil' niggas was on point and ready to die for him, but who was ready to die for me? Bezo thought as he looked down at Draco, who was now tongue kissing two half-naked women in the mouth. The molly had him second-guessing everybody. All this money made him feel like a target. "You good big homie?" Twan walked over, whispering in his ear, Bezo was biting down real hard, "Yeah, I'm good why you ask?" "Naw, I just see you looking crazy. Ain't none of these niggas go buss no move in here tonight. We got these niggas scared shitless." While Twan was talking, Bezo could see across the club in the booth that was on the second floor; Yellow Man was up there surrounded by his team. He was a slim tall red nigga with long dreds and a mouth full of golds. He was one of Kilo's main customers but refused to deal with him. After Kilo died and it looked Bezo like he had a good enough plug and was doing dam good without him or his work. Bezo called the bottle girl over who he saw earlier taking the bottle up to Yellow Man's booth. "Ayee what them niggas drinking up their ma," Bezo asked her, pointing at their booth. "Oh, they been ordering Hennessy Xo and Grey Goose all night." "Well, I want you to take them ten bottles on my tab and tell them it's from me." She smiled a flirtatious smile then went back to the bar. He watches as her arid two other bottle girls with buckets of ice and bottle made their way up the stairs to the booth out one of the buckets and began filling up cups around the booth "What was that about?" Draco asked, "Really nothing, wanted to let that nigga know who was really ballin', you know that was Rilo's man." "Yeah, I know that's why I ain't robbed his bitch ass yet, I know you wouldn't like that." "Yeah, let him live, he one of the good ones." "Yeah, I know, but you see that bitch ass nigga Dirt right there?" "I see him," Bezo said, they were in the middle of the club on the floor wilding out. "That's the nigga that's pushing the work through Cross Bush, his lil' niggas bussing hammer, he took the area from Pooh Bear, I want to holla at the nigga and see if he want to do business with us, if he don't wanna get down then you know what's after that. If I could get them niggas to start scoring all their work from us, then I don't got to set shop up over there, I could continue letting him run his area and doing what he do as long as he moving our dope, and look there go Pooky bitch ass. He been watching ah nigga since we stepped in, but fuck'em, he knows he a pussy. I'll catch up with him, but enough of these bitch ass niggas, let's get back to the party." Draco said as nine of half-naked women came walking their way. Twan looked up from the entrance of the booth, trying to make sure it was straight to let them up. Bezo nodded. Twan moved out the way, letting them through. He looked up at Yellowy booth, Yellow threw him a salute then disappeared behind the crowd of bitches he had in his booth. For the next hour, they partied hard with the bitches, more drugs, and drank more liquor. Bezo was full of molly now and still thinking crazy about everybody around him. Damn, I ain't doing this shit no more, he thought as they made their exit out the club. The other two goons were standing up front soon as they came out. Draco had two bitches following beside him. As they made their way across the streets and was about to get into the car, Dun, Yellows lil' nigga came running over, "Ayee Bezo!" He said with his hands up, showing he came in peace. "What up Dun?" Bezo said, walking over, Twan not far behind him. "Yellow wanted to send his respect and asked could be catch up with you later this week to discuss business, you got the same number, right?" "Yeah, it's the same, tell him to hit me up." "Ok, will do, you boyz be safe." He said, turning around then ran back across the street. Bezo got in the car with Draco and the two stripper bitches then they pulled out the parking lot behind the other traffic. It was so much traffic that Twan and the rest of the goons got caught up in it and was several cars behind them. "Dam, were the fuck them niggas at?" Draco said, looking through the rearview mirror. As they made it further away from the club, the strippers were in the back laughing, touching and kissing each other. Bezo could see through his mirror Twan swerving through traffic and driving all on the side talk to catch up with them; it brought a smile to his face. Just as he turned to face Draco again, his heart dropped because, beside them, the window came down, then a masked man hung out with a handgun and started firing shots into the car. "Go my nigga go!" As Draco slammed his feet on the gas, and the Beamer shot forward like a rocket. "Oh shit!" Draco said as the car tried keeping up still firing shots, the strippers were in the backseat screaming now. As the car was riddled with bullets, there was a loud crash that came from behind them right as Draco hit the corner. Bezo glanced over to see the Tahoe Twan, and the rest of the goons were driving slamming against the Impala that was shooting at them. "Oh, shit that's Twan them on their ass!" Bezo screamed out as shots went to rangin' out of the back seat of the Tahoe, and the Impala tried swerving off, but Twan kept firing out the back. "Bra I'm hit!" Draco said as he slowed down then pulled his hand from his side. Bezo could see the blood, "Man I'm getting dizzy, you got to drive, we gotta make it to the hospital." "I'm hit too!" One of the strippers said from the backseat then began crying and yelling hard. Draco slammed the car in park, and Bezo hopped but, as he climbed over to the passenger seat as soon as he got in, he threw it in the drive, then slammed his feet on the gas pedal already on the phone with the medics. He told them he was 2 minutes down the road, and two people were shot inside the car. As he pulled up, he could see several nurses and stretchers. He could see Draco going in and out, "Damn them bitch niggas got me bra, they got me good, I'm hit mere then once too, if I don't make it you know where everything at." "Man don't talk like that." Bezo said as the medics snatched him and the girl out of the car and rushed them inside. Bezo asked the other stripper if she was getting out, she shook her head then he pulled off before the police could come. When they made it to the shelter, when they were just pulling up, they ran to the car. Then began asking where Draco was, "He hit bra. I dropped him off at the hospital then got out of there. You know the police coming the other bitch got hit too, did you see who it was shooting?" Bezo asked. Twan said, "No, but we'll know in the morning. We killed the whole car. Why the fuck Draco pulled out like that, knowing traffic was crazy, I had to do the most to catch up with you big homie this shit crazy. We gotta get up to the hospital man; we gotta get up there."

"Knaw bra it's gone the police all over that mother fuckah asking a million questions if them niggas dead, plus bra hot bad. They go have to lock someone up so ya'll lay low, and I'm ah send somebody up there." Bezo got the stripper a uber, then he drove to his car and rented a room on the other side of town. It was 6 o'clock a.m. when he got in the room. He was full of molly so he couldn't go to sleep. This was his second time calling the hospital, and they told him Draco was in stable condition, Draco was hit in the side and in the shoulder. The girl was hit in the leg. He was waiting for the news to see who died, who was behind the attempt on his life because, on his homie Rilo's grave, they were going to pay dearly for it.

Chapter 22

Bezo was sitting on the edge of the bed and couldn't believe what his eyes were seeing and what his ears were hearing. It was 8 am, and the news report was reporting what happened last night. "2 dead and 3 others shot, 1 in critical condition, at the Tampa general hospital. I'm standing here in front of club Legit, where the shootings took place right down the road after the club was over. Witnesses stated they saw a black Impala pulled up next to a newer model BMW at the red light then began firing shots inside the car. As the Beamer sped away, the assailants in the Impala continued chasing them and firing shots, hitting Porscha Jones and Damion George, who's still in the hospital recovering from injuries. Witnesses also state as the Impala chased the BMW, a black Tahoe came out of nowhere and crashed into the passenger side of the Impala and began firing shots from inside the vehicle striking and killing both the driver and the passenger and leaving the other passenger in the back seat in critical condition. He is now in a coma at the same hospital as Ms. Porsha Jones and Damion George, these are photos of all the suspects and victims, and if anyone have any information on the suspects in the Tahoe were asking you to contact our tip hotline which is at the bottom of the screen or get in contact with detectives, this is

Shakedris Fisher with the Fox 13 news. Thank you and God Bless." The reason Bezo was on edge is because one of the cats that was dead was Dun, the same nigga that Yellow Man sent to talk to them last night, right before they pulled off. What the fuck was this about Bezo thought as he paced the room. I cannot believe this shit. This bitch ass nigga sent a hit for what, he could only think of one reason, and that was to get him and Draco out the way so he could control the city. That's the only thing Bezo could think of as he set back down on the bed then bounced back up, unable to keep his nerves in check. This bitch nigga, I ain't playing no more games with these niggas, no more games he said out loud slamming his fist into his palm. He received a text on his phone, he took it from the table and looked at it. It was from Elisha telling him good morning. He was going to text back but decided not to; he was not in the mood to conversate. So, he set his phone back down then picked it back up, calling Twan. He told him to meet him at the hotel alone, and he hope he wasn't still driving the Tahoe, he told Bezo he wasn't. No more than 30 minutes later, there was a knock on the door. Looking through the peephole first, Bezo then opened the door, letting him in. "Man, I haven't been asleep yet," Tawn said as he came in the room then turned around to face Bezo. "Yeah, I ain't been asleep either, you been watching the news?" "No," Twan said. "Well, that bitch nigga Yellow Man was the one who sent that hit." "Yellow Man, how you know that? I thought you was cool, right?" "Yeah, me too, but you remember he sent his lil' homie Dun to come holla at me last night before we pulled out?" Bezo asked. Twan nodded his head "Well, that's the nigga who tried to kill ah nigga last night." Twan face dropped. "How you know that?" "Because he was just on the news dead with another nigga dead too, but the 3rd nigga in the back seat survived." "Damn, all that shit was on the news?" Twan asked, Bezo said, "Yep, and I'm pretty sure Yellow Man know we properly found out who was behind the hit. So, from now on, ain't nobody safe, if that nigga could cut-throat me like that and I ain't showed nothing but respect to him and, Draco ain't never even stepped down on that nigga not once. So, this is coming straight from the top, and that's me." Bezo said, staring Twan directly in his eyes to make sure he understood what he was saying. "Everybody is food if they ain't buying work from us, then they get dealt with if they don't like it, they get killed. Leave Yella up to me. I want you niggas to put the fear of God in these niggas; I don't want nobody trying shit like that again. When Draco get out the hospital, we all are going to have a sit-down, because this is the takeover, no more games, no more half-stepping, no more bull shit, get down or lay down, that's it. If ah nigga selling dope and it ain't ours, take it and make it ours. It's thug shit from here on out, you feel what I'm saying." "Oh, I feel what you saying, and you can believe it's all the way on my nigga!" "Aight, let's get up out of here, get rid of that truck too." He nodded his head; they both left the hotel and went their separate ways. Bezo called Draco's baby momma to figure out what was going on with him, she told him that the detectives came around asking questions, but Draco refused to talk, and the doctors say he would have to stay in the hospital another three days to make sure everything was good. After hanging up with her, he picked the phone up for Elisha, who was calling, "Hello stranger, haven't heard from you in almost two days." "Ain't no way, I thought we talked yesterday." "Well, you thought wrong because I text and call twice yesterday, and I didn't hear back from you, but I'm glad to hear your voice to know your alright." "Yeah, I'm good but what you up to?" Bezo asked her. "Nothing, on break, on my way back in, but when am I go be able to see you?" "Probably tonight if that's cool?" "Yeah, tonight's good." "Well, I'll see you then." She said ok then hung up. Ain't no way in hell I was gon be able to meet up with her tonight, not with all this shit going on, Bezo thought to himself as he navigated through the traffic on the interstate watching his surroundings after driving around for over an hour he made his way back to the stash house where all the cash was. Only having 20 bricks left, he needed to count up and make a call to Ricardo. Pulling the duffle bags from under the bed, then the money machine from the closet he started the count up putting all the cash in piles, there was 4.5 million dollars. He owed Ricardo 2 million, he wanted him to send him 200 bricks this time, he wondered if he would have to pay for the other 100 straight, he didn't know, he would just have to call. After separating the 2-mill from the other cash, he stashed it throughout the house in different spots. He promised himself not to do no more of that molly shit because that just wasn't him. Bezo set down on the couch, pulling out his burner phone he called Ricardo, on the second ring it was answered, "What's up?" Ricardo said through the phone. "Needed to holla at you." "Already?" he said surprisingly. "Yeah but wanted to talk to you about something else." "I'm listen," "Well, you know the last package I got was one, but I need two this time, it's kinda of moving a little fast down this way and it's going to get even faster after I move a few pieces on the chess board around." There was a pause on the line for a while, Bezo had to look at the phone to make sure he didn't hang up. "You know what you're getting yourself into if you fuck with my cash? It's not gonna be pretty, long as you know that, I'll have two sent your way within the next few days." "You ain't got nothing to worry about, and I know what I'm dealing with and once I handle this package, no more doubting me just send what I need, and I'm sending what I'm supposed to send you, no more threats, we family right?" Bezo asked, then waited for him to respond, seconds later, Ricardo said, "Right, have the cash ready tomorrow at 1 pm, somebody will stop by." Bezo said, "Ok," then hung up, getting off the couch. Bezo walked to the backroom, lifted the mattress and pulled out every gun he could carry. Ak, Ar, Mach 11, Glock 9, Glock 40, Shotgun 12 gauge and double barrel. He put them all in the trunk of his car. He pulled off, making it back to Rilo's aunt's house. He parked in the driveway next to Draco's shot up BMW. There was a car cover on it. Once he was in the house, he tried again to go to sleep but he couldn't. Leaving the house getting back in the car, Bezo drove around town until he ended up outside the shelter. He parked the car arid walked inside the house; there were over ten people sitting around the living room, there were guns everywhere. Bezo could see Twan didn't' waste no time getting the team together. "What up big homie, I was just lacing them up about what we talked about earlier, and we were getting ready to move out. I got the drop on a couple of niggas, we gone stick at least three niggas up broad daylight just to send a message. But tonight, I know a couple of nigga that ain't go be down with getting down, so we gone go head and move them niggas out the way. You dig what I'm saying?" "Yeah, I dig it but I wanna talk to you about something else." Bezo said, stepping in the kitchen, "What up?" "I wanted to add more people to your team, put them on the payroll." "Add more people?" "Yeah, that ain't nothing but ten people in there including you, I'm trying to take over the whole city and this is a big city, so we need at least 15 extra heads for the bullshit I need you pulling off. It's all gone, pay off, everything you take, we split it, me you and Draco, but everybody else is on payroll. If they don't like it, they don't have to be a part of this because in the end, everybody go get rich and from now on, me and Draco should have security at all times at least two hittahs pure person, but give me a few days to get myself situated, but I want you to put two people up there with Draco asap at all time, I got to get more guns too so give me a few days and I'm ah load you niggas up bra. Within a month I want at least one trap in every hood, I know this sound like some movie shit but, I got enough money, dope and killas to make it happen, so let's get it." Bezo said. Then they walked back out to where everybody was at, Bezo shook all their hands one by one then left the house. Placing another call to Ricardo he requested a shipment of guns, Ricardo told him they'll be there when the work arrived. It was after 3 pm when Bezo finally laid down and was able to sleep. He had to get back up at 8 because he had a date with Elisha.

"Now look at him," Elisha said, pointing at the window of the house she just came out. Her son Coby was peeping out the blinds crying because she was leaving. "He acts like that every time I try going somewhere without him." "Ain't nothing wrong with that, he loves his momma." Bezo said as he drove away. Elisha had the entire car lit up with whatever perfume she was wearing. "If you don't mind me asking, what fragrance is that?" She smiled then said, "Oh this is Channel #9, my favorite. I got like 3 of the #'s, do you like it?" "Yeah, it smells good, I should of wore some cologne, but it ain't really my thing. But I see I gotta step my game up if I'm going to be hanging out with you and plus, I see you came out looking all good a shit. You did all this for me right?" "I guess," she said, looking in the mirror, applying lipstick to her lips. Bezo was watching her out the corner of his eyes. The skin-tight blue jeans she had on were breathtaking. The cream color 6-inch heels she had on were red bottoms, she also had on a silk red and white blouse and a simple gold chain with diamond earrings, she was dressed up for tonight. He didn't even know where they were going, but he didn't let her know. "I was thinking we grab something to eat from Red Lobster or Olive Garden then catch a movie, what you think about that?" "Whatever's cool with me, I'm just glad to be going out." "So, what do we call this, our first date?" Bezo asked and watched as she thought about it then turned to face him. "We can call it that." They got to Olive Garden, both ordered shrimp pasta and wine. "I think these breadsticks are so good." "Yeah, there good but them biscuits at Red Lobster, them shits melt in your mouth, I remember when I was doing time, this dude use to make biscuits and call them Red Lobster biscuits, he use to sale them for a dollar a piece, rumor was he made over $10,000 just off them biscuits in a two-year span." "I didn't' know you went to prison." Elisha said. "Yeah, I went when I was 18, I did a few years, don't ever wanna go back there." "I heard it's bad, I'm never going to jail, that's why I work and go home, do you got a job?" "Yeah," he said. "Where?" She asked, looking at him with a suspicious look. "It's a 24-7 job," "And what's that?" "Staying alive." She laughed then said, "Boy you crazy but ok, you just need to be careful," she said, pointing the fork at him. "Be careful for what?" "You know what," "No I don't, tell me," "Well, you pulled over

$20,000 out on me the first time we met and gave me 2gs like it was nothing and your phone never stops ranging at all, I know what that means I know what you do." "And what's that?" She looked around then leaned in closer to him, "You sale drugs, I believe but it could be something else I don't know but just be careful is all saying I hope you don't think I'm being nosey or you think you can't trust me and now your gonna stop answering my calls. But don't panic, remember I'm from where you from so I do have some type of street smarts." "Oh, I ain't trippin', because your wrong anyways." "I bet I am but this pasta is so good," she said, switching the subject, "You want some more wine before we go?" He asked her, she nodded her head and he poured her more. After covering the tab, they left the restaurant. Arriving at the theater 15 minutes later, buying a big box of popcorn and two large cokes they headed inside and found their seats in the back. "I haven't been to the movies in a long time, could you believe it?" "Me either," "It's been about five years for me," Elisha said. "Well, that's good because the last time I've been to see a movie I had to be at least 16 years old." "Boy quit lying!" Elish said, playfully slapping his arm. "I promise." "So you mean I'm the only girl you bring to the movie since you were 16?" "To be honest, me and my homeboy come to the movie to watch one of the fast and furious, I forgot which one, so your the first female I've ever took to the movies," "Aww, for real?" She said, snuggling tight against him as the movie came on. He reached over and put his arms around her. She looked up at him with a smirk on her face. They stayed that way the whole entire time. Only when she had to use the restroom, he took his arms from around her. He couldn't lie; he was having a good time. This was the first time he was completely relaxed ever since Rilo died. His mind was going a 100 miles per hour, not trusting nobody, even second-guessing his best friends Draco and Jacob. Having all that money made you think that way, at least that's what he thought, but Elisha's company was so cool he wasn't thinking about none of the bullshit right now. All the bullshit that was going on in his life was at ease when he was with Elisha. He didn't even know he was staring at her that hard until she looked over and ask, "What?" "Nothing just admiring your beauty," "You think I'm beautiful?" "Yep," he said, while she was still looking up at him, he leaned down pausing for half a second then placed a light kiss on her lips. She had her eyes closed, so he reached for her chin lifting it up then kissed her harder, she gave in then began kissing him back, they kissed each other for the next 20 minutes until the movie was over and everybody began leaving out, "Dang, I wanted to see what happened, you distracted me." Bezo said, smiling, "I distracted you, boy you the one started it," "I guess so," he said, wrapping his arms around her waist, pulling her close as they walked out the theater to the car. "I had a good time I can't lie, I needed that," "Me too," he said as they pulled off, they were silent for about 10 minutes. "You ready to go home?" "Are you ready for me to go home?" She responded, "Hell naw," "Ok than," she said, wrapping her fingers in his. They did little talking as he made his way through traffic back to the hotel he was staying in. "You bringing me to a room?" she asked, with a confused look on her face as they pulled up and parked, "I told you, I be staying in and out of hotels, don't worry, it's nice I always get the best." He came around and opened her door, then they walked inside, up to the elevator and rode to the 4th floor. They got into the room and she excused herself to go to the restroom. After a minute, he heard the shower running; he took the time to roll a blunt and call a few people back whose calls he missed. Twan told him he had something for him and found out where Yella stayed; he promised he would be getting back with him in the morning. Calling Draco's baby mother, she told him Draco was up but there were two young boys outside his room, they say you sent them, he told her he did. He talked to Draco for a while, letting him know what was going on why he was laid up. After their short conversation, he hung up and waited for Elisha to come out the shower. A few moments later, she did, walking in the room wrapped only in a towel. She came into the room and sat on the bed looking at him. He leaned in to kiss her but she held her hand out to stop him, "Look Bryson if we do this, I'm not trying to be just a one night stand, I'm grown enough to know what I want, I'm not saying we just got to up and be in a relationship but I don't just wanna give you a piece of me then I don't hear from you again. Because this city is not that big for you to hide from me, I'll hunt your ass down Bryson and it ain't go be nice." He liked the way she said his name, matter fact, she was the only one that called him Bryson, "Nobody ain't trying to up and leave you, why would I want to split from someone as sexy and cool as you," he said, leaning in kissing her softly on the lips, as she gave in and began kissing him back. She laid back on the bed as he got on top of her and began kissing her harder then began sucking and licking her neck, going further down he opened the towel and began sucking her hard nipples on her huge perfect breasts. She moaned as he kissed her all on her stomach and in between her thighs, he spread her lips with his fingers then began sucking on her clit. Placing his fingers inside of her, she was so tight and smelled so fresh. As he rose up and removed all his clothes, she leaned up to see him standing there naked; he had nine inches of hard dick standing up pointed directly at her. She mouthed, "Oh my gosh!" As she grabbed it with both hands and began squeezing it and pulling on it, "Dang, it's so huge!" She said, looking up at him then put it in her mouth and began sucking on it slowly, she kissed the head and licked it, she got him hot and ready and leaned back on the bed opening her legs, he leaned back down sucked on her for another 5 minutes then pushed himself inside her tight opening. Her eyes were wide as he opened her up then began moving in and out in slow motion, speeding up as she moaned and screamed his name, "This feels so good Bryson, oh my gosh, so good," he started moving faster and harder. "Damn this pussy good!" He said as he slid out and told her to turn around, she did and clapped her phat ass at him. He squeezed both cheeks as he slid back inside of her, he went all the way then came all the way out then started slamming up against her she was screaming at the top of her lungs, as she came, he turned her back over then threw her legs on his shoulders and push them up to her head and began diving inside of her for five straight minutes no break, making her cum another three times before he pulled out and came all over her pussy and stomach making animal noises as he climaxed hard. After he released all his juices, he fell back on the bed. Breathing hard, she laid there for a minute then got up, walking back to the restroom; she got back in the shower. She then came back in the room and laid in his arms; she leaned in, giving him a kiss on the cheeks then they both closed their eyes and then fell asleep.

Chapter 23

"These pictures look like porn," Toya said as she added the photographer Larry went through his computer looking at them. "That's what the critics say too, but if you're not scared to take a gamble and show the world and the industry all the beauty you have to bring to them. When I tell you you're going to be huge, I'm not just talking. Either I've photographed everyone from, Buffie, Maliyah, Keishia Dior, just to name a few and for this to be your first session, you killed it and your way more beautiful than they are, and I think these photos are perfect, so I'm not believing the bullshit your telling me you just have to take a deep breath relax and let's do the damn thing girl, let's show the world Queen." He said, leaning back in the chair and looking at her. She was still studying the pictures on the screen, "I can't lie, I am a bad bitch." "That's what I'm talking about, talk your shit girl." "Look at this picture," she said tapping the screen making it bigger, "My camel toe is so huge, can you edit it and make it smaller?" he looked at her as if she was crazy, "Why would I do that, this is what's selling they see this, everybody and their managers are going to be trying to get in contact with you, these bastards in the industry are so horny they would pay you tons of money just to show up to a private event, there throwing with hopes of screwing you later that night, but don't do it because word would get around then your brand would go down as well. I'm taking you, and Ryan is feeling this photo's as well for real and he's the boss and he usually gets what he wants." "Oh, he does?" Toya said, with a grin on her face, "Yes he does," Larry said again as he closed the laptop and told her he had to be getting to his next meeting. She told him she promised she would think about it hard tonight and have a real answer for them in the morning. She got back inside the Mercedes and headed back home. A week after leaving Terry with the blue balls, she promised to give him some pussy, and he's been begging for it for a week straight. He also wanted her to meet Looney and come by the studio to chill. She ain't seen Double R since he took her to get lunch. After she made it to the condo, she took a shower and threw on a pair of jean shorts and a tank top and waited for Terry to come up. She was tired of masturbating so she needed some real dick. She heard a knock on the door and went to open it; this was his first time ever coming up to her condo. "Damn what's up sexy, let me get a hug," he said, leaning in wrapping his arms around her squeezing her ass. He tried kissing her, she moved her head then pulled away from him, "Slow down horny man, let's sit down and chill for a moment." "Ok let's sit down," he said, looking around. "You have a nice spot, it's all hooked up. I like it," "You do?" "Yeah, I like it," he said, looking around, "I do too, the place came furnished, I was too lazy to go shopping for furniture." She came back with drinks in her hand and gave him one. "Did you bring some weed like I told you to?" "Yeah I got it." He said digging in his pocket, pulling out a big bag full of loud, she didn't have her long nails at the time so she rolled the blunt with her legs open with one tucked under her, and she watched as he kept looking between them. "So, when we go hit the studio TJ?" She said as she put her last finish touches to the blunt, dried it then lit it, taking a small drag from it she looked at it then pass it to him, "Shit we gon be able to hit it tonight, we basically live in there right now, I got another artist, Young Cat, real nice with the trap rap. I'm telling you this shit go be huge." "You should let me be in the video's if you think it's gone be that huge, I got cars too, you can use them if you want to or you go be using Phantoms and shit." "Oh knaw, we can use the Benz and your BMW truck, I was going to ask you about that anyways," he said as he downed the rest of the Vodka he had in his glass. She could tell he was losing control and wanted some pussy bad, let me stop playing with this boy, she thought as she finished the blunt then put it out in the ashtray. She got up, then pressed play on the stereo and began dancing in front of him, "Oh yeah like that," he said as she pushed him back on the sofa and began giving him a lap dance. She could feel his hard dick pressed up against her ass through his pants. She stood up shaking her ass in his face, unbuttoning her shorts she bent over and pulled them down, just enough to tease him. Every time he tried touching her, she slapped his hands out of the way. She didn't have on a bra under the tank top and her nipples were rock hard, she let her shorts fall down only having on the thong and tank top now, she pulled one of her breasts outputting it up to his lips, he began sucking on it like a puppy. After he finished with that one, she gave him the other one; she was dripping inside of her panties and was ready as she took off the top then laid back on the couch. She told him to get naked, and he did. His dick wasn't big but it was ok, she thought as he leaned down on top of her kissing her, then sliding her panties off, sucking on her pussy, giving her the same good head that put her to sleep the other night in the truck. After getting her even wetter and hot he slid inside, she took a deep breath, grabbing his ass cheeks, pulling him deeper inside of her. "Damn this pussy tight!" he said, looking down at her moving slow kissing her, looking down in her eyes, she looked up at him and told him to fuck her hard, she didn't want to make love she wanted to fuck. He said I got you then began fucking her faster and harder, she started screaming as he slammed inside her fast and hard, "Yes just like that, I'm finna cum, I'm cumming!" She screamed as her body locked up and began shaking, he kept pounding on her ass, he fell his self-cumming, she was so sexy and had all her shit together, he didn't mind having a baby with her, that would for sure lock her in the thought as he began cumming and shooting a heavy load inside her. He knew she could feel him filling her up. He was laying on top of her breathing hard as she rubbed his back and sucked on his ear, she was squeezing her pussy muscles around his dick, she did it until he was back rock hard and moving in and out of her again, she told him to let her get on top. He set back on the couch she leaned down then began sucking his dick fast and hard, as she squeezed his balls, she knew her head and pussy was great the way he was moving and moaning, she knew she was in full control as she kissed and licked him, she looked up at his face, his eyes were wide and his mouth was open, she got up and straddled him, easing his dick inside her pussy she began bouncing up and down lifting all the way to the tip of his head and slamming down going in circular motions giving him all she had as she came hard and felt him skirting inside her again. "Damn that was good," she said as she looked down in his eyes and kissed him on the lips. They took a shower and had sex again then got dressed, he put back on the same clothes, she got dressed in a Fendi dress and heels then they both headed out. Stopping by a place called Freddie's to get a bite to eat, then they drove to the studio that was on the other side of town, "You know how to sing or rap?" He asked her, "No boy, I don't know how to sing or rap, I just know how to look pretty." "And I bet that come easy for you?" "I don't know, what do you think?" "What do I think?" He asked, pointing at himself. "Yep," "Well, I think you the baddest bitch in the world, no disrespect, but I ain't trying to ease up on you, you got the whole package, phat ass, big breast, pretty skin, any face, green eyes, money, green energy, pretty smile, man you to live and die for on God plus you got good pussy and head." She slapped him on the chest playfully. "Shut up; I shouldn't of gave you any now you go want some all the time." "Hell, yeah if that's good with you. I'm trying to hit that shit every day, well at least eat it." "Nope that is not fine with me, that was a one-time thing." She said as they pulled into a parking garage and got out of the car. "This is where the magic happens," he said as they walked inside of the building. There was a woman sitting at the front desk, "Hello Mr. Jackson," she said as they walked in, "What up Tasha, what's going on with cha?" "Nothing, been an easy day, Looney and the crew are back in studio 3." He said ok, then they walked to the back, passing different soundproof rooms. When they got to Room 3, she could see inside. There was a white man controlling all the buttons and gauges on the board and there was a chubby guy in the booth rapping. He had on a lot of jewelry and added a blunt in his mouth. "That's Looney," he said as they walked in, he introduced her to the other two people that were in the room. After he finished recording, he came out arid embraced TJ and ask who Toya was. "Oh, this is a close friend of mine," he said, letting that linger. "Toya this is Looney and Looney this is Toya," he said, she held her hand out he took it and shook it, "Man run that shit from the top let them hear it," the white guy hit a few buttons and the music came blasting out the speakers. "When them real niggas love ya and the streets waiting for ya and them bitch niggas hattin' they can't do nothing for ya, I just put on my chain and turn on my strap, they say the streets been off well bitch I turn on the trap, I turn on the trap, I turn on the trap, I turn on the trap, yeah bitch I turn on the trap." Looney rapped through the speakers and it was sick, Toya said that he was really good. TJ looked at her like what I told you. After the song went off everybody began clapping and patting him on the back. "Man this shit go be big," TJ said, "Yeah, we almost got the whole mixtape done, three more songs, we got the single out I'm pretty sure we should be getting a lot of calls and you know, I got Gucci and Ti on speed dial," the white guy said. Toya wondered who he was; he had to be somebody to have Gucci and Ti phone numbers. Damn she thought as she set on the couch and listened to more songs. "My friend here has a couple of cars we can use too in the videos," TJ said to Looney as the music went off, "I keep telling you I got my own cars and you got cars too nigga, we ain't got to be on all that fake shit, but you the boss my nigga whatever you fills the best for us." "Ok cool then," TJ said, rubbing his hands together. "You ain't from around here ha Shawty," Looney said, looking over a tourist," She said, looking around the room, getting a laugh. "Knaw nothing like that, it's just if you was from around here I would have been ran into you, you know because know everybody and no disrespect to you or my man TJ here, you fine as hell and a nigga would have been had you on the scene, so I figured your new around here and my man TJ was the first too ran into you and believe me when I tell you, he's a good guy he's a good guy," "Thank you my nigga for being so polite," TJ said, holding his glance on Looney, long enough that he turned his head. For the next few hours, they recorded and re-recorded songs, got high and drunk, she didn't know how many drugs Looney was on but that nigga was feeling his self as he rapped and danced in the booth. She couldn't lie; she was filling his D-Boy swag. Around 12 am, her and TJ got up out of there, got something to eat and went back to her place. He bent her over the couch and hit her from the back fast and hard, cumming inside her again, she told him he had to go, she wasn't down with him spending the night. She took a shower and ate most of the food she had then laid down on the couch, damn today was crazy, she thought as she closed her eyes and fell asleep.

Chapter 24

Toya's phone woke her up. She turned over on the couch, reaching for it. "Good morning Larry," she said, stretching out on the couch yawning. "Good morning, it's 1o' clock in the evening, I've called you over five times, it must have been a long night for you last night." "Something like that," she said as she set up on the couch. "Well, I wanted to know what we were doing with these photos because we're coming up on a deadline and you promised you would have an answer for me this morning and it's 1o' clock now. So, what's up?" Wiping the cold out of her eyes, she yawned again then said she'll do it. "But I'm not signing no contracts, I'm not trying to have nobody controlling my life or my future but I will sign a check when the cash goes to rolling in." "I know that's right girl, well I'm going to contact Ryan and let him know it's a go and I'm pretty sure he's going to be contacting you, so get up and brush your teeth and wash your pretty little face, talk to you later." She giggled then said bye before she hung up. She hated hangovers. After taking two aspirins, she stripped out of her dress and got underneath the warm water, letting it run all over her head and down her back. To wake her up and relaxing her muscles. Damn he fucks the hell out of me last night, because I kicked his ass out, she thought as she washed her hair. I can't give him no more for a while because she could tell that nigga was the lovey dove type. But she already had told him she wasn't looking for that. That's why she put her pussy on lockdown, no more coochie for Terry, she said to herself. Getting out the shower drying herself off, she walked in the room laying back in her queen size bed with only the towel wrapped around her. She began looking through her phone, trying to find something to do today. There was a lot to do in Atlanta, she needed to go shopping. She needed more summer clothes, she didn't have her Facebook, Instagram or snapchat anymore and she missed it, but not enough to get herself killed. She knew people was out there looking for her, hopefully not the police for Rilo, her cousin and ex-boyfriends murder. Hopefully, they thought she got kidnap or some shit like that. She didn't even have a criminal record, she also wondered what was his best friend Bezo thinking. There was no way in hell he could ever think she could have done something like that. But she didn't know and she sure as hell wasn't tryna run into him anymore. Rilo told her stories about him, she knew he was dangerous and a vicious killah, but she wasn't worried, because she wasn't going back to Tampa never in a lifetime, but them niggas probably was bumbs by now being that Rilo's dead or maybe Bezo knew were all Rilo's shit was, he trusted him like that. I couldn't trust no one like that, no one was loyal, life showed me that, Toya thought as she reminded everyone, she's been through all the people that hurt her before she started hurting people herself, even the one person she thought loved her the most crossed her. She was molested numerous times by her stepfather who raised her since she was 5 years old until she was 13. When she had enough, she told her mother who kicked her out the house and sent her to live with her grandparents, who had a house full of kids, where it was even worse. She grew up having to suck her older cousin dick every night. Her other cousins use to steal her clothes and shoes and didn't like her because all the other boys liked her because she was so pretty. She was forced to grow up in the streets, depending only on herself. By the time she was 18 years old, she was already stripping, selling pussy, stealing, robbing and everything else that was under the sun. She knew all the good things and the bad things life had to give. So no, she didn't trust nobody and wouldn't give nobody the ups on her heart never ever, that shit hurts too much, she shook the thoughts out of her head and got back out the bed to get dressed. She put her hair in a tight ponytail and threw on one of her favorite sundresses and flip flops. She threw some cash and her phone in her Gucci bag then headed outside with her big Gucci frames over her face, she hit the alarm on the BMW then got inside. After a few minutes of driving, she pulled up to the mall then found somewhere to park. Putting her glasses back over her face, because she knew her beauty brought all types of attention but she was used to all the stares she got from passing people, sometimes it scared the shit out of her. How people just stared at her but for the most part, she was used to it and she knew her ass was jiggling like crazy under the dress she had on because she didn't have on any panties, but the old guy that was watching her when she passed creeped her the hell out. She walked from store to store, bought a few things to add to her collection, she stopped inside of Tiffany's to try on a few pieces, when someone came up behind her, "I thought that was you," a familiar voice said from behind her. She turned around to see Ryan staring down at her looking good like always. He was dressed in a crisp white shirt, Robin jeans and designer sneakers, like always his jewelry was sparkling. She could see two younger guys standing outside the door; she knew they belonged to him. "Where did you come from?" she asked, "From the store across from here," she looked over at the sign out front, it said Gucci. "I should've known you would have been coming out of Gucci, with your expensive lifestyle." "Is it something wrong with that?" "Hell, knaw I'm trying to get like that, I'm tryna ball too so don't think I'm hatin'," Toya said with a laugh, he smiled then asked what she was looking at. "Oh, I'm just window shopping, but I like these earrings and this necklace," she said, leaning down, looking in the mirror. "There's a bracelet that goes with this set too, mam, can I see this?" she said, pointing down at the gold and diamond-studded Tiffany bracelet, she put it on her wrist. "What you think?" she said, turning around facing him, striking a pose, "I think you look wonderful." "Not me boy, I'm talking about the jewelry." "It's nice but remember, it's not the ice that make you, you make the ice, but it's really nice, do you like it?" "Yeah, I love it," she said, turning around and taking it back off. After everything was off, he came over then told the lady to bag all of it up. She did as she was told, after ranging everything up the total came up to $8,300 even, he pulled out a credit card and swiped it. She set there looking as if stunned but she wasn't surprised, niggas like Double R love to flaunt their cash. He picked up the bag and gave it to her, "A gift from me to you, you know for gracing the cover of my magazine." "Are you serious, your putting me on the cover?" "Why wouldn't I?" He said as they walked out the store and the two young men followed them. "That's so nice, this is gonna be so crazy, is the magazine gon be big?" "You can bet your ass it's gonna be big in Atlanta, that's not a problem but I want to be respected in the industries as a man with a real agency, real models and a real magazine, the urban world is huge and it's a lot of people getting real money. I want some of it, I ain't lying and I'm branching everybody that's riding with me right along to the top when I get there, you can bet your pretty little ass on that." "When is the magazine coming out?" "Probably in another month or 2." "Their probably gonna think ima whore the way I'm acting in those pictures." "Let them think what they wanna think as long as you're getting paid, don't nothing else matter, watch how many doors open for you, and don't forget I told you either." "I promise you I won't." They were back outside and the Maybach she saw him driving previously showed up out of nowhere, one of the young guys open the back door and he got inside, before the back door closed, he looked back at her, "If its ok, I would love to take you out for dinner tonight, somewhere nice so we could discuss business." "What time?" She asked, "Let's say around 9," "If you don't mind I want you to wear that jewelry I bought for you, you make the jewelry look nice," he said, winking his eye then closing the door, as soon as he did, the car zoomed off. "Damn," she said to herself, that nigga is a certified boss. I wonder if he would act like TJ did if she gave him some pussy, she laughed at the thought then shook it out of her head. She caused TJ to let him know she wasn't going to be able to meet up with him tonight because she had a dinner meeting with another agent from a modeling company. He sounded disappointed but said ok, and he'll call tomorrow.

She put the finishing touches to her make-up in the mirror, her natural hair fell to her shoulders and she decided to wear it back in a tied ponytail. She liked how all the features her face had to give stood out. She placed all the jewelry he purchased on, plus a few rings of her own. She slid into the Tom Ford dress she purchased when she was in Florida then added her perfume to her finishing touch. Admiring herself in the mirror, red was her favorite color, but the way the creme colored dress complimented her eyes and yellow skin she knew he was going to be amazed when he saw her. She put on her heels, then set on the couch and waited for him to call. It was 9:05 when he told her he was downstairs. She was going to make him wait another 5 minutes but thought otherwise then headed downstairs on the elevator. He stepped out of the Range Rover when she came outside. "Oh my God, you have to be the most beautiful woman in the world tonight," he said as she spun around, showing off her dress. "You think?" She said as he stood back, nodding his head. "Where have you been all my life?" He asked as he took her hand, then led her to the passenger side of the SUV and let her in, closing the door behind her. "Ok, let's get out of here," he said as he got in and they pulled off. "I talk to Larry today; he says he wants to have another session with you," "Oh yeah," Toya said smiling, "Yeah but something different, maybe at the beach, something with a tropic background he was thinking white sand, different color trees and plants, animals and shit like that I never seen him so excited. I'm just glad to have him on my team, that's a blessing." "So, he's really that good." "Yep, he's great, real experienced, that's why I'm glad he's so into this project, I have him in control of the magazine, I think he could help me in a great way. When you're in this type of business, you can't be scared to take chances, you know what I mean, I know you were real uncomfortable with the pics but remember you gotta eat, you got to feed your house and your house is whatever you make it, your family, your crew, you, or whoever's under your roof. Home starts here," he pointed at his heart. "And there's no place like home, so you go to follow your heart no matter the situation, your heart never leads you wrong and I know what you're thinking, well my heart have led me wrong before, maybe in a relationship or with some guy you thought was perfect and you opened your heart to him and he broke it, but you live and learn, that's early in life and your heart learn so fast, it learns the first time so it won't have to go through the same pain again. But if you're an ignorant person and you're not listening to your heart, than that's on you. So again, follow your heart because it doesn't lead you wrong, I can promise." "So, what's your heart telling you about me and this magazine thing your pushing?" "My hearts telling me I'm onto something and my heart led me into that store that day when I first met you." "Is that right," "My love for grapes led me right in that store to get a fresh batch and there you were, looking stunning as ever." "Ryan, you have a way with words and speeches. I have to keep an eye on you," "Why's that?" "Just for my good, it's nothing major," she said as they pulled upfront of a building, got out and drove the SUV away. "This place is called Le Petit Bo finger." "Le Petit Bo fingers?" "Yes, it's originally from Paris, they have great food and the atmosphere nice." He made reservations, so they were led directly to their tables and wine was brought to them. He poured both of them glasses. "So, tell me, are you staying here for a while or are you in and out?" "Well, if I find something out here that'll keep me here, I won't mind staying but until then, my options are open," she said as she took a sip of the wine looking at him over the glass. "Sometimes you look all over the place and don't even realize all you need has been sitting in front of you the whole entire time." "Oh, is that right?" "Some people never know because they never look in the right direction." She smiled and left that in the air. "I looked you up like you told me to." "Oh, you did and what did you see?" "Oh, I saw a lot of good things about you, you have a lot of good things going on." "Oh, I do?" He said as he took a bite out of the food that was on his plate, "Plus I seen a lot of bad things too, should that scare me?" "Not if you like bad boys, plus you can't believe everything you see and hear, it could deceive you, I have a past but without my past I wouldn't be here. You know what I'm saying, I got respect from the streets and I don't hide that I'm a street dude, you need money and influence to survive in this game. I'm telling you to cut your throat to get to the top. So, if I got to be a monster to get to the top, well, a monster I am. You know what I'm saying." "Yeah, I know what you saying, I know exactly what you saying, I'm trying to turn myself into a monster. I'm tired of being ran over, I promise these streets is real, when I get them M's I'm go be a real boss watch and see, that's what I came to Atlanta for. Everybody that doubted me and told me I can't be shit I'm go show they ass, just watch." "It's hard to believe someone ever told your sexy ass you wouldn't be shit." "You wouldn't believe what I've been through in life," "It don't look like too much, I don't see a scrape or bruise on your pretty ass," "There all in here," she said, pointing at her heart with a serious look on her face. "I know what you mean. I have a lot of bruises on and in my heart as well, you have to just keep pushing and keep up, you know what I mean, what doesn't kill you only makes you stronger. I had to be at least 24 when I really knew what that meant. I lost my mother, the woman I love with all of me and I know she loved me with all she had, flaws and all, when she got cancer and she was dying, I didn't know what I was going to do. I didn't know what I was going to do in this world without her. But she died and I was left alone and I was doing time, all my friends left me, my girlfriend left me, that was the first time I felt alone and I broke, I cried for 3-days straight after she died but I realized that I had to be strong, stronger than I ever been in my life because If I wasn't, I would become a victim to the game and I refuse to be, so I was strong, in the mind, body and soul; so I live by that what don't kill you makes you stronger, we go through things all that pain and hurt, we don't get weaker we get stronger and smarter." "When it gets hard, we get smart, I forget where I get that from, but it's true." "When they go low, we go high, that's what Michelle Obama say." "And that's right, I can fill that." "You know somebody can learn a lot talking to you, your full of knowledge and good energy, do you ever think about giving speeches?" "Yeah, I thought about it but speeches can be too hard sometimes, they ain't meant for everybody, only my kind." "And what kind is that?" "I don't know, maybe the elite." "Oh, I like that, do you think I'm one of the elite?" "I think you are too, no lie, I've been peeping your swag and you got a lot going on, I wouldn't mind spending more time with you know, do this another time, this was real fun, I love talking to someone that'll listen than talk back you know what I mean, it's like you know the game I play or you play the I game I play." "Maybe I do," she said as they got up from the table then headed back outside. The Range Rover came and they got in and pulled away. "So, what do you say we do this again?" he asked as they pulled up to her building. "Yeah sure I don't mind, just let me know," "I will," he said as she got out and waved bye then closed the door. He waited till she walked into the building, then he pulled off. Wow, that was amazing, she thought as she rode the elevator up to her condo. She stripped out her clothes, took a hot shower then laid down daydreaming until she fell asleep.

Chapter 25

"That's the nigga mama house right there." "How you know?" "Because the bitch told me she drove a white Infinity truck and that he kept his cars at her house and there goes the Infinity and that's the HellCat right there, I only seen him in it one time but that's the same Challenger I promise, she say he stop by here every night and gets a plate of food, the bitch promise me this." "And who is the bitch?" "She use to be his fiancé but they split after he had a baby from her cousin and the bitch is a stripper now." "Oh yeah?" "Hell yeah." "Well, after this, remind me to kill that bitch too," Bezo said to Twan as they staked out Yellow Man's mother's house. She lived in a nice neighborhood right behind Wal-Mart. "So, what we gon do?" "I'm gonna knock on the door to see if she would answer, if she does and I walk in I want you to drive away. Watch from a distance and call me when you see that nigga pull up." Twan shrugged his shoulders but said ok. Stopping in front of the house, Bezo had on a dread wig and a beard on his face just in case there were cameras or nosey neighbors. He got out and walked right up to the front door and ranged the doorbell. After a few seconds, someone from the inside yelled out, "Who is it?" He said it was Malcom from down the street. "Malcom?" "Yes Mam, I know your

Yellow Mans mother and the police got him pulled over, down the road and they've just pulled a whole bunch of drugs out of his car, they got him in the back of the police car now, he told me to come down here and get you." With that said she unlocked the door and peeped out, without hesitation, Bezo kicked the door in, causing it to knock her back. Before she could get out a scream, he came in grabbing her by the neck and squeezed it tight as he shut the door back with his foot then locked it. He pushed her hard back on the couch, pulling out his gun. "If you scream or make any sound, I'm going to kill you. Now, is there anybody else in this house?" She shook her head still staring directly at him, "If you want money I got money, I got a lot of it, please don't hurt me," "Where's the money, let's go, let's go get it, any tricks you're dead, no second chances." He glanced over on the kitchen table, there was a plate wrapped in aluminum foil, so he knew Yella was on the way. He followed her to the backroom, "It's up there, I see my son put all his money in there, just take it and leave, don't kill me, I don't have no involvement with the streets. I told my son I didn't want nothing to do with what he had going on and I meant it." Bezo grabbed the chair that was under the desk in the corner of the room, there was a poster of Tupac and other rap artists on the wall and high school football trophies all over the room, so he knew this was Yeguas room. "Well, climb up there and get it for me and remember any trick I'm gonna kill you right here and right now." She did what he said and climb on the chair, lifting the door on the attic. Pulling a black duffle bag down and handing it to him, he set in on the bed. "Anything else up there?" She said "Yes," then pulled down two more. She got back down and stared at him, "You got what you wanted, now you can leave, please go!" He told her to sit down, then he took the zip ties out his pocket trapping her hands behind her and then tying her legs to the chair then he reached in his other pocket pulling out duct tape, putting it over her mouth, he got the bags and carried them to the front, then waited on Twan to call. It was another hour before his phone began to ring. Twan told him Yella was coming down the street. Bezo stayed where he was and that was pressed against the wall over in the corner next to the big screen television and the couch. He heard as a key went into the lock and the door opened, Yellaman came in followed by two kids, a little girl and a boy, "Grandma!" they both screamed running to the back of the house. Bezo wasted no time stepping out with the suppressed 9mm squeezing the trigger several times, hitting Yellaman in his face and head. The impact sent him crashing against the glass table, at the same time, he could hear the kids screaming in the back room. He guessed they ran across their grandmother; the little girl came running back upfront the same time as Twan came bursting through the front door. Bezo scooped the little girl up and covered her mouth, he told Twan to carry the bags to her mouth, telling Twan to carry the bags to the car and wait for him. Once he got to the back, he saw that the little boy was trying to untie his granny. He set the girl down then told the boy to not move, he looked at the woman then told her, "When I leave, they could free you. But, you shouldn't let them go upfront because it' isn't pretty. And like you said, your son chose the streets and this time he fucked with the wrong person so he deserved what he got. He said then ran out the house. He jumped in the car, and Twan sped away.

"How much you got over there?" Bezo asked Twan as soon as he saw that he was finishing counting the pile of money that was in front of him. "This is $553,000 even," he said whistling. Bezo nodded then put another stack of cash in the money machine watching as it flickered through. After it beeped, he hit the blunt then passed it to Twan, grabbing the money stacking it on the top of the money that was in front of him. "This is another $450,000, so it's a million in all, this had to be the cash he had put up for a rainy day," "I ain't never seen this much cash," Twan said. "What's the most you've seen or had?" Bezo asked. "Shit maybe $10,000 that's all." "Well, this is how we go split this, 4 for me, 4 for Draco and the rest for you." "The rest for me?" he said, looking shocked. "Yeah, that $203,000 all yours, don't spend it in one spot." "Man quit playing!" "I'm serious," he said as he slid the cash towards Twan. "And that's how it's gonna be from now on my nigga, your under new management just make sure everyone else get a piece of the cake but everybody can't eat like we eat, so they get there's on the back end, that's why we need to get these traps open in every hood."

Two days ago, the 200 bricks got there from California and over 30 guns and rifles with ammunition. Bezo was ready to do whatever he had to do to get full control of the city. Still telling Twan to hold up on the security he requested but made sure someone was with Draco the whole time he was at his baby mother's house. Draco wanted to get the hell out of there but Bezo told him not until he got healthier. His arm was in a sling and he had a shit bag. The doctor said he would need it for the next two months, he promised Draco he wasn't missing nothing; he was only getting richer as he set back on his ass. Jacob was supposed to meet up with him in the a.m.; he was already done with the 10 and needed 20 more. He didn't know what the hell

Jacob was up to over in his city but it looked to him he was doing damn good. Probably was doing the same shit they were doing over there. After splitting up with Twan, it was after 1o' clock in the morning and he decided to call Elisha. She didn't answer; he set the phone back in his lap. As soon as he did it started ranging, "Hello," he said, "You just called me?" "Yeah, what you doing?" "I'm a sleep boy, it's 1 in the morning," she said with a giggle. "I'm saying you don't wanna get up and come stay the rest of the night with me?" "No Bryson, I'm not finna be your late-night fling, I already told you that, I haven't heard from you all day, but you got the nerves to call me at 1 in the morning asking me to spend the night with you." "I be busy most of the times, but I promise I'll make time for you, I didn't want to have sex, I just wanted to go to sleep with you next to me tonight that's all." "Well, not tonight, so I'll talk to you tomorrow, lhopefully, so be safe out there Bryson." He said he would then disconnect. He ended up at the stash house where he put the cash up then fell asleep on the couch, promising himself he would get a new car or two tomorrow and somewhere decent to stay.

Chapter 26

"If you want them bulletproof, that's going to be an extra 50 grand a piece," the dealer said to Bezo as they looked at the Mercedes S550 and the Audi A8, "So, If I give you the extra 50 grand a piece to bulletproof both of the whips, how much is it going to be total?" "The best I can do is 280 and that's killing me, but if you got cash, what the hell with it, they can go." "Yeah, I can do 280, matter fact I got it in the car with me right now." "You got that much cash on you right now?" "Yeah, it isn't a problem, is it?" Bezo asked. "No not at all. Let's go ahead and get the cash and start on the paperwork now." After grabbing the bag of cash from the car, Bezo followed the dealer inside the building. After they set at the desk, he watched as he counted the money and gathered it together then disappeared in the back. After they came back out, they finished the paperwork, he promised Bezo he would have the cars shipped out to the shop and have them delivered wherever he wanted them within the next two weeks. After leaving the dealer, it was still early, not even 1o' clock yet; Bezo made his way through town until he got to downtown Tampa. He scheduled a meeting earlier this morning for 2o' clock; he was interested in leasing one of the condos in the building. He met the agent down the stairs and they rode the elevator up to the 6th floor, exiting the elevator, they entered the condo and he was shown around. This place was huge. Bezo thought as they looked around, it looked right over downtown, "You say you were asking $2,500 a month." "Yes that's the price, is that a problem at all?" He asked with a serious look. "No, not at all," Bezo had one of his associates fix up paperwork showing that he was a business owner and fake bank stubs showing where the cash would be coming from. So there would be no problem with him leasing this place. He asked when was the earliest he could move in. "The earliest is the 1st of the month and that's next week. Is that good enough for you, Mr. Davis?" "Yeah, that's right on time," Bezo said, rubbing his hands together. They made their way back downstairs. Promising Elisha he would meet her on her break, he navigated his way across town until he got to her. She was standing out front, waiting for him, looking beautiful as always. Every time she smiled that big beautiful smile it relaxed him. "You might not answer every time I call but your always on time," she said as she got in the car, leaning over kissing him on the cheek as he pulled off. "I want to run something by you," Bezo said, looking over at her. "What would that be?" "Well, I was thinking that maybe you're tired of being clustered up at your cousin's house and you want your own space; you and your son. I wanted to help you find somewhere decent for y'all," "That's really nice of you Bryson, but I don't need for you to fill as if you need to do that for me, I have a great job, and I've been saving money and looking for somewhere to stay as we speak," she said showing him her phone, she was on Zillow.com looking at different apartment complexes in the area. "Oh, I see you on your shit, but I want to help you out. Like you said, you didn't want no one in and out of your life, I was planning on sticking around and a little bit of help wouldn't hurt at all, you know what I'm saying, and I think you should be looking for a house, something with a back yard where your son could play and run, you know how hyper he is plus, I never met someone that's always declining help from a real good friend," he said, reaching out over touching her face lightly. "So you plan on sticking around?" "Yeah, why not?" "So that means you like me?" "Yeah, I like you a lot, your the whole package just enough for me, I can't have no other man claiming you not in this city." "So what you trying to say Bezo?" "I just said it, but wait don't get ahead of yourself, It's just a lot of stuff you don't know about me yet." "Like what?" "Well, how can I say it?" "Say what?" she said, adjusting herself in her seat so she was facing him directly. "Let's just say as of now, I'm a big name in this city and I want you to know what you're getting yourself into before you jump in headfirst." "What do you mean you're a big name, Bryson?" "What do you think I mean, your not crazy Elisha I believe you know what's going on, so it's entirely your decision to get involved with me, but I'm not really a fairy tale kind of dude, I am though if you live in the same type of world I live in." "I don't get it, you tell me you wanna help me out and you're sticking around but you also tell me you have some type of big deal around here and I need to be cautioned before I jump in head first dealing with you." "Yep," Bezo said, shaking his head, "Well, what type of big deal are you around here?" "A really big deal, I'm making a few adjustments right now just to make things a little better for me, and your one of the adjustments. Hopefully, you'll consider dealing with me because I do need a Queen on the throne with me." "Are you serious?" "I'm dead ass serious.

You can quit your job now, we don't even got to go back there; that's how serious I am, so know I'm not playing." "I don't believe this," she said, looking back out the window. "What isn't there to believe?" "You Bryson, you that's what, you're a real funny dude." "Funny in a good or a bad way?" "I don't know right now," she said as they pulled up at her job. They sat in the parking lot for a while until she looked up then looked at him, "What?" he said, looking at her confused, "I don't know why you bring me back here, didn't you say I could quit my job today?" "Yeah I told you that. You wanna get your car and I follow you home?" "No boy," she said, playfully slapping him on the arm. "I'm not gonna quit my job, I have to get back in there before I lose my job, but you're crazy," "What type of crazy?" he said, looking at her ass as she got out, "Crazy," she said, before closing the door, walking back into her work. Walking like she was on the runway, knowing he was watching her. "Damn," he said, gripping his dick through his pants, that's wifey, I got to his-wife that shit ASAP, he thought as he pulled off. Stopping by the stash house, Bezo grabbed 50 bricks to bring across town with him. He told Twan to meet him at the shelter. When he got there, he pulled up behind the house. He brings 5 bricks in the house with him. He had them in a black backpack slung across his shoulder. There were three other people in the house Bezo never saw, he nodded his head at them and continued down the hall to the back room. "Who them niggas?" he asked Twan as he came in the room, "All of them my cousins, they from Nuccio, real hittahs, slang that ion real good. Don't mind doing dirty work. I added them to the payroll." "Ok that's good, but this for you." He said as he pull the blocks out the bag, "And all of it's clean, I want 27 a piece, they go for 30, so you can sale them whole or break them down, it don't matter, just make sure I get mine," he said, looking at him with a serious look. "I got you big bra," "Aight, I'm finna get up out of here, you went over there and holla at Draco yet?" "Yeah, I just came from taking him some weed and drank, that nigga already be high as hell on the perks the doctor done prescribed him," "Yeah, I got to make it over there, I know he feel some type of way I ain't pulled up yet." "Not really, he ain't said shit about it." He gave Twan dap then headed out, making it to Rilo's aunt's house, where he stashed the work but brought 20 of them with him. He pulled up to the hotel where Jacob was at. Knocking on the door, it opens seconds later. Jacob was standing there looking fully alive or high, whatever it was, it had him hyper and happy. "My man!" He said, rubbing his palms together, "What up my nigga?" "Oh nothing much, just getting to it and it's been lovely I promised, It's even sweeter than I thought it would be. I'm just glad you're in this position, I don't know what I'll do without you!" "Is that right," Bezo said as he pulled out the blocks, stacking them onto the table. Jacob went to the safe then bring the cashback, "It's all there my nigga, all hundreds." "Just the way I like it," Bezo said, placing the cash in the bag. "You want something to drink; I needed to talk to you anyways?" "I'm good on the drink but what's up, I'm listening," he said as he sat down in one of the chairs around the table. Knowing Jacob and the shit that ran through his head, he wanted to talk to him about something crazy. "I was thinking about expanding my brand, you know, get my hands in different shit, I don't plan on being in the game that much longer anymore you know, I think when I turn 40, I'm going to retire somewhere nice, me and my family," he said, with a smile on his face, "I know your connected and I was trying to see if you could check the #'s out on the boy for me, you know that shit's getting big on my side of the bridge. I ran into the shit like a week ago when I took it from ah nigga and it did some pretty good #, but I don't have a connect on that shit and I would love to get my hands on that, that would be nice if you can help me with that." "I don't know but I'll make sure I check on it, I heard it's a lot of money in that game right there, Rilo never wanted to fuck with that shit," "I know but Rilo is not here anymore it's your time, you got to get it while it's good you know what I mean." "Yeah I know what you mean and I'm go try to handle that for you, I probably got to make a trip and have a face to face to do that my nigga," "Do it and watch how we shoot above the clouds and leave the game rich." "I got you," Bezo said as he stood up, indicating he was ready to go. Jacob showed him the door. He promised he'd keep in touch, giving him a dap, Bezo made his way back outside then got back in the car. Herion, he thought to himself, he didn't even know what a brick of that shit even cost, that was never his lane, never even consider fuckin with that shit, but he would make sure he checked on it for Jacob. Bezo made sure he dropped everything off and made sure the car was clean, he knew that the police probably was watching Draco's baby mother's house and he didn't want to get in no shit over there with the law.

Placing a call to Twan, he made sure he sent two extra heads over there to be on the watch while he was in the neighborhood, he wasn't trusting shit. He needed to trade this rental in anyways; he had the same one for too long as is. Draco was laid back on the couch, flipping through the TV when he came in. His son was sitting on the floor next to him, there were four people sitting outside the front door; 2

were already there and the other 2 Twan sent right before he got there. "Oh shit, what up nigga?" Draco said, straining to lean up, his son got up and ran over to him, "Uncle Bezo!" He said as he held his hands up, Bezo picked him up, then spun him around in the air, then put him back down. Kiesha came out the backroom to see what the commotion was, she was doing her hair, half of her head was done, "Oh, that ain't nobody but Bezo ass," Kiesha said, turning back around walking In the room. "You say that like Bezo ain't nobody girl," he could hear the other women saying to her as they disappeared. "What up nigga," Bezo said as he leaned down to embrace Draco before he set down next to him on the couch, "Man I'm all fucked up," he said, lifting up his shirt showing him the bag that was on his stomach, "That bitch nigga got me good," "Not good enough, you still here," "Yeah thanks to Twan crazy drivng ass, I see you put homie in position too." "Yeah, I told you shit was finna change, matter fact you the one to convinced me to change shit up, no worries though my nigga, you still my right hand man," he said, wrapping his arm around his neck scruffing his head, they both laughed. "I handle the one situation with our homebody Yelia too," Bezo said in a whisper. "I know, I seen the news," he whispered back. "He lucky your nice ass got him because the moma and the kids would of got it too, that's my word, bitch ass nigga try creeping ah nigga like that after ah nigga did nothing but show love, that's crazy bra, when I get right, it's a few niggas I got to pay a visit just because my nigga." "Oh yeah?" "Hell yeah!" He said, looking at him with that crazy face he always have when he wants you to know he's serious. "Can't play with none of these niggas no more, real shit." "That's what I'm trying to tell you, you really ain't got to put that type of work in no more, you bigger than that but hey," Bezo put his hands in the air, "But if you wanna be a goon all your days go right ahead or you could build your throne and you could eat like a fat cat and get rich my nigga, you feeling me this shit finna get crazy." "I know my nigga, I hear ya, I hear ya," he said, shaking his head. "That what I'm talking about nigga, I knew you had something somewhere in that big ass head of yours to think with," "Whatever nigga, your shit ain't that small either," Draco said as they both laughed. "I need you to pick my car up for me too; they finished getting it back right for me. I'm glad I had insurance but that shit just went up through the roof." "Oh yeah," "Hell yeah, Gieco they be scheming like hell," "Man you need to get that shit bulletproofed, I just ordered some whips up and I'm getting them bulletproofed now." "Oh you doing it like that, hell ya!" "Shit that was a close call, plus shit been crazy since you've been out of commission. I built up a team and put them on payroll, we got over ten trap houses now," "Damn, I only been down almost two weeks!" "Yeah, Twan move like that, I like that nigga, he one of us, when you see ah nigga bred like that don't never be scared to give that nigga a position and let him eat because somebody else would." "I know nigga, why you think I put him under my wing." "Smart move. That's why I love ya nigga, but everything good." "Yeah, I'm just ready to move around, this bitch killing me all she wants is money, she acts like that shit grows on trees then every time my phone rang I can't even answer it without this bitch over my shoulder; she acting like we together or something. If it wasn't for little man, right, I would of been somewhere else, real shit my nigga." "I hear ya, I know how hard Kiesha ass go." "Man that bitch be trippin!" "Just chill out my nigga." "Oh, I'm chillin, soon as I get a lil' better I'm out of here." "Kiesha go kill yo ass." "Yeah, right." "Hey, you remember Mr. Gilmore from the hood?" "Yeah, I remember Gilmore, he been dead for a minute now." "Yeah, that's him, you remember his granddaughter Elisha?" "Yeah, I remember Elisha your girlfriend when we was younger, she had the phat ass." "Hell yeah my nigga, you remember her, how about I ran into her and we getting along real good." "Elisha, I thought she moved away?" "She did but she came back and we been kicking it ever since, I'm thinking about locking her in, she got a son too, the lil' nigga about three years old, he cool as hell!" "Damn my nigga, I ain't never heard you talking like that." "I know, this shit real, I'm just adjusting a few things in my life right now and I can't be running around like I been doing, that shit for the birds you feel me?" "Hell yeah I feel ya, I got to find something to lock in because Kiesha ah make me kill her ass dead no bullshit my nigga that bitch is a trip bra." "Both of y'all be trippin but I'm finna get up out of here so just B-E-Z and let's get this money, I got some shit put up for you too, aight." Draco said aight, they embraced, then Bezo left the house. Two of his hittah follow him to the car and watch him until he is gone. Bezo looked at his watch, it was a G-Shock, Damn it's time to step up my ice game, he thought to himself as he made his way to Elisha.

Chapter 27

"What up lil' man?" Bezo said, looking down at Elisha's son, he was standing next to her in the doorway. He was there to pick her up. "My cousin wanted to meet you," Elisha said, opening the door wider to let him in. Coby was bouncing up and down next to him as he walked inside the house. "Give me some money, give me some money," "Boy move go sit yo ass down somewhere, always begging, I don't know where you get that shit from," Elisha said, grabbing him by the arm taking him somewhere in the backroom, coming back by herself. "It was past his bedtime anyways," she said as she came up to him, wrapping her arms around him and kissing him gently on the lips, "What was that for?" Bezo said, smiling down at her. "I thought you said I was your girlfriend?" "I said that?" "Yeah, basically you told me you were planning on sticking around, are you having second thoughts?" "Oh no," he said, leaning down, kissing her back on the lips. "That's what I thought," she said as she planted another kiss on his lips. "Is that Bezo?" A female voice said from behind them, he turned around and instantly knew who it was. "Oh Crystal, what's up?" He said excitedly, turning to hug her, "Oh my god, girl you've been talkin about Bezo the whole entire time, you talkin about some damn Bryson, boy how you been doing?" She said playfully, pushing him in the chest, he laughed, "You know me I just been chillin, livin the same shit new day, what's it been about three years, right?" "Yeah, it's been three years, I heard about Rilo, I'm so so sorry." "Yeah shit's all fucked up but life goes on and we gotta keep pushing." "I know that's right," she said with her head down a little bit. He could see Elisha looking at them like how the hell do yall know each other. "Oh, Chrystal used to talk to my main man Rilo, they had a really bad break up. I haven't seen her since. I thought she moved away or something like that." "Who is he talking about, the boy Rillo and you use to always talk about?" "Yep, the one that slept with my best friend behind my back, you could at least tell me Bezo, me and you were way too cool for that." "Hell I didn't know shit, this my first time hearing about that, I thought you just up and left, I didn't know what happened." "Boy quit lying because they dated for a while after we broke up." "Hey what you wanted me to do, everybody got to live there own lives, I never did nothing to you, we still cool, right?" He said, holding his hand out, she hesitated for a few seconds but took it. "I guess we still cool, gurl you better watch this nigga," she said, looking at Elisha, "Come on don't do that Chrystal," "Knaw I'm just playing, he one of the good ones." "He better because I ain't got time for no bullshit," "I know that's right." Crystal said as she disappeared in the kitchen then came back with 3 glasses and a 5th of Grey Goose. "You drink?" Chrystal said, looking at Bezo, "Yeah I do a little drinking, I don't like to get drunk though, that shit gives me bad hangovers." "Yeah, I don't like to get drunk either, I just get a lil' bit tipsy so one glass is enough for me," she said back. "So this what you do, sit around her drink Vodka and remenis?" "Yeah, we remenis about all you dog ass niggas, girl I'm so sick of there azz, I might get me a bitch, a lil' big booty hoe." "Gurl quit playing!" Elisha said, laughing. "No for real I ain't playing and Imah be the nigga in the relationship, switch my swag and all." "Naw, I can't see you being no stud," Bezo said. "Watch and see, Imah have me a lil' girlfriend in ah lil' bit," "Not me girl, I want a real dick, that plastic shit ain't go do nothing for you." "Oh I'm not taking the plastic, I'm giving the plastic a big 12 inch one too, I ain't playing," that got all of them laughing hard. "You got some weed Bezo, please say yeah?" Chrystal said, looking at him with puppy eyes. "I might got a little in the car, let me go check," he said, getting up walking out the door. "Girl you don't know who that is?" Chrystal said, scooting over closer to her. "Yeah I know Bryson, I grew up with him," "I don't think you know Bezo, you might know Bryson but Bezo is a made nigga. Rumors is he run the city now and he got all the money and bricks, plus his lil' niggas around here robbing and killing everybody. Another rumor is he was the one suppost of robbed and killed Rilo but me knowing him the way I do, I'm a 100% sure he didn't kill him, they were like brothers, way to cool with each other, but gurl that nigga got money a whole bunch of it and he's a real dude if he fuck with you then he fucks with you, no flim flim in between. But believe when I tell you he's a real dangerous dude, don't let that smooth talk and the layed back relaxed persona shit fool you, he'll bussah nigga ass real quick, but I think yall a perfect match, so consider him a come up." Chrystal said, sliding back over to her side; hearing him coming back in the house. "Don't believe everything she told you about me, I ain't that bad of a guy," he said as he set down setting the weed and blunts on the table. “Boy ain’t nobody talking about you,” “I was gone about 4 minutes, I bet you told her my whole life story.” Chrystal and Elisha looked at each other than burst out laughing. “What’s funny?” Bezo asked, looking at both of them. “You boy, that’s what’s funny, can I roll the weed?” Chrystal asked, already ripping the wrapper off the blunt. “What kind of loud is this?” She said, looking at the weed through the bag. “Oh its girl scout, straight pressure, if you don’t be careful that shit go knock you on ur ass.” “Oh I know about this shit you ain’t gotta tell me twice.” She got up from the couch and walked over to the kitchen, opening the drawer pulling something out then she came back sitting back down on the couch. “Whoever invented this was the smartest person in the world,” she said, holding up the weed grinder in her hand. “Oh yeah, I need to get me one of them.” “You can have this one, I’ve got another one somewhere, I just got to find it is new too.” She broke down the weed then began rolling the blunt. “I didn’t know you smoked,” Bezo said, turning around looking over at Elisha, “I don’t, never did, that shit just isn’t for me, I barely drink, but this is ok,” she said holding up her cup. “She’s so boring. I am in this bitch high by myself watching reruns of Martin laughing my ass off.” She lit the blunt with a pink Bic lighter she brought out with her from the kitchen. He watched as she puffed it like a bro then watched as she blew the smoke out her nose and her mouth at the same time. “Yeah, this some gas,” she said as she puffed it two more times then passed it to him. He hit it then tried to pass it to Elisha, “No, I’m good, I ain’t hitting that shit.” “Come on Elisha, it’s friday we ain’t got shit to do we might as well get high,” they all laughed. “Boy that ain’t even how he says it, referring to Chris Tucker in the classic movie Friday. She snatched the blunt out his hand then slowly put the blunt to her mouth. They watched her as she took a huge pull on the blunt then swallowed the smoke instead of inhaling it. Her eyes instantly got big and she began coughing really hard, Chrystal was balled up in on the other side of the couch laughing really hard as Bezo was trying to see was she ok, patting and rubbing her back. After an eternity of coughing, she came back around. When she looked up her eyes were red and watery, "You alright baby girl?" Bezo asked, "Hell no boy, I'm high as hell, I ain't doing that shit no more, hell knaw," Chrystal was still laughing, she was laughing so hard she was crying. "Girl you is so silly," Elisha said, now with a smile on her face. He knew she was filling the effect of the Girl Scout. Bezo and Chrystal finished the blunt and the bottle of Goose, they were watching Friday and all of them were laughing really hard. "I swear I had to be done watch this movie a thousand times, no lie," Chrystal said, clapping her hands together with every word she said, "I heard they suppose to be making the Last Friday." "Yeah, I heard that too!" "But they been saying that for some years now." "I can't wait til it come out, Imah be one of the first one to be in the theatre watching that bitch real shit." Chrystal said, still clapping her hands. "Why you clapping your hands every time you talk?" Elisha asked Chrystal, looking at her with Chinese eyes and a big smile, "You wanna order a pizza?" Chrystal said, ignoring what Elisha said, she grabbed her phone already having the Domino's app, she asked them what they wanted, then placed the order. Rolling another blunt, Chrystal and Bezo smoked it by themselves, trying to convince Elisha to hit again, she refused to. The pizza got there a little while after with hot wings and cinnamon breadsticks. Coby had to smell the food because he came up front rubbing his eyes, telling his mama he was hungry. "You hungry baby," she said, holding her hands out, he came over and got in her lap, she hugged and kissed him. All of them devoured the food together. Bezo and Chrystal smoked another one, after they finished, he told Elisha he had to be going. She asked where he was going, "Got to handle some business if that's okay," he said, leaning down to kiss her, she grabbed him by the arm pulling him back down. She kissed him harder, he leaned up, patting her son on the head, "Alright lil' man, B-E-z," he said then he gave Chrystal a hug after that. He headed for the door turning around, winking at Elisha who was blushing. Getting back to the car, Bezo drove off. Still thinking about Elisha, he had a smirk on his face, she just might be the one, he thought, yeah, she just might be the one.

Chapter 28

5 Days Later

Bezo backed up in front of the shelter; leaving the car running, he got out and went inside. Like always, the house was full of lil' niggas everywhere and guns; he ain't never feel safe here, anything could happen, the police could kick in the door, or this bitch could be shot up again at any time. "What up Bezo?" One of the lil' niggas said from the couch, "What up TY?" Bezo said as he walked to the back room where Twan told him he was at. When he walked in, Twan had cash all over the bed, counting it with one of the machines he gave him. "What up big homie?" "You know same shit, just a different day," "I feel you on that, but I already got this cash for you, a couple niggas bought them shits whole, I sold them for 30 a piece making me a quick 15 g's, this right here is 135 for you," he said, pointing at a pile of money that was on the bed. Bezo grabbed the cash, putting it in the Nike bag he had in his hand. "I'll have another 5 for you probably later today, just give me a little bit. But other than that, what's been going on?" "Oh really nothing, it's like since the nigga Yelia came up dead everybody been fallin in line. I put my lil' nigga Gino them on 24th and they doing #'s, I should have all that cash for you in 2 days. I got the nigga T-Raw wanting to spend 250 but he want 10 of them, I told him the best I can do is 28 because I got to make something, he told me he'll let me know, if he don't fuck with it then I'll just kidnapp, rob and kill his bitch ass." Bezo knew he meant it and didn't doubt him at all. "Yeah, fuck em', more money for us either way." He left the house and got back in the car then pulled off. Draco was moving around now and said he feels a lil better but Bezo still felt like he was moving too fast. Pulling up to Rilo's auntie house, Draco was already backed into the driveway in his BMW, painted black now, Bezo pulled up next to him, letting down his window giving him a dap.

"Damn my nigga, how you feelin?" Bezo said. "You know, just glad to be out of Kiesha house, that bitch crazy she ain't stop calling yet." "I thought you was go get the BMW bullet-proofed?" "Man I know you ain't talkin, I know that rental car ain't proofed up." "Well Imah be proofed up in a few days" "Well, when you get your shit than I'll get mine." "Yeah I bet you will." "Nigga you already think you bulletproof." "I can't think that nigga, I almost got took out the game, in this same car," they both started laughing. "So you ready to get back getting this money?" "Hell yeah nigga, I'm ready, that's what I wanted to holler at you about, but I was onto something else. Since I was lying down in that house watching that TV man you can learn some shit. I was watching gangland and the Vice Lord nigga was on that shit out there in Chicago and them niggas were getting a lot of money fuckin with that heroin shit and I know a few niggas around that fuck with that shit, we could saw this bitch up for real my nigga, you with the soft, me with the boy, we control the city, we could even fuck with that loud niggas ain't go have no choice but to fuck with us." Damn

Bezo was thinking to himself while Draco kept talking. Jacob just asked him about seeing if he could get that boy down to him, now Draco was asking for it too. He needs to fly out there to LA and have a real talk with Ricardo. He would have the money for him in another week or so, but he definitely needed to have that talk. "You see what I mean my nigga, nigga's ain't trying to flood the city like we trying to bra, that boy go get us this cash if you ain't fuckin with it bra do what you can to get it to me. I got my own cash, you ain't gotta front me nothing, I'm ready to pay whatever." Bezo told him to give him until next week and he'll let him know what it was. "I'm helping Elisha and her son get somewhere to live right now. I told her I wasn't trying to move in right now. I'm not ready for all of that shit right now, I got this lil' condo I supposed to be moving in a lil bit got tired of living in and out of these hotels you know what I mean." "Yeah I do, that's why I've got my own shit, can't let none of them hoes nowhere I stay. That bitch Kiesha would have been tired to move out the projects into my shit." "Yeah, on the real, I been meaning to hollah at you about that, you need to move your gurl and your son out that shit for real, you don't know what type of shit could happen, shit might look sweet right now but believe me, niggas go clapp back ina few, that's why we got to be locked and loaded each and every way." "Yeah, that's right my nigga." "I know, that's why I'm getting my shit together now other than what else been going on." "The nigga Twan been getting it in." "I know, I talked to him earlier today." "You see the progess?" "Yeah I see it, and there's a whole bunch of lil' niggas around I don't know either." "Yeah we had to bump up security, shit we need more people when this heroin shit starts flowing." "You think so?" "Hell yeah!"

Bezo said, after a few more minutes Draco pulled off. Bezo stashed the money in the house, not wanting to ride around with all that cash. He came back out leaving to meet Elisha. She wanted to show him the house she found; she texted him the address. He put it in the GPS, then he headed that way. It took him over 45 minutes to get to Valrico, then another 5 minutes to the house that Elisha was looking at. It was a nice neighborhood; all the houses looked new, no more than ten years old. "About time you got here," she said as he walked up to the front door where she was standing with the landlord. "Drove fast as I could, the traffics bad out this way." "I thought it was better today," Elisha said as she led him through the house, showing him the bed and bathrooms. "The kitchens huge too, I love the island that's in here and look at the backyard, there's a pool and a clubhouse were Coby and the friends he meet could play and there also a Jacuzzi, she says they just installed, I think it's wonderful, what do you think." "If you like it then I love it and if it's what you want, let's get it." "Your serious?" She asked, looking up at him as if he was gonna smile then tell her he was just playing but he didn't, he just asked to talk to the landlord. "How much are you asking?" Bezo said, looking down at her, "Oh, $1200 a month, plus a $1,000 deposit." "How much do you want to sell the house for?" He asked, still looking down at her, "You want to buy the house?" "Yes, if that's not a problem." "Well I'll be damn," she said, sucking her teeth. "My father left this house behind for me and my brother, so we just rented it out. I never considered selling it, but if you give me a moment to contact my brother, I will, he's in Omaha on vacation right now," she said, then walked away to get on the phone. "What happened?" Elisha said as she walked up and wrapped her arms around his waist, leaning up, she gave him a kiss on the lips. “She's trying to see how much her brother wants for the house.” “She already told me $1200 a month.” “I know but I'm trying to buy it.” “Your trying to buy it?” she said, looking confused, “Yeah, ain't no use paying $1200 a month, then when it's all said and done, you still don't own.” The landlord came back over,” “Hey man, the best we could do is 200 thousand cash money,” Bezo moved his head from side to side, contemplating what she said. “200 is to steep, I can do 150 and it's all cash, I could have it for you today.” “150 all cash?” “Yes,” he said. “Well it's a deal,” she said, shooting her hand but for him to shake and he did it. Elisha stood back looking stunned, never seeing nobody even talk about that much cash and this nigga just came right in here and bought the whole goddamn house. He walked over, placing a kiss on her forehead. “I guess you need to start looking for furniture,” he said, looking around the house. “Damn Bryson, you just bought a whole house; this is crazy!” “And it's yours,” he said back to her, “It's mine?” She said, looking up at him, pointing at herself. “You heard what I said,” “Why would you do something like that.” “I don't know, just thank God, I know you've been partying every night and day asking God for a blessing, now you finally get one, you start asking where it comes from plus I think you deserve it,” he said, placing another kiss on her lips. “Wow man, this is way crazy. I need to sit down,” she found a chair then set down. She began fanning her face as if she was about to pass out, she started crying, “Oh my God, than you lord, you are so good,” “Yeah Gods good,” the lady said as she came back up to team. “Wanted to let you know we could get the paperwork started whenever you guys were up for it.” “Yalll can handle that, just call when you ready for the cash." Bezo said, kissing and hugging Elisha again rather than shaking the landlord's hand. He got in the car and drove off. Another day of blowing cash, he thought to himself and it felt good to do something good for such a good person. The condo would be ready in a few days. He drove straight for the airport, he had to catch the next flight to LA He had a meeting with Ricardo. "Right this way," one of the guards said as Bezo got out of the car and walked up the steps, walking the same way through the house as they did the last time. Ricardo was walking around the pool with a cigar in his mouth; a huge muscled Rottweiler followed behind him every step he took. Bezo walked over to him, watching the dog the whole time, "My good friend Bezo, what brings you way to LA, good news I hope," Ricardo said, extending his hand, Bezo shook it. "Always good news with me, I was getting ready to hit you up to run what we did back again, I have 4 mill that I owe you plus I was thinking of something else I would like to put my hand in, it's beginning to be a booming business in my area and I didn't want to miss out on the fun." Bezo said while staring up at Ricardo, "Follow me this way," Ricardo said as they began walking until they got to a mini-bar on the other side of the pool where he poured them both drinks. "You want a cigar?" he asked as he handed him the drink and they sat down. "Knaw I'm good, I don't even know how to smoke them thangs." "You know they start tasting better the richer you get, they get more expensive too, you know what I'm saying," he said, blowing out a cloud of smoke from the cuban cigar. "You should start smoking now because every rich man eventually start loving them and my man, your rich and your gonna get even richer than you ever thought you could." Ricardo handed Bezo a cigar and lit it for him; he watched as he puffed the cigar like a pro. "Good, right," Bezo nodded his head. Ricardo set the matches on the table then told Bezo to let him hear what he had to say. Bezo got straight to it. "I was trying to get my hand into the heroin business." "That's a dangerous business you are talking about getting in." "I love dangerous." "My type of man, I love dangerous too, being dangerous got me all of this and much more to come, money and violence is the only way you can get someone's full attention and I hand out both of them like it's nothing. I live real fast and real dangerous, so dangerous is fun arid I love it too my man." he said, taking another sip of the whiskey then puffed his cigar. The boys gonna run you 65 thousand a pop and from now on I charge you only 18 a pop for the girl, just to show you that I appreciate the good business you brang to me." "Expect it to keep coming as well, I don't plan on slowing down either. I believe I can take over more than just my city, the way my mind thinks I can probably control the whole entire drug flow in Florida." "And that's the way you got to think, if you're not thinking that way then you're not thinking big at all. I will send you 25 bricks of boy down there to see how you like it. Remember, this is a dangerous business and your opening up a different door and you better be ready for what's on the other side." "Don't worry I'm always ready."

Chapter 29

"I need yall over there shaking ass, you throwing money homie and you just keep standing right there next to him looking pretty, just keep looking directly into the camera," the director said as he instructed everybody what to do, this was Looney's video shoot for his single, "Turn on the trap," it's been getting heavy spins in the club and even radio play. Toya stood next to Looney as he danced and rapped, his shirt was off, he had a body full of tattoos and bruises, you can tell he's been out there in the field for real, Toya thought as she watched him. She wondered was all that jewelry he was wearing real or was it really his. After the director yelled out cut, they all took a break. "What you think?" Looney asked as they walked over to a clapping Terry. "Yo my nigga you looked like a real star. This shit is finna be so easy." "Who you telling." Looney said, givng him dapp. Toya and Terry was spending a lot of time arid she knew he was really feeling her even after she told him numerous of times she wasn't looking for nothing serious, but they were fucking on a regular now. "You love the camera too?" "Yeah, that shit was fun I can't lie, I wish I knew how to rap, I'll be shooting a video every week." "When these niggas see you in this video, everybody go be checking for your fine ass," he said, squeezing her azz, as she smiled, everybody knew they were fucking and he wasn't trying to hide it. "So what else you got planned for tonight?" He asked as they sat down on the couch. "I'm going straight home after this, I'm so hungry and tired." "I'm coming over tonight, right?" "No, not tonight, I'm tired and all you trying to do is hump on ah bitch all night." "Come on, don't do me like that," he said. "How you want me to do you, I'm telling you the truth," she giggled. "Oh, you think that's funny don't you." "No I'm not laughing at you." "Then what you giggling about?" "Ok, yo funny ass Terry." "What's funny about me?" "I don't know, everything." "Oh, you done made me out to be some type of funny nigga?" "Yep, just like Kevin Hart," they both laughed. "Oh that's cold," "So, when are we going outside to shoot with the cars, that's gonna be fun?" "I don't know why I paid the director to figure all that shit out, I like the way he works. I need to book him for the other videos as well. Give me a second," he said as he got up off the couch and headed where the director was. Looney came over and sat on the couch next to Toya, "My fat ass needs to exercise, I'm tired as hell," he said as he threw a pill in his mouth and gulped a bottle of water. "Boy yo ass be tired because you be on all them drugs." "Oh no, that was just a aspirin, I'm starting to get a headache because I'm not on enough of drugs right now." "Yeah right," she said, digging in her purse, "You wanna hit this?" she said, pulling out an already rolled blunt. "Hell yeah, please put some fire to that quick too," he said, impatiently. "Ok boy, just chill," she said as she lit the blunt, hit it a few times and passed it to him. "What the hell you do, I never got the chance to ask you, I see them phat ass cars you rollin in and that 63, damn there a 100 racks and that BMW nice too." "You know I try but the culture is way different in the A, everybody's riding Bentleys, Maybachs and Rolls Royces and shit." "Yeah but most of that shit be leased or rented, so don't get caught up in that lifestyle because nigga be flawsen when you see me riding like that, that means I really got it," he said, passing the blunt back to her. "Shit all them cars you got I done counted 4 of them already, you got the old school Chevy on them big rims, the Mercedes, the truck and SUV, you riding too shit," "Yeah you could say that, I ain't complaining but I see you and my man TJ done locked in ha," "That's what he trying to do, but I told him I'm not on that lovey-dovey shit right now, but I guess he's just the lovey-dovey type, he cool though," "Yeah he's a good nigga, if it wasn't for him I would of been dead or in a jail a long time ago, so, two thumbs up to that nigga, you ain't got no more trees?" he said as she took the last puff of the blunt. "Yeah but you got to roll up, I got these long nails on," she said, digging in her purse again. Like a real pro, he broke the' blunt and the weed down in record time, rolling it up then, put fire to it, he called one of the lil' niggas over that was with him, and told him to fix a drink up and bring it to him. "So you think that, you could make it big in the rap game?" "Really I'm just trying to make it big or small as long as I can get a ticket then I won you know what I mean, all this shit a game you just gotta take it how it comes to you." "I know that's right," she said as he tried to pass the blunt to her, "Naw I'm good I'm already high' as hell and you need that shit more than I do." His homie came back with a double cup with purple liquid in it; she already knew it was syrup. He took a sip of it, then leaned back on the sofa. Terry was still over talking to the director, "So how did you and Terry meet?" She asks him as he hit the' blunt and took another sip on the lean, "Shit through the game you can say, he use to fuck with one of my partners, but both of them niggas are there own bosses and shit ain't work out for them, than one thing led to another and my other partner end up doing some cutthroat shit crossing out TJ and a lot of niggas didn't like that shit, plus me, So I chose sides and kept fucking with TJ, I lost a lot of money behind my decision but it is what it is because if you'll cut throat somebody like TJ then you'll cut throat a little oh me. But TJ is a nigga with a vision and I'm just trying to see it how he sees it, he thought I should rap one day when I was free-styling on this beat and the next day I was in the studio and this shit's moving fast." Toya was wondering who Looney and TJ, the other partner that crossed TJ out. She had no clue at all, this was the most info she even knew about Terry, she knew he had to have some type of money and she knew his hands were in the streets. He wasn't fooling anybody with the lil' job he had at the dealership. Since she's been dealing with him, that nigga done pulled up in 5 different cars and trucks and the two different presidential rollies he was sporting, they weren't cheap at all plus Looney's a real street dude, a real gangsta but he listens to Terry and takes orders from him so she knew TJ had to be somebody out there in the streets, she thought to herself as she watched Terry finish talking with the video director, then head back over to the couch were her and Looney was sitting. He set in between them, kissing her on the cheek, "What you up to?" He asked, Locney lift the cup and blunt up in the air, "You see it my nigga." "I should of figured you azz was getting higher than a girraffs ass." "Naw my nigga that I ain't high enough, I'm tryna get G-9 high, matter fact, I'm trying to get Space-X high, way up there on another planet," Toya began laughing. "You get high and that's all you want to do is laugh." "And eat, where the hell is the food, I thought you said they were going to have food on the set, I haven't seen not a chicken wing in sight." "You wanna run and grab something to eat real quick?" He asked her. "Yes please." They both got off the couch, Terry asked Looney did he want something, he shook his head, they turned around to leave, but she turned back around to get her purse and caught Looney staring at her ass with a lustful look on his face, she didn't say anything just turned around and caught back up with Terry. After getting in his Porsche, they drove for a while until they came to a stop at a soul food restaurant. They got out and went inside, ordering at the counter, they were taking their food with them, "Ooh I want to try the candy yams," "Yeah there real good, I love them." "Well, what about the turkey and the blueberry cornbread?" "Oh, the turkeys good but I never tried the cornbread." "Well, that's what I want and a sweet tea." "I'm just gonna get some wings and a drink," he said then placed the order. They found a seat and sat down, as they waited for their food. "So how's the modeling thing going?" He asked as she looked through her phone, "I told you I was working with a different agency now, I took pictures and they were going to use me as the cover artist." She always tried to avoid this conversation but he always brought it up ever so often. "The Smooth magazine didn't work out for you?" "No it didn't, how many times am I going to have to tell you that." "I'm sorry, I forgot, but what's the other agency called?" "Double R," she said, still having her head down in her phone acting as if she was more focused on what was going on in her phone than the conversation they were having, but she could see that he was really really bothered when she mentioned Double R. "You said Double R?" "Yeah, that's what I said," she replied, placing her phone back in her purse. "How the hell did that happen?" He asked, looking over at her with a shocked look on his face, "Hold up, did I miss something?" She asked, looking at him, confused. "The Double R thing, how did that come upon?" "I met a photographer in the grocery store who shoots for Double R and he asked to shoot with me and he loved the pictures and wanted to use me as the cover artist, said that it would be good for business, would get me a lot of exposure." "You got to be fucking kidding me," Terry said as he stood up then started pacing in front of her, she stood up and asked him what was the problem. "Double R, that's the problem, you can't do this magazine with him." "Why?" "You just can't, it's too much bad blood," "It's too much bad blood. I don't understand?" "Well, I'll put it like this, you have to choose sides because this nigga is no friend of mine, and he's a fucked up dude and I don't want no dealing with him, nobody around me that's dealing with him, that's how bad the blood is, it's a fucked up situation and your not from around here so you don't know what's going on and for you to be dealing with him and me just isn't gonna work so you have to choose sides, right now, you fuckin with him or you fucken with me?" "Your talking about Ryan right?" "You damn right that's who I'm talkin about," This was the first time she saw him angry, she never saw him angry at all. "Wow, this is too much for me right now, I'm not understanding," she said. "What is it your not understanding, it's either me or Double R, plain and simple." She only stared at him in disbelief not saying anything. "Toya, are you hearing what I'm saying?" "Yeah I hear you." "Well you need to be calling him now canceling whatever yall got going on, I can get you any magazine, I know a lot of good people, I didn't even know that nigga had a magazine." "You got to give me some time to think about this Terry." "Give you some time to think about what? I don't understand," "Just give me a day or so to figure this out." "You should already have it figured out, but since you don't I'll make it way easier for you." He said then turned around without another word, he walked out the door not turning around once. She watched as he got into his car then drove right away; she couldn't believe the nerves of him, this nigga just left her. She pulled out her phone and called his phone, it went straight to the voicemail, she tried it again she was blocked, this bitch ass nigga, she thought as the women with their order came over with their food in bags, Toya took them then set down. She ordered an Uber and waited for it to come. She shook her head again because she still couldn't believe this nigga just left her like she was some random bitch in the streets, then again, fuck that nigga, she didn't need him. The Uber pulled up and she got in, she got dropped off to her building then called a tow truck company to go pick up her cars to be dropped off there as well. After eating her food, she searched her purse for her weed then cursed herself out when she remembered she left it with Looney and Terry was her only weed plug. Now ain't that about the biggest bitch in the world.

Chapter 30

Double R backed his Range Rover into the garage then got out of the SUV walking inside the house. Double R made it to the back room where the 6ft tall safe set in the walk-in closet. He pressed his palm against the screen, then pressed a couple of buttons and waited for the combinations of locks to release; then he opened the safe. There was a stack of Kilos of cocaine inside of the safe. He grabbed the black duffle bag and stuffed it to its capacity, zipping it up afterward. There were stacks of money inside the safe as well, he filled another duffle and closed the safe back up. Placing a few phone calls, he stepped back inside the garage, placing both bags inside a hidden compartment that was in the back of the-Rover. Getting back in the SUV, he pulled back out the garage waiting till it closed, then he drove off making his way across the city until he got to his old neighborhood in zone 6, where he owns numerous homes. He pulled up to a white brick house, where he waited for the young gentlemen with a red bandanna hanging out his back pocket to open the fence, and he backed into the yard. When he got on, he retrieved the bricks then walked inside the house, where there were a house full of young niggas and guns. One of them was watching the monitors, this was his trusted goon,

Gunna, he came over and embraced him as he set the duffle down on the table. "What up big homie?" "Shit just got back into town, got to meet up with a few people, I know the streets been dry, so it's gonna be a lot of traffic comin trough here today, I already place a few calls to let niggas know everything was good, so it should be a few niggas pulling up in a second. "I'm going to be leaving all these here with you; it's 50 of them. Just call me if you need more, and tell that stupid ass nigga to tuck that flag in his back pocket out front, he ain't got to let the whole damn world know he's a blood, that's stupid, real niggas get money. Tell him if he wanna gang bang don't do that shit here because we are running a business here and don't need the extra heat." "Yeah, I got you, plus the problem you had last week before you left, that's done, I took care of it myself." "Ok good, that's what I needed to hear." After he made sure everything was situated, he pulled back out of there and headed downtown, where he needed to meet someone else. He parked the Range Rover, retrieving the money from the back. He then got inside the new E300 Mercedes, it was all black and tinted; he drove until he got to the hospital. He parked inside the parking garage next to a dark green Nissan Altima, Double R got out retrieving the bag then got inside the Nissan, were an older white man was sitting behind the wheel. "That's 500 thousand right there." "It better be," "All the fucking trouble I'm keeping you out of and the crime rates rising around here, it's my ass that's on the chopping block here Ryan," the DEA agent said. "Well, that should keep me out of trouble for a long time." "Yeah, it should but you need to tell your goons to stop shooting up the whole fuckin city." "How do you know it's my goons?" "Because who else is going to allow there people to act like some animals every time someone owes them money, you got to help me help you or were going to both be in some deep shit, when you were in cahoots with that Terry guy, you were moving way smoother, you ran him off, now it's your way or the highway and my man, that type of attitude is not gonna keep you around for a long time, mark my word and be careful out there and move a little smoother, I know you think you got it figured out, but this isn't the wild wild west." "I hear ya." "Don't just hear me make some adjustments and cut back on the murder and the shootings, elections coming up and there going to be looking for someone to be making an example out of, don't' let it be you, Mr. Reynolds." "I got you," he said as he got out the car then drove off. He always had the chills when he met up with agent Coleman, one of the guys that helped him climb to the top. He helped boost his career as well, setting a few pawns in place for him to knock off from time to time, it was an all part of the game, he believed. He didn't give a fuck, either way, it went as long as he was free and alive, everybody could fall as he made his way to the top. Larry was sitting at the table in the office when he walked in, going straight to the refrigerator. Double R grabbed a bottle of water, then sat at the table next to Larry and asked him what he was doing. "I'm putting the finishing touches to a few of these pictures. I wanted to add this girl, Black Diamond, but wanted to talk to you before I did, what do you think?" He said as he slid the computer over to him, scrolling through the pics. Black Diamond was a tall dark skin, thick, beautiful girl, "Yeah, she is a go, have you talked to Queen? I've been calling her and haven't heard from her in a few days," Double R said. "Yeah, that's kind of weird. I can't get in contact with her either, I was trying to talk with her and get her back in front of the camera." "Yeah, that's a good way of thinking, I'll get in contact with her," he said as he stood up walking to the back where the booths were. One of the models was just finishing up a shoot. The photographer was leaving out and she was getting her things together, "What up Jewels?" Double R said as he walked inside the booth. She was standing there in nothing but a pair of thongs and a Victoria Secret bra, "Oh hey Ryan, What you up to?" "I was on my way out until I saw your fine ass over here looking sexy like always." "You think so," she said turning around making her phat ass bounce, "You know I do," he said walking up to her pressing up against her wrapping his arms around her, she could feel his hard dick on her ass. He kissed her gently on the ear, "Ooooh you better stop before you get in something you can't handle." "And what's that?" He said as he slid his fingers inside her panties then began playing with her clit. She began moaning and grinding her ass up against him as he continued to play with her clit and suck on her neck. She turned around, taking his dick out of his pants as they kissed, then she squatted down, placing his dick in her mouth and began sucking the tip of his head until it was rock hard. She continued to suck it and pull on it with her hands until he was hot and ready. He pulled her up then turned her around, she gripped the stool as he slid inside of her then began pounding on her real fast. She began moaning and screaming, it didn't take him long to cum as he pulled out and came all over her ass. He found a towel out of the piles of clothes that was on the floor, then he washed his dick and her ass off. She turned around and they kissed really hard again. He promised her a slot in the magazine. He walked out the booth back to the front where Larry was still working on the pictures. He told him he was heading out and would catch up with him later. He got back in the car, texting Queen while he pulled off. Why the hell wasn't this bitch answering, he thought.

Toya sat on the couch throwing popcorn in her mouth while watching movies she ordered off Net-Flix, not even glancing at her ringing phone. It wasn't anybody but Larry or Ryan, Terry didn't even call, not once. She tried calling him twice more but she was still blocked. Damn, how the hell did she trick herself with feeling some type of way about this nigga when she told herself it wasn't nothing but a fuck thing but something was there, if it wasn't, she wouldn't be sitting at home feeling all moody and shit. Still not having any weed, she substituted it for red wine, and for the last two days, she's been here drinking and eating junk food. Her phone rang again; she still didn't look at it. Then moments later, there was a knock at the front door. It startled her because nobody ever came there but Terry. She got up from the couch and walked over, looking through the peephole and said oh shit to herself, Ryan was standing on the other side of the door smiling. How the in the hell did this nigga get up here and how the hell did he know where she stayed. She opened the door, "What are you doing here Ryan?" She said, still having the chain attached to the door. "I'm just coming to check on you since you're not answering your phone for me or Larry. It's good to see your alive, I thought we left on good terms the last time we spoke." "We did," she said. "So what happened? Are you having a change of mind in working with us? You didn't sign any contract or anything like that so we do need you to at least sign a permission form so we could release the magazine with you in it." "What if I don't want to do it?" She said, rolling her eyes. "If you open the door I can come in and we could sit down, if that's alright with you, Ms. Queen." She stood there for a second, staring at him as if she was considering what he said. She closed the door then released the chain, letting him in the condo. She walked back to the couch, sitting down, grabbing the condo. She walked back to the couch, sitting down, grabbing the bowl of popcorn, throwing one in her mouth. He came in behind her looking around, seeing the bottles of wine, the balled-up tissue and the movie she was watching. "Oh I see what's going on here, your sitting up in here pouting because someone broke your pretty little heart." "I don't have no heart to break FYI Mr. Ryan or Double R, whatever you want to call yourself." "You can call me Double R." "I thought only your friends call you Double R?" "I thought we were friends, the last I checked." She didn't say anything; she threw another popcorn in her mouth. "So, who's the guy your crazy over, I didn't even know you were involved with anyone here, I'm kind of jealous now." "First of all, I'm not crazy over no one and there's no reason to be jealous over him because he's already jealous over you." "Jealous over me?" "YEP," "Now this is getting interesting," "There is nothing to explain, I just got myself in a fucked up situation fucking with two people who obviously don't fuck with each other." "So you say to the guy that's jealous of me, we know each other?" She nodded her head. "Well, who is this guy?" He asked. "You really wanna know?" She said, looking over at him. "Yeah why not." "His names Terry, Terry Jackson, everybody calls him TJ." She could see the shock on his face with the mention of his name. "You gotta be kidding me, how the hell do you know TJ?" "I met him at the dealership when I was buying the BMW." He laughed.' "I forgot that funny ass nigga had a job at the dealership, that nigga is a fuckin joke, you in here pouting over that nigga, I wish I would of knew this shit, awww man this ones going down in history. Let me guess, he got pissed off because you were working with me and he decided to stop fucking with you?" She nodded her head. "Just know your not the first one. He cuts off everybody that wants to do better for themselves. Niggas aren't finna come up fucking with that nigga, I ain't come up until I cut that nigga off, I got bigger dreams and goals and I ain't just talking when I said I want to reach the top, I'm trying to reach that bitch for real. I'm saying what you benefiting fucking with that nigga, he ain't got no magazine or no modeling company, I could put you where you wanna be and connect you to all the right people. You need to get into contact with so you can get where you need to be and don't let all that good boy persona shit fool you. That nigga got his hands in everything moving around here, I bet you didn't know that, did you?" She shook her head. "Well, he ain't what you think he is and he's one of the biggest drug dealers in the city and he controls the whole North Atlanta. I bet you ain't know that either, that nigga is fake as fuck." She watched him as he was steaming from the other side of the couch and she remembered what Looney said about one of his partners cutting and throating Terry and he chose sides. She thought this was her best opportunity to really figure out what was going on. "Well, he told me you were good friends until you went behind his back and cut throated him." She saw his eyes get bigger and his mouth drop open. "Damn that nigga told you some shit like that?" "Yes he did and that's why Looney said he don't fuck with you anymore." "Looney bitch ass, I don't give a fuck because that nigga don't fuck with me, who the fuck is he. The best thing he got going on is that music shit he into right now and if he keeps running his mouth like a lil' bitch, I'll make sure that nigga don't get no more play around this bitch, I don't know what the fuck wrong with them niggas. Talking about I cutthroat somebody if his bitch ass would of got aboard, we would of all been heading to the top but he wanna sit around and move pieces on the chessboard that don't make no sense then when I take the lead he gets pissed off and say I cutthroat him, that's bullshit. Niggas had to move out the way, he didn't want to come in, he stayed outside, and I blew up bigger then he thought I could ever be so fuck that nigga, you don't need him or whatever he got to offer I promise you. Fuck with me, and we'll go to the top however you want to get there, that nigga crazy for even playing with someone as beautiful as you, you know what I mean, from what I see you got a lot going on for yourself, nice condo, nice car, nice clothes and heels. Plus, your independent, you came here independent, you ain't come here to jump right into a relationship and definitely not with a nigga like that, you got to have fun, your beautiful, you have options. You got dreams and goals, don't you?" "Yeah I got goals and dreams." "Well you ain't go reach them sitting in here pouting and drinking this cheap-ass wine, that shit bad for your health, you need to get yourself together and let me take you out some were nice tonight because this ain't go cut it, you can't just sit up in here hiding out. Imah show you how to have fun, so get yourself together and answer when I call and fuck that nigga TJ, consider losing him as a come up, not a setback." He said as they walked to the front door. She let him out, then closed and locked the door back up. She set back on the couch then got mad at herself because she let him leave without asking if he had any weed.

Chapter 31

"That's 10 of them right there, all clean so you can step on it a lil' bit or do whatever you wanna do with them," Terry said as he handed his worker the bag full of bricks of cocaine. "This the 250 I owe you, I should be getting at you in a few days with what I owe you for this." The worker said, slapping the bag; Terry nodded his head. Walking back outside to the Escalade, he made his way across town to the studio where Looney was waiting for him; they were already recording when he walked in. There were a couple of groupies in the room smoking and drinking and looking pretty. "Hey Tj," one of them said as he walked over to the engineer and asked what was going on. "Not much, just going over a few things, adding alibis and trying a few hooks to the free-styles he did the other night." "Ok that's good, let's stay on top of all that, always, you know what I mean hard work pays off." "Yeah I know what you mean." After a few more sets, Looney came out of the studio reaching for one of the blunts that was in rotation, inhaling a huge cloud of smoke, then refilled his cup. "What you think, you see how I redone that part of the song?" "Yeah I think it sound better too, maybe you should do that to some of them other songs too." "I was thinking the same thing also." Looney sat on the couch between 2 beautiful girls with short dresses on. Leaning over sucking and licking the one on the left neck, while his hand disappeared under her dress, she did nothing but giggle. The music was blasting inside the studio and all the girls were up dancing now. "I like this song; this could be a stripper anthem, I can see myself now throwing my ass to this song," the red girl with the braids said as she bent over shaking her ass, having no panties on as she showed them all she had to give. "Damn!" Was all Terry could say as he watched them begin to strip out their clothes. The engineer got up and closed the blinds on the window. One of the girls came in front of Terry and unzipped his zipper, pulling out his already hard dick and began sucking it. One of the other girls were eating the other one out while Looney fucked her hard from the back. The engineer was sucking on the titties of the girl getting ate out. They had it heated in there for over an hour and a half. Terry told Looney he was headed home to get dressed and would meet him at club, "Next," later tonight. He got back in his truck and made his way back to his house, which was a newly built five-bedroom home in a new community that was gated. He grabbed both bags of cash out the back seat, then made his way to the bedroom where he set the bags on the bed. He stripped out of his clothes, then took a hot shower; he got back out with the towel wrapped around his waist. Walking inside his walk-in closet, he chose a pair of Balmain jeans and T-shirt, and a pair of designer shoes. After getting dressed, he put on two Cuban links and his Hublot, he put the Glock 9 pistol on his waist then grabbed the keys to the Bentley Continental he barely drove, tonight he was feeling good. As he stuffed over 20 thousand dollars cash in his pockets, not bothering to put away the cash, he left the duffle bags sitting on the bed as he exited the room, then the house. Getting inside the two-door tinted Bentley, Terry hit the garage remote pulling out, he hit the button again then watched as the door went down. Making his way through traffic, stopping only to refuel the Bentley, Terry got to the c club within 45 minutes. He parked right in front of the club. Without being searched at all, he made his way through the crowded floor to the booth that was already poppin. Looney was drinking out of the bottle of Ace of Spades and throwing money around the booth. Two of the five girls were naked and dancing. "TJ what up my nigga?" Looney said as TJ walked over to him, giving him a dap and embracing him. "Shit you know me, looking good, smelling good, I see you got this bitch jumping though." "Yeah I'm finally ready to perform in the next 30 minutes, I want them to hear the new song to see how their club reacts to it." You already know how they gonna react, quit acting like you don't know your a star, Big Looney Loon, your name already trending nigga." Terry said, throwing his arm over his shoulder. Taking a swig out the Ace of Spade bottle, watching the crowd, he could see a few niggas out there he dealt with from time to time. He was never in the game for stretches at a time, only half of the year, he'll flood the city with everything they needed then back away from the game the next 6 months, never giving the feds long enough to build a case on him. Rather than hanging out in the streets and hitting the clubs every night, he rather work on other things and invest money. He was working at the dealer right now, learning all the in's and out's because one day, he was planning on running and operating his own luxury car dealership, selling and leasing everything from Benzes to Rolls Royces. Niggas without a vision didn't see what was coming at them head-on. Terry was smart enough to take heed from watching how the streets chewed niggas up then spit them right out and he refused to become another citistic. That's why he cut all ties with his long time friend, Double R. They grew up in the same neighborhood, went to the same school and fuck the same hoes. He went to college but Double R went to prison, always one foot ahead of the game. While up in college, Terry found a plug and began flooding the city with the purest cocaine it ever saw, putting Double R on as soon as he came home. He made it to the NFL but not long after he got injured. He came back home headfirst in the game, not giving a fuck. He and Double R were on top of the world. Until he got power struck and didn't want to abide by the same rules they abide by the whole time, it was never to take their business out of town. But he did anyways, and he and Double R ended up catching two murder charges. Terry spent a shit load of money on a lawyer and had a few people moved out the way to allow him to beat trial. After getting out, his wife divorced him and ran off with another guy. A few months later, they both came up dead and the heat worsens. The feds were popping up, asking questions about murders and drugs and some robberies. Knocking off a few of there packages on the road and Terry could feel the heat, so he told Double R to fall back for a few months to enjoy life and spend a little bit of the money he was sitting on. Instead of falling back, he went behind Terry's back, contacted his plug in Texas, placing an order for 200 bricks to be sent down. He met up with the driver of the package shooting him in the head then robbing him for everything. Terry didn't know what happened until there was an attempt on his life. He had to kill and get rid of both bodies, one of the men that broke in his house to kill him, he recognized as one of the plugs nephews. Placing a call, he wanted to know what that was about. Not believing his ears, he called Double R right away to find out his phone # was blocked. If it wasn't for the war that was going on between his plug and the Cartel back in Mexico, he would have been dead. His plug and his plug's family was killed in the midst of the war. Instead of waging war on Double R, he wanted to talk to him, so he sent KD and Mario, 2 of his trusted soldiers, to talk to him at a club he recently opened. One thing led to another and KD and Mario were killed; that was the last straw. Instead of retaliating, Terry fell all the way back and everybody that was in the middle of that shit they chose sides, only a few loyal niggas continued dealing with Terry. Out of fear, the majority of everybody kept dealing with Double R. Terry followed Looney on stage with their crew and groupies right behind them as soon as Looney stepped out the crowd went crazy. He performed his single that was hot right now, then two other songs. Terry set back admiring his lil' nigga work as he bounced up and down on the stage and the crowd went crazy. He was looking over in the booth that was next to the stage and locked eyes with Double R. He was puffing on a phat cigar smiling at him as his jewelry sparkled, there were a few women in the booth with him but the one that caught his attention was Toya standing next to him dancing to the music like she had no care in the world. Seeing the shock on his face, Double R wrapped his arm around her and pulled her closer, whispering in her ear. He watched as she turned towards him with a fuck that nigga look on her face. He couldn't believe this bitch he thought as he turned away from them but he was boiling inside, wanting to snap that bitch neck. After Looney got through performing, they walked back down to there booth. "Loon you see that shit?" "See what?" He said, looking around. "Look up there in Double R's booth and tell me who you see." Looney looked for a few seconds; his mouth fell open. "What the fuck!" "Yeah, crazy right, these hoes ain't shit." "I don't understand, what the fuck happened, I thought you were a thing my nigga. The last time I saw yall together shit was good for her to be over there with that nigga. That's some cold shit my nigga." "I guess that bitch chose up. I stopped dealing with her when I found out she was doing business with him, you know he got that modeling agency and a magazine suppose to be dropping soon and she was featured in the mag and modeling for him, I told her to choose who she wanted to fuck with she didn't know at the time, so I made it easy for her, I left that bitch at the restaurant the other day we went to get something to eat from the video shoot." "Oh that explains why she sent the truck to pick up her cars." "Yep," Terry said, watching Double R booth as clouds of money began raining down on the crowd. He could see Toya having the time of her life as she danced and threw money he could see Double R pressed up against her. "Damn," he thought as he tell his stomach turn. Looney was still looking confused also, he shook it off then money and poppin bottles until the club ended an hour later. They made their way outside, he was parked upfront so they posted beside the Bentley hollering at bitches and catching up with niggas from the city. He watched as Double R came out the club surrounded by a crowd of people, his arms wrapped around Toya. Damn this bitch was bad, she had long curly hair on her head that fell down her back and the white Fendi dress she had on hugged the shit out her body, showing off all her curves. She only glanced over at him for a quick second as the Wraith pulled up and they both got in and the car pulled off. “Damn, that’s a cold bitch T.” “Yeah, fuck it doe, I’m out of here, I’ll catch up with you sometime tomorrow,” he told Looney as he got in the Bentley with one of the groupies then pulled off. He promised himself not to even think about that bitch no more but he knew deep down in his heart that wasn’t even possible.

Chapter 32

"That was crazy!" Toya said as they pulled away from the club. "You talking about the party scene or the look on your boyfriend's face when he saw you with me?" "He's not my boyfriend and I'm talking about the whole night, it was just so crazy, I was not expecting to see Terry or Looney tonight. How the hell did that happen, I know he think I'm so fucked up but it ain't even like that." "It don't matter because you ain't fuckin with that nigga no more is you?" He said, looking over from the driver seat. "Hell knaw, after that nigga left me stranded like a anything ass bitch, I could never fuck with someone like that again." "At least you got something to think with because these bitches out here don't know what to do or where to go. You want to stop somewhere and get something to eat?" She said, "Yes," and they stopped by the waffle house, then pulled up to a massive house a couple of minutes later, he stopped in front of the huge gate, placing his palm on the screen then the gate opened. They drove down a long driveway until they stopped in front of the mansion arid he shut the car off. "Damn, this house is so fucking big!" She said as they walked up the stairs and entered the house. "Yeah, I bought it over three years ago, it was owned by someone who played for the Atlanta Hawks, I love it, it's just right, makes me feel proud about myself every time I wake up here in the morning, I be like this some real boss shit," he said as he showed her around the house; all the rooms and game rooms, even the six-car garage where he had a Lambo and a Rari parked. "Damn, what's that?" She said as they walked inside another room. "Oh that's a stage," he said, hitting a switch on the wall and a pole came out the floor lifting until it locked in a socket that was on the ceiling. "I have a few strippers here from time to time when I'm throwing parties. When you finish eating, there's a shower in here and a change of clothes that will fit you," he said as he walked out. After she ate, she walked up the stairs and found the shower and the pajamas. She took a quick hot shower then got dressed. She walked out and he was fresh out the shower too with a towel wrapped around his waist. She could see his dick print through the fabric as she looked down, he told her to come here. She did as she was told, he leaned down and placed a kiss on her lips. She only stood there so he pulled her closer, wrapping his arms around her then began kissing her harder, squeezing her on her ass. "Who told you I wanted to have sex?" She asked as she moved his hands off her ass. "You did." He said, looking confused. "I did?" "Yeah when you didn't tell me to take you back home," she laughed at that. "Oh so you automatically thought that meant I wanted to give you some pussy." "Or you wanted some dick," he said, gripping his dick through the towel. She said, "Boy you a trip." Then she walked over to the bed and set down. He followed behind her, stopping in front of her. She was looking at his ripped up body and the gunshot wombs, and the tattoos that covered his body. She rubbed her hand down his chest, looking up at him smiling. She unwrapped the towel and it fell to the floor. His dick was right in her face and it was big, long and black. She gripped it in her hand and began to massage it as she stared at him in the eyes. "What you want me to do with it?" She asked as he moaned. "I want you to do whatever you want with it," he said as she kept pulling on it and massage his balls gently in her hands. She put his head in her mouth and sucked on it like a piece of candy, causing him to make a sound like an animal. She began sucking harder arid, trying to put it down her throat. She was moaning as she slopped all over his dick and licked it up. When he was rock hard and ready, she let his dick go and leaned back on the bed. He wasted no time with pulling her pajama shorts down and tried to place her whole pussy inside his mouth, forcing a deep moan out of her as she arched her back. He began devouring her clit, making her cum instantly. Her body locked up and shook hard, he stood up and rubbed his dick across the lips of her pussy to get his head wet then he slid inside of her tight wet pussy. He was in awe how good her pussy was as he eased in and out, opening her up. She leaned up, gripping his ass cheeks, pulling him deeper inside her as she looked at him with her mouth wide open and a look of pleasure in her eyes. He began pounding on her even harder and faster as she screamed and told him to fuck her, turning her around, he began sucking on her ass hole and popping his thumb inside of her. She began throwing it back instantly, he just stood there and let her work, he felt himself about to cum and he grabbed her ass and began pounding her hard as she screamed out his name, he came inside her feeling his juices leave his dick and fill her up. He was breathing like a dog as he laid back on the bed and she began sucking his dick again until it was back up. She straddled him and began riding him, taking him on the ride of his life. He tried to hold on but couldn't and he came within the first 2 minutes, cumming inside her again. As she laid on top of him and squeezed her pussy muscles around his dick, arid began rotating until he was hard again. She fucked him crazy until he was sound asleep; he went to sleep dreaming about her. She was the first bitch in a long time that he came in and he did it three times, this was the best sex he had in his whole entire life. He didn't know it but he was in a world of trouble dealing with Toya.

Chapter 33

"Damn, this shit is finna be so crazy," Draco said, rubbing his hands together, looking at the 5 bricks of herion that was on the table in front of him. "And you can do whatever you want with them, there the same way I got them, you can cut em' anyway you like em'. I don't think you should use fentanyl. It's bad for business right now, a lot of people dying and going to jail for that shit. That Dominican Rat Poisen a friend of mine says that's best and I got ah nigga finna break one down then I should have it down pack in a lil' bit. I can already see the takeover. These niggas don't even know how I'm finna fuck the city up." Already meeting Jacob earlier, hearing the same speech and excitement, he was glad to make both his homies happy. He left Draco there to handle his business, getting inside the new bullet-proof Mercedes. Then took 1-4 to Kennedy cruising through downtown, arriving at his building, he rode the elevator up getting off on his floor. Only living here for the last week, he was already comfortable here, he even furnished it himself and helped furnish the place he got for Elisha. She was calling now asking him to come over; she didn't understand what his reason for buying her house and not wanting to live there with her was. He said he would, just had a lot of business on hand at the moment and didn't want to be in and out of there, plus he couldn't really be locked down at the time either because that wouldn't be good for the way he conducted business. She said she understood but he didn't know if she really did. He dumped all the cash he made that day on the counter. Collecting over 250 thousand from Twan alone today was good but Jacob coped 20 bricks of soft and 5 bricks of boy came in like a cash coal with 850 thousand dollars and Draco grabbing the 5 bricks of herion said he wanted to deal with that only and didn't want him to deal with no one else in the city, because that was a lane he was go fuck with and open it wide open. Bezo agreed to only deal with him with the boy. He didn't know about Jacob and that would be a problem. He stuffed the cash inside the safe he installed in the condo. When he got back, Elisha was still calling his phone, so he took a shower and got dressed in a new Ralph Lauren outfit and shoes he bought earlier. He also purchased a few new jewelry pieces. He headed back downstairs, hitting the alarm. He looked around the parking garage before he pulled out. Over the last few months, his life changed tremendously, thinking about his man Rilo every day and not a day went by that he didn't. He was making a promise to God when he found out who did it, he would destroy them and everyone around them. He lit the blunt and inhaled deep. From his spot to Elisha's on the expressway was only 20 minutes. He pulled up in the driveway behind her Toyota Corolla and got out the car. He walked in without even knocking, Coby took a liking to him and was used to seeing him all the time, so when he walked through the door, he ran up to him and Bezo picked him up flying him through the air like an airplane. Elisha was looking from the kitchen with a smile on her face, "What up, what we got in here?" He said, walking over, placing a kiss on her lips. She turned back around and said, "Fried chicken, white rice, string beans, macaroni and cornbread, I baked a lemon cake too, it's my autie recipe, you go like it, watch." "Got damn gurl, you tryna make me move in forreal ha?" "Yes I am and I don't know why you did all this nice stuff for us," she said, pointing back and forward between her and Coby. "Then you tell me where a thing is but you're not trying to be here as I live here because you aren't ready yet. I understand what your trying to tell me but I don't understand it at all at the same time, I'm lost and you come in here dressed all nice, I hope you don't think your leaving here tonight, not tonight Bryson, you got to stay here." "Ok I don't have any problem with that, you act like there's a problem," he said, leaning down kissing her again even harder on the lips. They began kissing passionately until they remembered Coby was in the room. She told him to sit down and she began serving the food after they held hands and said grace they dived straight into the food. "I told you that boy is so greedy," Elisha said, smiling as she pointed at the way Coby was scraping the mac n' cheese off the tray. "I see why he is digging in it like that, this mac is the bomb," Bezo said, pointing at it with his fork. "Might be the best mac and cheese I ever tasted." "Forreal or you playing?" "No I'm forreal you got something going on here and this chicken is on point to ain't it lil' man," he said, facing Coby who was still scraping his plate. "It's good mommie," he said, smiling. After they finished eating, they watched a movie in the living room on the flat-screen TV. Coby set in between them on the couch. Halfway through the movie, he fell asleep and Elisha carried him in the bedroom then closed the door behind her. "Finally some alone time," she said as she slumped back on the couch, laying her head on his lap. "So what you been up to today?" She asked, "Same thing every day, making sure I'm able to make it back here to you," he said, leaning down kissing her on the lips. She had on a sundress, so he reached over, placing his hand underneath as they kissed and he began playing with her clit with his two fingers. She opened her legs wider then he began rubbing it faster and sliding one of his fingers in her tight hole. She began moaning and rollin her body. She turned over, reaching for his zipper pulling his dick out she began sucking it slow and deep as he placed his hand on top of her head. She was quick at learning the motion; he wanted her to stroke it. She began making slurping sounds and sucking hard on his head while she jacked him off, he reached behind her, lifting her dress all the way up exposing her phat ass, he began rubbing it then slipped his fingers back in her pussy. She leaned her head back, losing her breath in total passion. She pulled his pants all the way down then straddled him, placing his dick in her tight hole. It took a few seconds but she eased down on top of him and began bouncing up and down at a slow pace. He pulled the front of her dress up then began sucking on her breast. She began riding him faster and harder; she whispered that she was about to cum. He grabbed her ass cheeks and spread them as he began pounding her hard while she was still on top of him. She began screaming as she climaxed all the way to the top, he wasn't finished with her. He laid her back on the couch, placing her leg behind her head. He got as deep as he could then slammed into her like a head-on collision. She had to bite the pillow to keep from screaming and waking her son up. He continued pumping until he felt himself about to cum, he thought about pulling out but considered otherwise and kept pumping even faster as he felt himself reaching the top and she did as well as she reached back pulling him deeper inside of her and began humping him back. His eyes rolled behind his head as he exploded like a bomb right inside of her and juices shot everywhere. He was panting hard as he laid on top of her and fell asleep.

While Bezo was home getting pussy, Draco was inside his trap house surrounded by his goons watching the fiend he gave a tester to nod out on the floor. This was the 5th person he let test it and every last one of them passed out on the floor then woke up and claimed that was the best shit they tasted in a long time and word got around fast because his phone was ringing and there were fiennes outside the house knocking on the door. He spread out packages to his workers and told them how to sell it and what to sell it for. They had two spots inside the Robles Park projects and it was already doing # with the crack they were pushing through the complex, but he was tryna turn all the feints out on this china white. Twan walked in with a smile on his face when he saw Draco, "What up big homie, how's it going, I see you forreal with that other shit," he said as he looked down at the fiene struggling to get up. "Yeah, in a lil' bit this should be a steady flow then all us can eat off this shit. I'm trying to put it together now but I see you doing good to on the real this the way I like to see you and when the rest of you niggas act like yall want some money yall can roll like Twan, now lets get to it," he said, clapping his hands and everybody started moving, bagging the drugs up and walking outside to take their position on the block. "What up with JC, I heard he didn't want to get down but he still moving blocks." "Man I think that nigga the police, every time I roll down on that nigga I swear it's a shit load of weird cars go-fee- poppin up and parking across the street. He goes to looking and talking crazy so I left that nigga alone, it's better that nigga than me if them is the people." "Yeah they been said that nigga was the police but Imah pullup on him and have a sit down with him." "I'm telling you it's something that ain't right with that nigga, I ran it by Bezo and he told me to leave it alone." He looked over at Twan with a cold look on his face, Twan through his hands up then said, "Hey your the boss." Draco liked the way that sounded. He walked outside, followed by his goons and got inside the BMW. Ever since he saw the Audi and the Benz Bezo purchased, he swore he was going to get the BMW bullet-proof but never got around to it. He took MLK all the way to west Tampa, where he parked and walked inside another trap that was there. He broke down a quarter bird of heroin and showed them how to bag it up and suit. After he left there, he walked through the projects followed closely by his hitters until he got to Tracey's house, one of the known heroin addicts in the city. If he told you your shit was good it was good. He watched him melt the powder down on a spoon then suck it up in the needle; he found a vein to shoot it in. He passed out across the floor and didn't move for 5 minutes straight. They thought he was dead until he popped up out of nowhere and said, "Man, you got that blue magic, that Frank Lucas, man that shit is crazy, let your uncle get another bump of that shit, I ain't really get the whole effect of that shit," he said, struggling to get to his feet. "Nigga you ain't my uncle and look at you, you can't even stand up," Draco said, laughing. "Well at least leave a little bit of that shit around, I could hustle with. Let a nigga get ah job nephew." "Knaw I ain't going to do that, I don't wanna kill you about my money Tracey," he said, throwing a gram of heroin on the table. "Spread work," he said as he turned around and walked out, followed closely by his goons. He stopped by his baby mother's house to get some good pussy. He had a couple 100 thousand stashed there, he took it with him. He didn't want to have to fuck her up or having the sticky fingers. He left his car at the shelter then hopped in the new mini-van he purchased. He never showed no one where he lived but Bezo, that's why he left his hitters back at the shelter with his Beamer. He grabbed the bag of cash then walked inside the apartment. It was fully furnished and paid up for the next two years. He moved the bed out the way then lifted the carpet; he had two safes built in the floor. He opened one of them then began placing the stacks of cash inside. He had over a million dollars, the 400 thousand dollars Bezo had for him made him think even highly of Bezo, but he really wasn't feeling the way Twan was carrying himself self and now he was running the way Twan was carrying his self. He was running around the town, putting down like he was the next nigga up. He really didn't like how he let JC continue to move, how he wanted to and not break the crew off. That was a big no-no, and he was taking his position. Draco laughed at the thought of Twan even trying to swang ion like he did. He put everything back how it was then he went to the kitchen going in the refrigerator he grabbed a can of beer and stood over the counter. Pulling a plastic bag out his pocket, he licked the molly out his palm after he poured it in his hand. He could feel the drug working immediately. As he finished drinking the beer, he went back outside and got back in the mini-van, calling ahead to the shelter, telling his lil' homies to be ready to ride. When he got there, they were waiting inside a stolen Expedition. He parked the van and jumped right into the backseat. He told the driver to drive. This is what he loved about his team, they were on go no matter the situation, they only took orders and followed direction. All of them dressed in all black with assault rifles across their laps; he knew he could get anybody wacked tonight if he wanted to but Draco had only one person in mind. They drove for a while until he told them to stop in front of a two-story wood house. He told them to wait for a minute as he got out and looked around. There wasn't anybody wandering out on the streets, so he felt comfortable enough to proceed with his plans. He opened the door and told them to get out. After telling two of them to watch the back of the house, the other two followed up the stairs to the front porch, where he began ranging the bell uncontrollably until he saw the light come on inside the house. When the door opened, Draco forced his way into the house, knocking the old man in pajamas to the floor. Walking to the back room, he snatched the old woman out the bed, placing a gun to her head, then the next room were two young boys who were sitting on the bed, he told them to get up and not make a sound, they did and he directed all of them to the front of the house where the old man was already tied up and gagged. He waited for the rest of them to be tied and gagged and seated next to each other on the couch. Draco pulled out his burner phone, took a few pictures of them, put in a phone number and sent a quick text, letting JC know he had 30 minutes to get to his parent's house, "Alone," or all of them would be dead and if he even thought about trying any kind of tricky shit, he would murder them in the most brutal way that he could imagine. It took under 30 seconds for his phone to start ranging and JC to be on the other end, screaming, crying and begging for him not to hurt his parents or his kids. He was on the way and wouldn't try anything stupid to jeopardize the lives of his family. Draco told him he was waiting then hung up the phone. He then set down on the couch across from JC's family, "It's all up to your son if you live or die, you better hope he don't try nothing stupid because all of us are going to die tonight." The old woman closed her eyes and bowed her head; the young boys began to cry. Draco shrugged his shoulders then began strolling down his timeline on JC. Moments later, he could hear a car pulling up in the yard and the car door opening and closing. He wasn't worried because he knew JC was being surrounded, searched and walked to the front door. There was a knock on the door and one of Draco's men answered it, JC was pushed in the house. He was looking petrified as he saw his family in real life held hostage like this. "Please man, anything you want just let me know, they ain't go say shit, I promise. I'll give you whatever you want, that's my word, he said while on his knees looking up at Draco. Draco shook his head then told him to stand the fuck up and quit acting like a bitch in front of his family. He did as he was told then followed Draco to the kitchen, the set down at the table. Not saying anything for a while, Draco set there and let him wander for a while. Then after eating the apple he took off the table, he threw it in the trash then washed his hands on his pants. "Look JC, I don't know why it had to take all this to get your attention but I see that you love your family and you'll do anything for them." JC nodded his head, "But you've been a very bad boy, you continue to do what you want to when you know things have changed dramatically the last few months and everyone have paid ties and are abiding by the rules me and my friend Bezo have set. I know Twan have talked to you a few times and you and whoever you're involved with have spooked him. Most people think your working with the police that's why your not scared or should I say wasn't scared, but obviously, things have changed and you don't know what's gonna happen tonight, but I only wanna make things better for you not worse, so I got a onetime proposition that could help me and you both, I don't wanna rob you, I don't want to hurt you, I only want to make things better for the both of us." "Anything man, I promise, just let me know what it is and I'll do it," JC said. "I don't want to have this talk again JC, this is a onetime thing that's my word." JC nodded his head. "Well, here it goes, I need for you to continue selling your drugs however you're selling them, but I also need for you to sell my drugs as well. A different drug from yours, I'm trying to open a new lane here and I think you could help me with this. So I'm gonna give you a kilo of heroin and you're going to sell it however you wanna sell it but your gonna bring me a hundred thousand dollars back off every kilo, it's good, so maybe you can squeeze you a little extra in somewhere. I want you to sell the shit out of it and make sure everybody knows you got it and it's good because like I said before, I'm trying to open a new lane here, and I believe you're the best guy for the job since you feel like you can do what you wanna do. 100 grand every kilo, or we won't have this conversation again, the next time you're gonna be making funeral arrangements. So, no games, you still get rich and do what you want to do but your helping me in the process, is that a deal," Draco said, extending his hand across the table. JC took it and shook it and said, "Deal." Draco dropped the brick on the table, and without another word, he and his men disappeared out the house and drove away.

Chapter 34

I never thought about having this much money, Jacob thought as he ran all the cash through the machine and stuffed it in a black duffle bag. When he was finished, he moved the bookcase, which was in his study room, and stuffed the bag in the wall next to the other bag that was already there. After putting everything back exactly the way he found it when he came down there. He walked back upstairs where his wife was just finishing breakfast and his kids were waking up, walking in the kitchen, wiping the sleep from their eyes. He walked behind his wife and placed a kiss on her neck then spun both of his kids in the air one at a time. After the food was done, they sat around the table as a big happy family. His wife was a white woman and his kids were bi-racial. She was a stay at home mom, while he worked and made sure all the bills were paid. She knew about his past troubles and convictions and believed that he was a changed man. But little did she know he was so deep in the streets, it even scared the shit out of him sometimes. He and his family lived over an hour and half from where he conducted business and ran the streets. The heroin that he got from Bezo the other day was almost gone and it was in high demand. He didn't know how good it was until one of his people told him he needed to break the shit down because it was so pure niggas were still stepping on it 3 and 4 times. Bezo told him about the rat poison and he cut what he had left and doubled everything up and it still went like hotcakes. His lil' cousin, P, was having the time of his life as they took over the streets and did what they wanted to. P was in his new Impala when Jacob pulled up alongside him and let the window down, handing him a half a brick of boy through the window. "Hey man, I was thinking about something last night," P said as he grabbed the packages. "What's that lil' bra?" "Shit we need to be opening some spots and breaking this shit down because we'll get more money singling this shit rather than whole selling this shit, we need to be getting every dollar while we're hot." "I understand what you saying, but I'm good with getting what I'm getting now you know what I mean, we made away so we can eat and were doing just fine right now so let's just continue to move how we've been moving, get rich and full because this shit don't last forever and remember I told you that," Jacob said as he rolled the window up and drove away. He pulled up to the mall tucking his .38 special on his waist before getting out of the car. He put his jacket on, then made his way inside, walking around for a while. He grabbed a few things for his son and his daughter then saw a nice MK purse his wife would like. After he left the Polo store purchasing a few shirts, he made his way to the Apple store purchasing two new iPhones then headed out after he figured that was enough shopping for today. As he made it across the parking lot, he scanned his surroundings, just a habit of his. As he opened the back door to the vehicle, he could see a movement from the corner of his eye and he could see two younger guys coming from behind a parked car in the crowded parking lot. He noticed both of them were holding guns, he dropped the bags and reached for his waist coming back up with the .38 squeezing the trigger but not before the shorter of the two lifted up his Glock and began firing shots in his direction hitting him in the center of the chest, sending him crashing back against the car. If it wasn't for the bullet-proof vest, he knew he would have been dead instantly. But one of his bullets caught one of the shooters in the shoulder and he was holding it, firing wild. The bystanders in the parking lot were screaming and running as Jacob regrouped and squeezed off another well-placed shot, hitting the one that shot him in the chest in the head. The one with the Gsw to the shoulder turned around to run, firing backward, hitting the cars in between them. Jacob aimed and squeezed put his last two rounds hitting him in the back, watching him tumble over dropping the gun. He knew the hollow rounds ripped through him and he wasn't getting up again. He picked his bags up and threw them in the car. He hurried up to start the car then peeled out the lot. The car was shattered with bullets, his chest hurt like hell, he didn't know how in the hell he was going to explain this one to his wife, "Fuck!" He said out loud as he banged on the steering wheel.

"So what do you got planned for today?" Bezo asked Elisha as he gently rubbed his hands through her hair. She was laying with her head on his chest, after having morning sex. "I was thinking about going shopping with Chrystal," she said. "Since you came in my life, we haven't been spending no time and she's been bored ever since I moved out." "Oh yeah?" He said. "Yeah, me and my cousin is real close, when I moved away she use to come to visit me every summer way up there in the ville." "I would come with you today but I have a lot of stuff I got to handle but I should be finished and I'll stay here tonight, I had fun." "Oh you did," she said, leaning up kissing him on the lips. They had sex one more time before they got up and took a shower. It was too late to cook breakfast and Coby was already up eating cookies, drinking milk and glued to the T.V. watching cartoons. "What you watching lil' man?" Bezo asked, bending down, taking one of the Oreo cookies from the rack. "Scooby-Doo," he said, with a mouth stuffed with cookies. "Ok then lil' man, Imah see you later alright, so be good." He nodded his head and continued watching T.V. Elisha followed him all the way outside, up to the Benz. "This show is a nice car," she said as she rubbed her hand along the hood. "You think so?" "Hell yes, it's so big and expensive, it look like it's made for a boss like you I guess." "That right baby," he said, giving her another kiss before he got in the car and backed off. It wasn't even 11 o'clock and he had 12 missed calls 3 from Twan and 2 from Draco, they were the only calls he returned. After smoking the blunt he had left in the ashtray, he was starving. Stopping by Mcdonalds, Bezo ordered a #5 with a large Sprite. He decided to back up in the parking lot and devour his meal. After he finished eating, he set behind the dark tint and rolled another blunt. While looking across the parking lot, he saw Yellaman's mother and kids walking to the door of the establishment. He felt a certain type of way inside, he didn't know if it was guilt or something else, he didn't know but he pushed it aside as he lit the blunt. Fuck that nigga, he tried killing me first for nothing, his mistake, one that cost him his life, he thought as he smoked the blunt and navigated through the city. He knew he told Twan he wanted security at all times but thought better of it and only needed it when he was around. He called ahead and let them know he was pulling up in a second. Twan had purchased a new Stingray, all black with red rally stripes and he was parked out front next to Draco's BMW. He walked in and they were playing NBA2K on the huge flat screen in the living room. Draco had put bullet-proof windows throughout the house and was having everything tidied up even the bad plumbing. "Yo what up Bezo?" Twan said as he pressed buttons on his controller and focused on the screen. "Shit, what up with you niggas?" "Oh you know, beating the shit out of this nigga, he go be broke before he leave this bitch today." Draco said as Bezo looked at the pile of money on the floor. "Man them niggas betting a thousand dollars a game!" Sosa said from the couch. "And I'm up 5 games, going on 6 if this nigga don't tighten up on his back strokes." Draco said, Bezo laughed and set down the lazy boy. He waited for them to finish with the game which took 2 hours. He spent his time chopping it up with the youngins and getting caught up with what was going on in the streets. When Twan won all his money back, Draco refused to keep playing and swore he let Twan win because he didn't want to hear him crying all day. Bezo got up from the couch and walked towards the back room, followed by Twan and Draco. "Man when I tell you that shit moving so fast it's crazy," Draco said as he sat on the bed. "Yeah the coke booming too, all the traps doing big numbers and more niggas wanna fuck with ah nigga." "You acting like they got a choice," Draco said, looking at Twan like if that was the craziest thing he could ever say. "Yeah. You are right about that, niggas scared shitless I'm having the time of my life out there." "Just don't get caught up in the hype and get tricked, stay focused lil' nigga," Bezo said as he looked at Draco then asked him, "Why did he put the herion in the same trap they were selling hard and soft at?" "I thought you were trying to start your own lane and didn't want any of us dipping dur fingers into the cookie jar until you got everything moving the way you wanted it, but you stopped the flow of the way we been eating to make your pockets fatter, that seems ah lil' selfish to me, so if you don't want us nibbling in your bizz and swerving in your lane, I don't need you shutting down shop, you need to be opening up shops and adding extra workers, not putting a stop to the coke flow until your shit get to pumping." "It wasn't even like that Bezo." "Well how was it?" "Shit we already got like 20 traps what's 3 or 4 of em' moving the herion?" "No nigga, 5 or 6 and I heard how you did JC that was sick right there," Bezo said laughing. "Damn nigga, who you getting all your info from?" "I got ears and eyes everywhere," he said seriously. "I bet you do but JC chose to move ah lil' bit of work for me in exchange for him and his families life, that nigga was scared as hell!" "I bet he was but be careful with that cat, I don't trust him, he probably was better off dead." He turned to Twan and asked who he had worked with in dirty game because he heard they had a spot over there. "I got 2 lil niggas named Preston and Darryl over there holding things down. Real good niggas nothing to worry about, they make sure that paper right everytime." "Yeah but I heard their selling a lot of trees over there too, you know about that?" "Yeah I know about it, I didn't think it was a problem just a little extra cash on the side." "You think I didn't want any extra cash on the side." "It ain't like that, I just coped a few pounds and told them niggas to move them for me." "Yeah to open your own lane right?" Draco began laughing. "Come on Draco!" Twan said, he did not like that he was in the hot seat. "I think' both of you wanna go off and do your own thing and forget about what's going on here. We got something magical going on here and it's not time to start trying to figure things out for yourselves, that's how dynasty's get broken apart because everyone on the team want to do there own thing but a team doesn't work like that. I hope yall haven't forgot who's the QB here because the QB control the game and makes sure everybody get the ball, but you niggas tryna build your own team and control the ball and that's not gonna work because were'gonna end' up playing against each other and battling for the championship and the championship is getting rich and when I got on I made sure both of you, you got rich just like that," he said, snapping his fingers. "So for you niggas to both go off and do your own things that isn't right and that's losing focus, so Twan I don't want you doing anything like that again without talking to me first arid Draco you need to stop doing whatever you want to and make sure you open all them spots back up what you shut down other than that, why were you niggas calling me all morning?" "Shit I think you wrapped everything up," Draco said. "Not with me I needed them squares, hopefully you bring them with you because I still got a lot of people calling and I'm down to my last one." "Yeah give me a few hours I got to make a few moves then I'll meet you back here." "That's a bet," Twan said as he walked out the room. "How come you can't take that car to get proofed up, you dont' think somebody else will try to wipe yo big head ass out arid your son and Kiesha, did you find somewhere else for them." "Damn Poppa Bezo, why you drilling a nigga so hard?" "Because if your already ready you ain't got to get ready, thats what a old wise nigga told me once." "And were that nigga at now?" "Shit he dead." "So I guess you could never be too ready." "You right about that but I can gurantee I ain't go make it easy for one of these bitch ass niggas to kill me like everybody else getting killed." "And how's that?" Draco asked. "Slipping like every other nigga that got wacked in the streets, they were slippin and slippers don't count, so get proofed up and move your family up out of that shit, you know how Kiesha is, she be on every scene and if them niggas can't get you there going after the people that's closer to you, you should know better than anyone else, look at what just happened to JC." "Yeah you right, I got it my nigga, but enough of that, what's going on with you and Elisha?" "We trying to figure things out right now, she wants me to move in with her but I can't do that right now not really trying to be locked down but I'm feeling this relationship thing, makes you feel like you belong to something, you know what I mean, something other than the streets." "I don't know why you are playing, you should go ahead and put a ring on that thing you know you want to." Draco said. They both laughed at that. After they finished talking, Bezo told them he needed to head out. After leaving the shelter, he drove straight to the stash house where he held the drugs. After Ricardo dropped the number down to 18, Bezo didn't even touch them anymore, he sold them how he got them, for 25 a pop, letting Twan and whoever else get theres on the back end. Only putting 10 blocks in the bag he locked the house back up and headed back out meeting Twan, dropping the squares off to him. He then headed across town to meet Jacob who was waiting for him at a Starbucks. When he walked in, Jacob was sitting at a table in the back corner. Instead of being dressed up in his regular preppy clothing, he had on a Nike jogging suit. "Damn what up man, you look different today," he said, after he set down. "Yeah shit a lil' crazy for me today, right now got into some shit earlier and it got ugly had to smoke 2 niggas in public but it was self-defense. If I wasn't wearing a vest, I'm pretty sure I would of been smoked because the lil' nigga got 2 good shots off hitting me in the chest," Jacob said unzipping the hoodie, he didn't have on a shirt underneath and there was a big ugly bruise spreading across his chest. "Damn that shit got to hurt like hell." "Yeah it's kind of sore but I'll live, I'm pissed off because how them niggas come at me right in the middle of the parking lot at the mall earlier today in front of everybody. Them niggas ain't care if they were seen or not, they didn't even have suppressors on there gun. Lately I've done so much fucked up shits to niggas, I don't know who the hell the hit could of came from. But I'll tell you one thing I'm finna fuck the whole city up until I do find out who tried getting me killed, they shot my car up too, I don't know what the hell I'm going to tell my wife." "Your married?" "Yeah I'm married, I thought I told you that?" "I don't remember hearing it, that's crazy, your wild ass got a wife." "Kids too." "You got kids too, ain't no way!" "Yeah man, that's what I'm saying, I got to find out who after me and dead that shit before it get out of hand because I can't get my family involved in this shit." "You already got your family involved when' you got involved, that's just how the streets go this shit, ain't fair, that's why you gotta be ready so you don't got to get ready." "Oh you can believe I'm ready, I'm super duper ready, I was made for this shit." "Yeah but you worried about your fam finding out about your shysty ass ways, she didn't know she was marrying a gangsta," Bezo said laughing. "Come on man this shit ain't funny, I came over here to holla at you about some real shit and you laughing at ah nigga." "Aight aight my nigga I got you," Bezo said, trying to stop laughing. When he stopped,

Jacob took a sip of his coffee then proceeded to speak. "Like I said, I don't know who these mother fuckers are but they tried killing me and I'm going to need that reinforcement I was telling you about. The way I'm looking at it this shit is gonna get real ugly, I'm going to need your help because I believe this shit is gonna blow through the roof and I'm trying to put a lid on it before it does." "You know I got you, just tell me what you need, I got guns and goons on deck, whenever you need them just let me know and I'll send them over, but how did you like the one thing, is it doing good?" "Oh yeah, I'm going to need another 5 in a day or two." "Damn that shit that good?" "Jacob nodded his head. "You ever think about buying a bullet-proof car, if not I think this would be a good time for the new whips I got there bullet-proof, I can't afford to be killed right now. I got to much shit to do." "Bullet-proof ha!" "Yeah, I think you should consider getting all your cars proofed, especially your family vehicles." "I never thought about that, I already took my car to the shop. They say the quickest they could have it ready is in 2 days. I told them to paint it white instead of it's original color. I do need to get it bulletproofed because that's the car my wife and kids ride in. I don't even know what the hell I'm going to tell her when I come home in a different car." "Tell her you got in a car wreck." "I thought about that because I got the bruises on my chest but where did I get the new car from and where is the family car, I'm thinking about not even going home until I get the car out of the shop." "Damn it sounds like your more worried about your wife kicking your ass then niggas trying to kill you." "You got that right, I ain't worried about no amateurs like the ones from earlier doing shit to me but the wife could be a real pain in the ass. So I don't need that in my life right now but them bitch niggas knew I was at the mall, I don't know how, did they follow me, did somebody see me in there than call them, I don't know but if they followed me there were did they start tailing me from, plus all the shit I've been doing I never showed my face and if I did the person that saw my face ain't here to tell nobody it was me. That's what driving me crazy." "Well you know what you got to do, lay low til something pops up, other than that keep doing what you doing, getting money, and money solves problems, throw some money around and I'm sure something ah pop up." "I got my lil' cousin P out there running the streets, I hope he's straight, I ain't hollered at him yet so Imah be getting up out of here," Jacob said, standing up looking around. Bezo did the same and they walked outside together. "You drop a lot of cash on this thing, ha man!" Jacob said as he looked at the Mercedes, "Yeah plus another 50 grand to fully bullet-proof it." He kept drumming that in the heads of everyone he dealt with. "Yeah I believe I'm gonna have to bullet-proof all my cars, it's better to be safe than sorry, let me get that number." Bezo dug in his pocket for his phone then gave him the number. After getting back to the condo, Bezo took a shower then walked back in the living room with only a towel wrapped around his waist. Sitting down on the couch, he began flipping through the channels on the T.V. Stopping on the news, he listened to the reporter talking about the crime rate skyrocketing in the Bay area over the last couple of months. Robberies and murders were a daily thing. There was a shooting today at the St. Pete Mall that left two dead and the other suspect fled the scene in a red car. No one could get a description or a license plate number, so if anyone got any information please contact CrimeStoppers we need help from the community because this is getting out of hand. She was saying when Bezo changed the channel until he found a good movie on Fx. He set back relaxed in his own space feeling like the king he was, the only thing missing was a blunt. He got up walking to the kitchen where the Swisher Sweets and the weed were sitting on the island. After he got threw rolling, his phone began ranging. It was Elisha, she was wondering where he was and she wanted to spend some time with him if that was ok. He told her he would be over there in a little while, she wanted to know what a little while was, he told her in about an hour then she made him promise. She told him Chrystal was over there and she wanted him to bring something to drink and smoke, he laughed then said ok. He set down for a minute, finished the blunt then got dressed. Switching the Benz for the Audi, he made his way over to his second home and that was Elisha's place. When he came in, like always, lil' man ran up to him and he picked him up. He carried him over to his mother where he placed a kiss on her lips and Coby giggled and swiveled in his arms. "Yall look like a big happy family, this is so sweet," Chrystal said from the couch. "And please tell me you bring some weed and blunts." "Damn I forgot," he said and watched her smile turn to a sad face. "Knaw I'm just playing," he said, digging in his pocket, throwing the blunts and the bag of weed to her. "You got to grab the Ciroc out the back seat, I forgot to grab it." Bezo turned around as she made her way out the door hitting the unlock button on his remote. "You miss me?" Elisha said, wrapping her arms around him, kissing him harder. "Yeah I miss you," he said kissing her back and squeezing Coby tighter in his arms than put him back down on the floor. He ran to the back room. "He really likes you Bryson." "I know, I like lil' man too, I'm glad y'all came into my life you know what I mean, it makes everything better." "Who you tellin boy, my life is 100 times better since I met you." Chrystal came back in the house closing the door behind her. "Dang man, that car is so nice. I had to sit in the back seat to see how the celebrities are feeling when they are getting chauffeured. There's so much room back there. I need to get one of them, might take me 5 years of stacking my cash because I know that type of Audi got to be at least 100 grand." "Knaw it ain't that much." "Yeah right nigga, I got a coffee table full of Dupont Regestries, I know exactly what that car cost, big money Bezo," she said, deepening her voice making all them laugh. After Elisha put Coby to sleep, they gathered in the living room, smoked and drank all the Ciroc while Chrystal told them jokes and made them laugh. They convince Elisha to hit the blunt again and she didn't cough that bad like she did the last time and instead of ordering pizza she went in the kitchen and baked some cookies and brung a bag of Doritos back to where they were sitting. "Now these are my favourites, the sweet and spicy Doritos are the best thing they could have done and the Dorito tacos at Taco Bell. I'm in love with them but I gotta watch my weight. I'm getting a little bit older and I don't want to be skinny with a big ol' stomach like I got a beer belly or I'm pregnant," Chrystal was saying as she stuffed the chips in her mouth. Elisha was eating the chocolate chips real slow like they were the best thing in the world with a smile on her face. "Here baby, you got to try these," she said leaning over putting a piece of cookie in his mouth, he sucked her finger as she did. "You better stop boy before you start something you can't finish." "Come on baby you know I can finish anything I start, you know better than anybody," he said as he leaned over sucking on her neck, she only giggled and threw another piece of cookie in her mouth. "Yall so lovey dovey and good for each other, you might as well put a ring on my cousin finger and make this thing all the way official." "So you can bring your girlfriend to our wedding?" "Yep because I'm through with men like I said before, but I don't know, I guess all men ain't that bad," she said looking at him. "Oh now all men ain't that bad, but about a month ago all men were dogs with shit loads of fleas." "They are most of them anyways, I still feel like that but the way you came and swept Elisha off her feet, this is some fairy-tale type shit and if you break her heart and make her cry, I'm gonna cut your balls off my shelf and hang them on the wall like a stuffed animal." "Damn like that!" "Yeah just like that," she said as she popped another Dorito in her mouth. "And I'm going to help her and we go hang them right on this wall above the T.V. but I don't got to worry about that do I baby?" "Not at all, I don't want nobody but you, so no, you don't have to hang my balls on the wall." "I know baby," she said, leaning down kissing him again. "Damn Bezo, I didn't know you were this sweet." "I know, you don't know a lot of things about me." "You think I don't, you just like your trifling ass friend Rilo, God Bless the dead." "I thought you just said I was a good man." "I changed my mind." They both laughed. After smoking another blunt they went to the back room. Chrystal grabbed a blanket and a pillow, said she was sleeping on the couch, there was no way she could drive all the way home. After Bezo made love to Elisha she fell asleep on his chest. He felt right at home but didn't want to call it that, right now but sooner or later he would for her and lil man.

Chapter 35

"You don't even know if it was him who sent the hit or even if those were his people or not," "I don't know, you're right about that, but somebody gotta pay for this. If not, who did do it might think they could do it again," Jacob said as he put on his vest then tucked his gun on his waist. "So we go hit as many people as we can. Then that would even the odds. We get rid of the competition and maybe even the ones that tried killing me. We got to stay on top of shit like this if not then we're slippin, and guess what, slippers don't count because if you slippin that's your ass." Jacob said, handling P a vest to put on. When he was finished, they headed outside and got into the stolen vehicle. P got into the driver seat then they pulled off. Still uneasy about the whole situation, P asked him if he knew if he had any idea if Trav had his goons with him tonight. Because they both knew how Trav rolled. "I heard he's gonna be alone." Jacob stopped all that firepower that nigga got. "Man you scared or something," Jacob asked him. "You talking about how that nigga roll, fuck how that nigga roll, if he do got his goons with him then that's better, we can kill all they ass tonight. We ain't got to worry about them niggas later. That's how I see it." "Well fuck it, if you like it, I love it," P said, finally giving up trying to talk some sense in this nigga head. They drove the rest of the way in silence. When they got there, P parked across the street from the house where Trav was supposed to be coming tonight; the house was yellow and white. There was a fence that went all the way around the property, "That's the house right there," Jacob said as they set back in their seats behind the tinted windows watching the front of the house. "This is supposed to be the stash house; the only person that lived there was his granny. And she's really old. He stops by here once a week to check on her and to stash his money. He supposed to be by himself." "And you say a good friend told you this," P asked, "Aint that what I told you?" "Im just saying how would whoever told you any of that know for sure, he must be in the loop with these niggas," "Man just know whoever told me I trust them, if I didn't we wouldn't be here watching this niggas granny's house right now." He said, sitting back in his seat and started back watching the house. Nothing happened for over an hour and P was still thinking this was a bad idea when two SUVs came around the corner. He knew it was a really bad idea, then they watched the trucks stop in front of the house, one was a Mercedes, and the other was a Tahoe. Trav got out of the Mercedes. Three other men got out and pulled out two huge duffle bags. He said something to the taller one that was standing next to the other two. He nodded his head. Then Trav turned around, then started walking towards the house. Jacob reached in the back seat and came back up with the AK-47. Before P could ask what he was doing. He was jumping out the track firing shots from the coppa; it sounded like a helicopter was cranking its engine. He mowed Trav down in the front yard. Right on the lawn, the other three men tried ducking behind the trucks. But not before Jacob caught one of them in the back of the head and sent him slamming against the truck with the back of his head blown off. After regrouping, one of the man popped Jacob running back behind the expedition. P was already out crouching behind the driver side's front tire. He could feel the truck rocking from the impact of the slugs. "Hey, I'm gonna fire from this way, to try to get there attention on me," Jacob said over the gunfire. "When they start firing in my direction, you take one of them out. I'll get the other one." He said then started firing the rifle again. The two men ducked back behind the truck. Jacob stopped firing for a second, and when he did, a head popped up. P pulled the trigger and hit him in the center of it. His head exploded and he dropped like a sack of potatoes. Jacob didn't waste any time he came around the truck pulling the trigger, firing recklessly, penetrating and riddling the Escalade with bullets, forcing the last man to run around to the other side of the truck. When he came out, P started firing, striking him in his upper body, dropping him flat on the pavement. Jacob ran across the street and picked both of the duffle bags up then ran back over and through the ruffle and the bags on to the back seat he slammed the door then hopped into the passenger seat, he slapped the dashboard and told P to go. "Lets go nigga," he said again when he looked over at P. P pulled the trigger and sent a slug through his head. His brains flew out and splattered all over the window. P reached over him, opened the door and then pushed him out. He closed the door back then slammed his foot on the gas. The back tore ran over Jacobs's dead body. But P kept going. He didn't even look back. He checked the rearview mirror when he was down the road to make sure he was in the clear, he looked back at the duffle bags then at all the blood and brain matter that was on the window. He pulled a cigarette out of his pocket and lit it, then kept driving.

Chapter 36

Thirty minutes later, P pulled into the driveway of Jacobs's stash house. It was an old wooden house. Jacob was renting it in his own name, which was stupid, P thought as he carried the bags into the house. The place was fully furnished, and it smelled clean as if someone recently cleaned it. He knew Jacob did because he was a clean and a neat freak. Plus, he wanted control of everything. But he didn't know the first thing about being a boss. A boss would never use his real name to lease a house where he stashes his drugs. Second, he wouldn't ever pull no stupid shit like he pulled tonight, putting both of their lives in danger. P was up to here with his bullshit; he was tired Jacob felt as if he could talk to him and treat him however he wanted to. P was the one out in the streets, making all the money. P was the one setting niggas up to get robbed. P was the one making sure shit was in order. But P was the one always getting the shit end of the stick. He was talking to himself in the third person. Jacob never split nothing down the middle with him. It was more like 90/10 Jacobs way. Even when he started to buy all of that coke from his plug, he would never let him cash in with him. But he wanted him to save all the drugs. Then when he, did he got only a small percentage of the prophets, and if it wasn't for him, Jacob would have never known about selling heroin; it was his idea after he took some from a nigga when they did a robbery. Jacob agreed to let him purchase his own after the finished selling the brick they took, but when he saw how much money they could make. He later changed his mind and decided that he couldn't let him open his own trap, that it wouldn't be smart, so he bought a few bricks and told P to only sale ounces no break downs. He was tired of that shit. So when he saw him running back across the street with them bags. He decided then it was time for Jacob to be taken out. His time was up. And how P had the juice. He thought as he took the top off the pool table, he removed the bricks Jacob had stashed there. When he took them all out, he put the top back on. He picked the duffel bags up and set them on top the tale. Then unzipped them. When he saw all the cash that was inside of them his heart stopped and he grabbed the edge of the table to keep from falling because his knees were weak. There were bundles and bundles of cash with all 100 bills. This had to be over 5 million dollars cash, he thought as he looked down at all of it. He zipped the bags back up and thought that it would be best if he got the hell out of that house. He put the bricks into another bag. Then took them and all the cashback out to the car. He got in then drove to his house that he shared with his grandfather. No one knew where he lived so he thought that it would be safe enough. When he got into the house, he carried the bags to his room then set them down on the bed. He started to regret even killing Jacob. But then again, he didn't even give a fuck, fuck em, he thought. That was a whole lot of cash in there, and he knew Jacob had more of it put up somewhere, he was sure it was at his home he shared with his wife and kids. And he was sure his wife didn't know anything of it because he pretended to be a whole different person when he was home with them. But little did they know Jacob was on low down dirty motherfuckah. He walked and pulled one of the bricks out then ripped it open. He scooped some of the powder up with his pinky then snorted up his nostrils. He felt it shoot through his veins immediately. He needed to get to that other cash, he thought. He knew if Jacob's wife did know about it, he could beat it up out of her or threaten the children's lives. If she knew where it was, she would cough it up. He was sure of that but he would also need a plug. He knew that Jacob and Bezo were close friends; that he knew for sure. He met him once. When Jacob went over to pick up a single brick but something happened and now that nigga was the real plug. He blew up and Jacob blew up as well. "But I was just a puppet." P said to himself. But not anymore, he thought as he unzipped the bag and looked at all of his newfound treasure. Not any fucken more.

Chapter 37

The next morning, Heather rolled out of bed and looked at her phone. There was still no caus or text from Jacob. She tried again but it went straight to the voicemail. What in the hell is going on, she thought. Something had to be terribly wrong because she tried his cell over 20 times. He didn't call back, not once. She walked out of the room, then got the kids ready for school. When they were ready, she drove the short distance and dropped them off. Afterward, she went to the grocery store, picked up a few things then headed back home. She tried Jacob the whole time she was out. He didn't answer; she parked, then got out the car and walked back towards the house. When she put the key into the lock, she felt something cold and hard against the back of her head. "One mother fucken word and bitch fill blow your fucken brains out right here. Now open the door and step inside," the masked men said, pushing her into the house. He closed the door behind them, then pushed her onto the couch. She was in complete shock as he tied her, then covered her mouth. He started yelling at her and asking her where the cash was. She didn't know what he was talking about. "Where is the money, I'm not gonna keep asking you, and if you keep playing stupid, I'm gonna start cutting off your pretty little toes." He then snatched the tape off of her mouth. "I don't know what your talking about," she said through sobs. He slapped her then cover her mouth back up. He snatched her from the couch the started dragging her across the floor down the hall. "Oh you wanna play stupid," he said, then started kicking her. "If you move a fucken inch then I'm go do move than kick you, I'm go blow the back of your head off." He promised her then he started searching the house every inch of it, destroying things throwing them around. He went down to the basement. After being in the house for over an hour, he saw that there was a back shelf full of books, he went over and tossed it over on the ground, everything went tumbling over. He saw two duffle bags stuffed inside of the wall. "Jackpot bitch," he said to himself, stepping over all of the books and climbing over the bookshelf. He retrieved the bags out of the wall; they were heavy; he knew that they had to at least have a few million in them. He ran back up the stairs. Heather was still in the same spot, she looked confused when she saw him with the bags. "Oh you didn't know your husband was a drug dealer, a big one at that. Oh he was a killer too, a cold-blooded one at that. Living right under your roof, sleeping right next to you and you didn't even know." He said, looking down at her. She started crying and trying to wiggle away. She was sure he was gone kill her because he got what he was looking for. The back of her dress was risen up, and her panties was wedged between her cheeks. The sight of it made his dick hard. He squeezed his head through his teams. He set the bags down. Then undid his pants and let them fall to the floor. He snatched her panties completely off of her than straddle her. He spits on his hand, then ran it across her pussy, then forced himself inside of her. She could not do anything but cry as he slammed into her. He fucked her like a Jack Rabbit fast and hard until he came, he pulled out and shot all over her ass. When he regained his breath, he took her to the bathroom and made her take a shower, just like he and Jacob did before on one of there robberies. After she was good and clean, he tied her back up. Then left the house carrying both bags, he through them inside the truck then drove away. He turned up the music then wt a blunt. This was crazy. His whole life had changed for the good overnight. Literally, he was rich, richer than anybody would of ever thought he could be. Now he was to go make sure everybody knew who was the new sheriff in town.

Chapter 38

2 Weeks later

Twan was backed in at the auto zone on Hills Borough. He was in a black Chevy Silverado, with light tinted windows. It was after 7 PM and he was waiting for one of his lil homies to pull up. He watched as a Sedan pulled up and stopped next to him. He unlocked the door when Katman, his lil homie, got out and walked over. "What up big homie," he said when he got inside the truck. "Shit tired as hell ah nigga been up all day trying to get this shit together." "Yeah same here but I got this for ya," Katman said, handing him a wad of cash. "It's all there. You ain't ever got to worry about me being short for real for real." Twan put the cash in the glove compartment but would count it later that was law. He reaches in the back then gave him a quarter-brick of hard. "That's nine ounces, I'm making you up of mines like you always do." "Say less," Katman said, gave him dapp then got out of the truck. Twan pulled off and headed straight home. He had an apartment on 127th. No one knew where he lived. He never brings any bitches here. He brought everything in the apartment, it is poorly furnished but he didn't mind because he never lived in one spot too long. 6 months then he was on the next. He sat down on the couch then counted all the money he made tonight. He piled it up on the coffee table that was in front of him. When he finished, he grabbed his weed then started looking for the blunts. They were no were to be found; he could have sworn he brought them in with him. He cursed himself out, then headed back outside because they had to be in the truck. When he got back to the truck, he unlocked the doors then searched the inside; they weren't there. He jumped in, started the truck and pulled off, the store was right down the road; he wanted to grab some snacks anyhow. He pulled up to the 7-11 and parked at the gas pump then walked inside the store. He grabbed a few bags of chips, some candy and a 2 liter of Sprite. He walked to the register, paid for everything and purchased $30 of gas plus a pack of swisher sweet. He walked back out of the store with his things in a bag. A blue new Honda Civic was pulling up to the pump next to his truck; it had tent on it. The driver door opened and Draco's baby mama Kiesha got out. "Hey Twan," she said as she headed towards the store, he said, "What's up." While watching her ass. She had on some small tight white cotton shorts, the back of her ass was hanging out and her ass was phat. Dam, he thought as his dick jumped inside his shorts. He unscrewed his gas cap then started pumping the gas. He watched as she came back out of the store. He could see her entire pussy print, it was bursting through the fabric. "Dang, that's your truck too, Twan?" she asked as she walked to the gas pump. "Yeah I just got it, you like it?" "Yeah, it's nice, I just got this car. Draco crab ass act like he couldn't buy me a new one, so I had to stack my cash and wait to my income tax check came then I got this," "Oh, I didn't know you and Draco was still together," he said testing the water's, "We ain't, he just my sorry ass body daddy. I don't even be fucking that nigga no more," she said but Twan knew that was a lie. He asked her did she smoke and she said yeah. "I got some tree's at the crib if you wanna smoke real quick," he knew he was crossing some dangerous lines. But with a smile on her face then said, "Ok," then he told her to follow him. Twan pulled off. She pulled out behind him. When they got back to the complex, they both parked then walked up to his place. When they walked in, she saw all the cash on the coffee table. Twan scooped it up and ran it to the back room. He came back up a few moments later. She was sitting on the couch. "Dam boy want give a bitch shit. I told him to let me hustle because everybody fuck with me in the project. But he want give me nothing but his ass to kiss. With his ugly ass," she said. "Yeah, but he takes care of you and his son like he is supposed to do and you shouldn't want to sell drugs anyhow. You are so beautiful that you are supposed to be somebody's wife at the crib cleaning up and cooking and shit like that not trapping," "Yeah, whatever, that shit sounds good. You niggas just be rapping telling a bitch anything, have a bitch sitting there why yall running around fucking all these other hoes. I ain't waiting on no nigga, I'm trying to get that bag by myself. I'm not waiting a lifetime to be saved by a no-good ass nigga, fuck that not me, lit the blunt." "See, that's the problem with you Niggas, yall think oh bitch can't get no money. Like bitches ain't hungry like we ain't got a desire to get rich, I wanna eat to. I wanna pull up in foreign cars, rock jewelry, and designer clothes to, I'm a hustle. And watch what I tell you, I'm go get rich." Twan was watching the entire time she was talking and smoking the blunt. She had some big ass titties, he thought. He watched as they bounced around while she was talking. Her shirt stopped right above her navel and it was pierced. She was sexy as hell. Her dark skin was smooth. She had a pretty face and her teeth were white. He didn't know why Draco ain't keep his dick inside of her. But if she was his baby mama he sure as hell would. "You ain't never thought about dancing," he asked her. "Hell yeah I thought about stripping, a bitch could dance too." "You can't dance," he joked, "Yes I can, a bitch ain't got all this ass for nothing." She said, then leaned over and slapped it. "Well, let see," he said, grabbing his remote then pressed play on the stereo. He reached in his pocket the pulled out a wad of cash then told her to dance. "You want me to dance right here right now?" "Hell yeah, right here right now, yall talking about you know how to dance let see plus I got all this cash you want it or not." "Yeah I want it," She said then stood up from the couch. She handed him the blunt then started moving her body to the beat. He threw a few bills at her and she started bouncing her ass in his face. She bent all the way over, making one cheek jump at a time. He squeezed both of them then put his face in between them. She started taking off her clothes the more cash he threw. Now all she had on was her thongs. Her breast was out and they were pierced. She put them in his face. He began sucking on her nipples. She smiled down at him and most of the cash he pulled out was now on the floor. She put one of the legs on the couch. Putting her pussy in his face, he pulled her panties to the side then started licking and sucking on her flesh. He pulled her panties all the way off then turned her all the way around. She bent back over, and then he started eating her ass and her pussy from the back. She had to grip the table to keep from losing her balancing because he was devouring her; shoving his fingers and tongue inside of her. He pulled his dick out and set her down on it. She was tight, warm, and wet. She started bouncing up and down in a circular motion, he was gripping her ass as she did her thing. She leaned all the way over and grabbed her ankles. She came all the way up and dropped all the way down on his dick. He grabbed her, then flipped her over on the couch. He threw her legs behind her head then slid back inside of her. She dug her nails into his back as he slammed into her. He pounded away. He didn't even consider pulling out as he came and shot a load inside of her. She was shaking underneath him. This was the third time cumming, he fell on top of her breathing hard. He almost fell asleep. Until she taped his arm and told him to let her get up. He rolled over and she got up then walked to the restroom where she wiped herself off. She got back, dressed then scooped all the cash up off the floor and put it inside her purse. She leaned down and kissed him on the cheek then told him to just call her if he wanted to do this again. She walked out the door, locking it behind him. Dam that was crazy, he thought as he set up. He was regretting giving that bitch all that cash. That was over three thousand dollars. He gave her that just for some pussy. But he couldn't lie, Kiesha had some good pussy and she put on a dam good show for a nigga. But for real, all the excitement came from just knowing that he was fucking Draco's baby mama. He knew Draco would kill both of their ass in a heartbeat if he ever found out about that shit, but he didn't even care he was gone fuck that bitch every chance he got, because Draco was acting like a bitch.

Ever since Bezo gave him a position, he could sense that Draco didn't like it at all. Because every chance he got, he tried talking to him any kind of way he wanted in front of everybody like he wasn't a killer too. All of the time, he put his life on the line for that nigga. He even saved him from being killed. If it wasn't for him, both him and Bezo would be dead. But he handled up and did his job and saved them niggas like he was suppost to. Twan didn't get it, who else was supposed to hold shit down why he was out of commission. Bezo needed his help and that's exactly what he did. He built the team up better than he could've ever done. And now he was acting like a bitch. But Bezo played fair and made sure he got his fair cut. And he treated him with respect. And Draco didn't like that at all, not one bit, he could see it all over his face. He wanted Twan to know he had more rank than him. Draco was 29 years old, only six years older than Twan but he treated him like a little kid. And he wasn't feeling that shit anymore. That nigga felt like he was god and since he started booming that boy, can't nobody tell him shit, that nigga think he frank lucas with the blue magic. Twan didn't know why they all couldn't just get along, get money, and see eye to eye. He was pushing bricks too, he could save bricks with the best of them. He was pushing them all over the city even a few niggas out of town was coping from him. He thought as he got up from the couch then got into the shower. He got out and dried off, wrapped the towel around his waist, walked back in the living room, set on the couch and rolled another blunt. He was go keep fucking Kiesha and he knew it was dangerous. But dangerous was his type of game but he wasn't sure if he was ready for Draco type dangerous and all the other crazy shit that came with it.

Chapter 39

Bezo was just walking into the house when Twan pulled up in the driveway behind him. This was their new spot, only Twan and Bezo knew about it. He left the door open and Twan came in behind him. Bezo set down on the couch. Twan came over gave him dapp. Then handed him a Nike bag full of cash. "I got ten bricks for you out there in the truck. Bezo was moving a little differently since Jacob got killed. He tightened up on everything. He had just talked to Jacob a few days before that. Then he got himself killed, that shit scared the shit out of him and he was refusing like hell to go out like that. He saw the headlines on the news. He got gunned down in a shootout four other people got killed. They believed somebody else was there but they got away. A few days ago, Jacob's cousin, P, started calling. He wanted to have a sit down with him, but Bezo kept putting it off because he didn't really know that nigga. Plus he feels a little uneasy about the whole dam situation. He was just been careful, trying to stay free and alive, he was basically living at the house with Elisha and Coby and they both were loving it. He was loving it too, he couldn't even lie. Bezo got up from the couch. He ran outside, got the bricks then came back in; Draco has up to 10 bricks now. That made him busy all the time so he was barely there with them. He gave Twan the bricks then watched as he ripped one of them open and started wiping it up over the stove inside an aluminum pot. He saw him and Draco do it so much he had it down packed.

Business on every block on PayRoll. Bezo was doing so good Ricardo wanted for him to fly in next week to attend a big party he was hosting. He didn't really want to go but he couldn't tell him no. His phone rang and he looked at it. It was Jacob's cousin again. This was only his third time but Bezo was getting tired of this nigga. "Yo," Bezo said, putting the phone to his ear. "What up bra," P said "I know you probably tired of me but I was really needing to talk to you." "Yeah I told you I was go call you when I got some time, I should be back in town tonight then I'll hit you up then. I'll find some were for us to meet." "Yeah, yeah that's good. I swear you wont be wasting your time. You know I got mad respect for ya. Jacob told me a lot about you. I know he had to mention me because that was big cuz and we were together all the time, you know what I mean." "Yeah I hear ya but I don't like talking over this phone, I'll call you at 8o' clock and let you know were to meet me." Bezo said, "Ok I got cha," P said. Bezo hung up before he could say anything else. Bezo told Twan he was heading out and to hold the spot down. He'll catch up with him later. He got into his car then headed to his condo. He hasn't been there for over 3 days. He felt good as home when he walked in. He walked to the back and just threw the bag of cash onto the bed because the safe was completely full, he couldn't even close the door. He promised himself to get a new one. He also promised to take Elisha car shopping today. Her car broke down on the interstate the other day he had to pick her up.

She had his Mercedes right now and she was loving it. All she did was shop after he convinced her to quit her job. She switched up his whole wardrobe, all he wore was designer now, Gucci, Louis Vuitton, Fendi, and all types of other shit he couldn't pronounce. She got her and Coby swag right as well and Chrystal was right there on every shopping spree. He pulled one of the Cuban cigars form the box and lit it. Ricardo turned him on to these things and this was the place he came to clear his mind; to reflect on everything else. He always thought about his nigga Rillo. He sent a few thousand dollars to his sister yesterday. He wanted to do more for them but they wouldn't allow him to, they almost always declined his help. He didn't know if they knew what was going on in the streets or not. But he knew ever since he got the throne shit have gotten way more scarier. Because he ran a vicious team and he was getting niggas walked every other day. So he had to move and think for everybody around him because he was the head and the leader of his team. He would meet with P later tonight just to see what he needed to say, even though he didn't want to. But that was Jacob's lil cousin, the least he could do was talk to him. But he wasn't trusting him because shit was cut-throat right now. "And Jacob was dead because he was slipping and slippers didn't count?" He asked the cigar, then turned the T.V and switched the channel to M.T.V. There were newly released music videos playing. There was a new rapper from Atlanta name looney, his new song was all over the Radio and this was his new video soon as it came on his phone started ringing. He looked around but it wasn't on the couch. He must have left on the sink in the restroom. He got up from the couch and retrieved it. There was a missed call from Elisha. He called her back and she wanted to know where he was. "I'm on my way to you," he said to her. She said ok then hung up. He walked in the room and grabbed the bag of the bed Twan had gave him. Then headed back out the door, he took the elevator down to the parking garage then got back into the Audi. He called the dealer last week and ordered a 645 BMW fully loaded and bulletproofed brand new for Elisha. It was gonna run him one hundred and fifty thousand dollars. But he didn't care, it was just some money. He stopped by the flower shop and purchased a dozen red roses for Elisha. A few minutes later, he pulled into the driveway, Coby came running out. He ran up to the car and tried getting into the back seat. Bezo turned around and opened the back door for him. Elisha came out and got into the passenger's seat. He leaned over, handed her the flowers and gave her a kiss. "Aww these are so pretty." She said, bringing them up to her nose, smelling them. She leaned back over and gave him another kiss. He backed the car out of the driveway. Then took 1-4 all the way to 275 where the dealer shop was right off the exit. When he pulled up, they were immediately met by Henry Falken, the same salesman that sold him the Mercedes and the Audi. "Hello Mr. Byson, how is it going?" He said as Bezo got out of the car. "And is this the lovely wife and child," he asked as he shook Elisha's hand. Bezo got the bag from the back seat and handed it to him, telling him to keep the change. Elisha grabbed Bezo's hand and they walked in hand in hand. When they got into the building, he took them over to a triple black 645, it was on the showroom floor. "Fully loaded, and bulletproof just like you wanted it," Faulken said, showing them the car. These things are in high demand. This is the third one I sold this week. But they weren't as exclusive as this one. The other ones were basic.

And this one isn't basic at all. "You wanna take a look inside," Bezo asked her. "Oh my God Bryson, is this my car?" She asked him, "Yeah you like it right?" "Yes I like it," she said then went over and got into the driver seat, Coby followed behind her. "You must really love her," Falken said as they watch Elisha and Coby look around the car. "Yeah she's cool." He and Falken walked over to Falken's desk and the cash was counted up. He ran it to the back and told Bezo to give him one minute. When he came back, they started on the paperwork. They were finished within an hour. The car was pushed off the showroom floor and brought outside, Elisha and Coby followed out behind it. When it was outside, they got right back inside the car. Faulken walked alongside Bezo. He was thanking him for the good business that he brought to the dealership. "And whatever else you need just let me know, if it's not here I'll get it here within 24 hours no matter the make or model, you know what I mean you take care of me, I'll take care of you. What are you anyway, a rapper or something." Bezo turned and look at him without saying a word. Faulken held up his hands. "You know what, I'm sorry for even asking you just keep bringing your good business and I'll keep with the good service." "That sounds much better," Bezo said then shock his hand. Bezo got into the car. He told Faulken he'll be keeping in touch then he pulled off, Elisha followed behind him. Forty minutes later, they got back to the house. He made a few phone calls then played in the back yard with Coby for a while. Elisha was in the house talking on the phone with Chrystal about her new car. Once he and Coby came back in the house, he looked at the time and told her that he had to be going. He promised her he would be back later tonight, he gave her a kiss then left the house. He drove the Mercedes to the spot where he told Draco to meet him. He was already there sitting on the couch when Benzo walked in. "What's good," he said then shook Draco's hand. "I need for you to take a ride with me and tell me what you think about this nigga. He's Jacob lil cousin." "Yeah I know Jacob that's your homeboy from St. Pete that got killed right?" "Yeah him. But I got a meeting with his lil cousin P who was moving shit with him and I'm assuming since Jacobs dead, he wanna continue to do business. I don't really know him but he is Jacob's cousin, and I don't want to just leave him hanging. He has to be an alright dude because Jacob didn't mess with too many people. I never heard him mention no one but his lil cousin. But right now I'm just no trusting shit," "You ain't suppost, to" Draco said, "That nigga could be the police or just a snake ass nigga tryna rob. You gotta be careful bra real shit." "Yeah I hear ya," Bezo said, "Just bring some more lil niggas with you to just be around just in case some shit pop off." He texted P and let him know where to meet him at. He set the phone back down table. "I need another ten of them things to bra." Draco said to Bezo. "Then shits moving so fast if I tell you the type of money I'm making you wouldn't even believe it because it's unbelievable. The last two weeks been crazy. Niggas from everywhere shopping with me. Plus Robles park is a cash cow, you wouldn't believe how many people on that shit." "I bet it's a lot of hoes on that shit to," "Hell yeah, bad btiches to them hoe's be hitting that shit then nodding off, as soon as they do, I'm pulling my dick right out and putting it in their mouth, you all ready know me nigga." They both started laughing then walked out the house and got into Bezo's Mercedes. It took them over 30 minutes to get to the hard rock casino were Bezo had got a suite for tonight on the 5th floor. P text and let him know he was outside. Bezo gave him the room number then waited for him to come up. Bezo was sitting on the couch when he knocked on the door. Draco got up and answered it. P walked in, Draco patted him down taking the gun from off of his waist then he patted his chest to check for wires. P stood there with his hands up the whole time. When Draco was done, he told him to have a seat. He walked over to were Bezo was and extended his hand Bezo took it and shook it. "Good to meet you," Benzo said to him as he poured himself a glass of patron then passed the bottle to Draco. He took it and started to drink from it. "Don't mind him, he's a good friend of mine, anything you have to say you could say around him, everythings cool." He assured him. Bezo lit his cigar with a high top fade with waves on the top of his mouth and two at the bottom. He looked to be about 24. P took a deep breath then said, "Alright, you already know what happened to Jacob." Bezo nodded his head. "I was there" P said. We was trying to rob this nigga name Trav, and shit went all the way bad. But I got away with the cash. Plus I still had all the work cuz had leftover. I use to go in with him when he shopped with you." P lied and hoped Bezo didn't know he was lying. "And now since he's gone I don't have any way to continue supplying the city because I don't have a plug. And I got a lot of cash and I need to re-up; niggas in the city waiting on me. Me and Jacob did a lot of fucked up shit to a lot of niggas. And now with Jacob gone, they might think it's time for them to try talking the city back. And me without any work would be the best way for them to do that but I can't allow that not with all the work we put in, it ain't," he said looking at Bezo with pleading eyes. Bezo looked over at Draco and he struggled with his shoulder. "How much are you trying to spend?" Bezo asked him. P looked back at Draco then looked down at the pen, a paper that was sitting on the table. "I rather write it down." He said, grabbing the pen and paper. He wrote something on it then passed the paper over to him. Bezo got it then looked at it. He blinked then looked at it again because he thought he was reading it wrong. He wanted to purchase 50 bricks of cocaine and 10 bricks of boy. Bezo handed him the paper back. P put it in his pocket. "You know the numbers?" Bezo asked him, "Can you write them down for me?" Bezo shrugged, set his glass down, wrote down the numbers when he was finished he slid the paper over to him. P looked at it then nodded his head and set the paper back down on the table. "I can have that to you whenever you want it," P assured him. Bezo told him he would give him a call. They set around and small talked for a few more minutes then Draco gave P back his gun and showed him the door. "So what did you think." Bezo asked him. "Shit I don't know yall go tall secretive and started writing shit down." "Yeah I know, that shit was kind of crazy. But let's get up out of here." "Go ahead I'm going to stay back, this room is exclusive to let it go to waste like that, I'm tomorrow." Bezo said alright then gave him dapp and left. When he left the room, Draco went back over to look at the paper that was left on the table, when he turned it over and saw the number, he was in complete shock. It read 1,950,000. "Shit," Draco said then set the paper back down. He didn't know but he just might have to look into P a lil more to see what was really going on. He finished the bottle and picked up the phone dialed a number, when It was picked up. He gave Kiesha the room number and told her to come through.

Chapter 40

While the heat was cooling down, P had purchased 3 more spots to hold down all his cash. And all the work he got from Bezo a few days ago was some good shit, he thought as he tasted the cocaine. He knew it was all pure as his face went numb, he broke down a few Kilos, then made a few phone calls. So niggas could come pick them up. He cut the boy with rat poison then distributed it only to a few hoods. When he was done, he parked his newly purchased Meroed then got into his Maserati granturismo sport, and pulled away. He arrived at his house and pulled into the garage. It was crazy how things had turned around for him. And all of it was positive. He was now the man in charge of the whole damn city with an iron fist. Something Jacob weird ass couldn't do. Some niggas is just better off dead, he thought as he dressed in his new Balenciaga outfit and put on all his new jewelry, which were 3 cuban link chains, a few diamond rings and a brand new audemar piguet. When he was done, he stuffed his pockets with cash and put his gun on his waist then headed back out the door. He pulled on Seminole where everybody was posted up. He parked the Maserati and got out. "Oh shit that's P," he heard somebody say from around smoking and drinking. He walked over and gave them all dap. "Damn my nigga you shitting on everybody in the city." "One I'm doing it right now, I ain't playing with these niggas." P had on more ice than anybody out there and his money was hanging out of his pockets. But everybody knew how vicious he was to even think about robbing him or coming at him like he was someone to play with. They all knew how he got down and everybody knew his cousin Jacob and how sick that nigga was. They all knew they were the ones around here robbing and killing everybody. But no one had big enough balls to confront them. "So when you Niggas ready to head out?" P asked. Because the whole hood was supposed to be hitting the strip club tonight, he looked down at his AP knowing damn well he couldn't see the time because it was fun on the ice. "It's 11:30 right now, we can headout at 1o' clock, the club should be poppen then," GG said. P said, "Aight," then they started shooting dice and smoking weed. When it was time to go, P pulled out with everyone following behind him. When they got to the club, he paid for everyone to V.I.P park there wips. He walked in the club surrounded by his goons. They purchased 2 booths in the V.I.P section, 20 bottles and $20,000 in one dollar bills and as soon as everything arrived, they started poppin bottles and throwing money, every bitch in their booths were butt ass naked. He didn't know how the DJ knew his name but he was shouting him out over the microphone as they threw money around, dam this shit crazy, he thought as he bounced around and sipped from the ciroc bottle. Young Jeezy came on over the speakers and the club went crazy. This was the life, he thought. This was the life he deserved and he didn't have anymore regrets for smoking Jacob bitch ass or doing what he did to his wife, fuckin' her. The only thing he did regret was not killing her white ass. The last song came on. He rounded all of his people up with all the hoes they would be taking back to the suite he had on the beach. When they got outside, they waited for the valet to go get their cars. The Maserati was the first to arrive. He got in with a red bone bitch he met in the club. He pulled out then waited for his crew to catch up but a fight broke out right there in the V.I.P area so they were on hold. He felt uneasy about sitting there so he pulled off and would just meet them at the hotel. He got on the interstate and got the Maserati up to 150 miles per hour. He slowed down then got off of the interstate. It took him another 5 minutes to pull up to the miurious hotel. Instead of value parking, he found a spot in the parking lot and pulled into it. He was about to get out of the car until he saw a black Tahoe pull into the hotel and start coming his way. "Are they with you because they have been following us since we left the auto," "Oh yeah," P said. As he turned the car back on and tried backing up but the SUV blocked his path. P slammed on the gas and slammed into the truck. He pulled out his gun and started firing through the back window. The doors flew open on the Tahoe. Then they started backfiring at him, riddling the car with bullets. The girl was screaming at the top of her lungs. He felt himself get hit in the upper thigh then in the back twice. "Shit," he screamed turning in the seat so he could shoot back. He glimpsed at the girl she had taken one to the back of the head and she was dead. He couldn't get any shots off because there were too many coming his way. Then the shots suddenly stopped and the truck sped off but some one started shooting at them. He looked up to see the security guard firing as the truck sped away then ran over to make sure P them was good. He asked if they were ok, P said he don't know and told him to call for help because he was hit. He called for help. When the paramedics got there, they both were taken out of the car. He was put onto the stretcher. When he saw his home boy pull up, they hoped out and asked him what was going on. He said he didn't know. But he promised himself he would find out, because he needed to, because he was too rich to be dying right now.

Chapter 41

Toya woke up in the massive bed. She opened her eyes and looked up at the roof of the mansion. It feels as if double R had kidnapped her. But she didn't care, she could live like this forever for the rest of her life. Yesterday, double R had took her on a all day shopping spree in new York. They got back last night. They were both exhausted and went straight to sleep. But double R was already gone. He left her a note for her on the dresser next to an envelope full of cash. He told her he needed to run off to handle some business but she should go shopping and she could use whatever car she wanted. She smiled and headed to the shower. This nigga double R was a trip, she thought as she got under the water. Ever since looney dropped his video everyone was checking for her. But double R put cuffs on her and made sure everyone knew who girl she was. He even took her out of the magazine. She really felt some way about that. Larry did as well, he almost quit. But double R convinced him to stay. He told toya that she was his girl and he didn't want her in no magazine like that. She didn't need any exposure any how, because he was the exposure. He took her with him everywhere he went. He wanted everyone to know that they were a couple and she didn't remember even agreeing to be his girl. But she couldn't lie, Ryan, double R, who ever the hell he wanted to be, he was a sweet man and she didn't see no flows in him yet, not one. He always told her she was the baddest bitch in the world. And ain't no other girl ever fucked him like she did, she was something special and he wasn't never letting her go, not in a million years. She got out of the shower, put on a robe then walked down stairs. She made herself breakfast then took backup stairs to the room. She set on the bed then turned on the TV. Looney was starting to be a big thing and his video was always on every time she turned on MTV videos. She could tell Ryan didn't like it because he knew T.J was on to something. She hasn't heard from him or seen him since the last time she saw them in the club. But that was ok with her. Fuck that nigga, she thought as she charged the TV the watched the view while she ate her food. When she was finished, she got dressed then grabbed the cash off the dresser double R left for her. She put it in her purse. She took the keys for the Maybach off the counter then headed outside. She made it down the long driveway and waited for the gate to open, when it did, she zoomed through. She admire the neighborhood as she drove through it, everybody had mansions out here. She didn't know how in the hell she could have possibly pull this off; walking up in mansions, riding foreign cars with over a million dollars in her bank account. She started without a dime. She thanked no one but God for this because he knew exactly what she was through and exactly where she came from. She pressed her foot down heavier on the gas and the Maybach shot forward, it moved like a yacht out on the ocean. She never smoked in any of his cars but she had an eighth of white window and she needed to blow real quick. She pulled up to a gas station, parked at the pump and ran into the store for a pack of blunts. She came back out, got into the car and started rolling the blunt. As soon as she finished, someone knocked on the window and she jumped. She turned to see looney smiling, looking in at her. "Boy you scared the hell out of me," She said, rolling down the window. "I thought this was you over here," he said. "How you know this was me," she asked him. Because this double R Maybach, everybody knows this car and he ain't letting nobody drive his wips. I seen a female behind the wheel, I said that got to be Toya and I was right. And I know you don't fuck with us no more but dam I ain't did nothing to you." "Boy I am not beefing with yall, I don't know what T.J told you but whatever it was he he was lying and he left me in the middle of Atlanta in a got dam restaurant, like I was some random ass hoe. Just because I was working with Ryan," "I see yall doing more than just working now, Double R got your ass cuffed. I ain't never seen that nigga like this. I heard you finna get married." He said, smiling, showing all the diamonds on his gold teeth. "Who told you some shit like that?" "Know I'm just playing you wifey doe, he getting you push the Maybach," "I don't care what you wanna think. But I'm finna blow this," she said, holding up the blunt. "You wanna smoke with me?" "Hell yeah," he said then got inside the car. "I seen the video," she said, lighting the blunt, "I thought y'all was gne take me out of it. You know like edit." "Knaw I couldn't allow that you were the baddest bitch on the set. I don't know what you and T.J got going on but I don't got nothing to do with that. So just so you know we still cool." He said as she passed him the blunt. "Ok I can dig that." She said as she looked pass his shoulder out of the window. She wondered was that his Bentley two gas pumps down. "What with T.J, he doing good though?" She asked.

"Oh yeah, he doing dam good. He moaning a lot of shit happen for us right now. I know you probably heard of Jay Ratchet by now. He got some hot shit on the Radio, that his artist to." "I bet he hates my guts now that I'm around here fucking with his suppost to be enemie but it wasn't even like that at first. I swear me and Ryan ain't have anything going on but it is what it is now." "Yeah fuck it. It is what it is just like you said but this is some good weed, were you cop this at." "Shit I don't know, Ryan got it for me." She rolled down the window and throughout the roach. "Well it's been nice seeing you hopefully, I'll see you around again knowing you got the cuffs on you." "Boy whatever," she said, smiling, looking over at him. She always admired his swag. Everything was hood about him and he was definitely a real street dude. He was also always on the chill. She had to admit, he was a real cool dude. "Let me get your number." She said, "So if I'm out and about I could hit you up plus I know your ass is always blowing." He gave her his phone and she put her number in it. "I might be out of town doing shows next week." She said ok then told him she would catch up with him whenever they both had the time. He got out of the car and she watched him walk back over to the Bentley and then sped away.

***

After leaving the mall, Toya headed back to Double R's mansion. Just as she was getting out of the Maybach, he came pulling down the driveway in the wraith. He parked the car then came over to her. He leaned down then gave her a kiss, "What you been up to sweetheart?" he asked. "Nothing much just went shopping, I was bored, were you been?" "Just handling a few things but I'm all down now wanted to spend the rest of the day with you. I let you sleep in because I knew that you were a little jet-lagged. But if you can get dressed in something more comfortable I want to take you somewhere and this place is one of my favorite places in the world. I go there to clear my mind. I think you would love it." She didn't know what the hell he was talking about. But she said ok then they went into the house were he bend her over the bed and fucked her real quick. They both took a shower then got dressed. She put on some blue jeans and a pair of black polo boots. Double R had on a crisp white t-shirt blue Levi Jeans and a pair of brand new white Timberlands. They went back out and got into the range rover. "You like the way the Maybach drives?" He asked as they drove down the driveway. "Yes," she said. "It's like a dream come true; all of this is like being a dream come true. I'm having the time of my life right now." He nodded his head and continued to drive. Half an hour later, they build up to a tall white brick building. They got out and walked inside. Soon as they came through the doors, Toya knew exactly what this place was. This was a firing range. There were handguns and all types of rifles hanging from the wall. They knew exactly who Double R was because they came from behind the counter and embraced him like they were lifelong friends. He told them what they wanted then they were led back to their booth. Double R told her to cover her ears with the ear muffs they gave to them. She watched as he loaded the rifle got into his stands then started firing at the target, over and over again. She watched as he dropped the cup then reloaded the gun. He told her to come over so he could show her how to do it. She told him she didn't need his help that he could step back. She adjusted the riffle, stood straight, then started pulling the trigger. He watched in complete shock as she dropped the cup. Slammed another one, cocked the gun then started firing again. When she was done, she set the riffle down, looked over at him and asked him how did she do. "Dam," was all he could say, then he asked her who taught her, "My granddaddy," she lied. "Damn you a bad bitch for real." He said then kissed her on the lips. "You know I'm fucked up about you, right?" "You are?" "Hell yeah," "Do you tell that to all of your women or just me?" I don't have nobody else all I got is you queen." "Don't be lying to me Ryan because I'm nobody's fool." "I ain't trying to play you." He said to her. "I hope your not," she said, then kissed him on the lips and squeezed his hard dick through his jeans. Then she turned around, walked back over to the booth, picked up the handgun, and started firing at the target, hitting it with every round.

Chapter 42

Looney backed up the Bentley in the projects then waited for his lil cousin, Rondo, to come down. When he got in the car, he handed looney a brown paper bag full of cash. Looney handed him a bag full of cocaine. Even though his rap career looked promising, this was his bread and butter. T.J was telling him he needed to aim out and just focus on the music. He would love to, but right now, he just couldn't do it. He made a few more stops. Then he made his way to the studio where T.J was waiting for him. He wasn't gonna tell him that he ran into Toya today because he knew he was feeling some type of way about that bitch. And he was tryna fuck that hoe anyways even if he had to pay; he had to have that bitch. He knew that pussy and that head was good. T.J stayed bragging about it. He parked then went inside the building. T.J was sitting on the couch and Ratchet was in the booth. He was from zone 6 east Atlanta. He had a name in the streets for beating a murderer about three years ago. "What it do lil bra." T.J said as looney came in, "Shit nothing just ready to hit the booth. I see Ratchet doing his thing right now," "Yeah we tryna finish this song up, then you are in there for the rest of the night. We got a few shows in full. We should be hitting the road pretty soon. So get your shit together for a real bra. I need your head all the way in the game and you know what I'm talking about. We need to get this real money. Just watch all the hard work go pay off. You and Ratchet, both of you niggas go be stars. You up first then him up next, I am ready to get labus hitting my line trying to kick out some paper. But we already got the paper they were talking about. We build our brand up then they ain't got a choice but to come at us direct, watch and see. I'm a mastermind when it comes to shit like this." "Yeah I feel you big bra on all that but I needed to holla at you about something," "Holla at me about what?" "I need to grab five of them. I got a few plays I need to be getting at," "Come on man Loon, you need to be chilling out," "I am, I usually get at least ten from you but I only want five. I just need to get this cash you know that and I just bought the Bentley I need to get that cash back as soon as I do in putting this music first I'm go be all in with it." Loony said. T.J thought about it for a moment then told him when they got up out there, he would run and go get the bricks for him. "But you have to put this music shit first bra." "I know big homie." "I'm glad you do," he said. Looney set his cup down then set back on the couch. He knew T.J's intention was good and he always had his back. He was always there for him no matter the situation. It's been plenty of times when he fucked all of his cash up and didn't know what he was going to do or who he was going to call when everyone let him down and turned their backs on him. But not T.J, he was always there to lift him up when he was down. Like once when he told him not to be trusting his baby mother like that and don't be leaving all of his cash at her crib. But he didn't listen. And one day when he was in the projects, the police rushed them and he had a gun on him, and they caught him with it. He violated probation with the new charge then got sent off to the prison. He caught 3 yrs and had to do 65% of that. But his baby mama ran off with all his cash with her new boyfriend, which was his cousin, Kenny, and they had a baby together when he got out of prison. T.J put him right back on his feet and made sure he never fell off again. And when that bull shit happened with Double R, he took T.J's side and showed his loyalty. That's why T.J looked at him like he was a lil brother and didn't want nothing but the best for him. They sat there for the next 30 minutes until Ratchet finished up and he got inside the booth and recorded a few songs. When he was finish, he told T.J and Ratchet he was gonna be getting up out of there. But hit him up because he needed to get them things from him. T.J said he was gonna hit him up in about an hour then they could meet up at Looney out Gloria's house. Loony knew T.J wasn't coming into the hood with work on him. So Gloria's house was good because she didn't live in the hood. T.J set there with Ratchet for another hour then he left the studio and head straight to his house were he went into his escalade, he left there and drove to his stash house were he picked up five bricks threw them into a bag then headed back out. Thirty minutes later, he pulled up to Gloria's house and called Loony to let him know he was there. 5 minutes later, looney pulled up in his Bentley, he go out with a bag, ran over to the driver's window and handed it to him. T.J gave him the bricks; Loony ran back to the car and sped off. TJ shook his head then said a quick prayer for him and hoped that he stayed free alive and safe. Because of how fast that nigga was living, he was gone need all the blessings he could get.

Chapter 43

Toya stepped out of the Maybach as the valet opened her door. She was wearing a Raisa Vanessa set, paired with Christian Louboutin sandals. Double R came around, taking her by the hand. He was in the black Celine suite, with Celine boots and sunglasses. They were escorted into the 5-star restaurant. He made reservations, so they were also escorted to their table. A bottle of Moet and Chandon, Double R poured her a glass. She was used to this everywhere they went, especially in Atlanta. He was treated with much respect, and he always left behind a huge tip. "Mr. Reynolds, what would you and the lovely lady be having tonight?" Double R ordered for the both of them. The server wrote down their orders then turned around and walked away. "Cheers to the good life," he said and raised his glass "To the good life." Toya said, then tapped his glass. "I have a party that I was invited to next week by a good friend of mine out in California. I want for you to join me, after we leave there, we could visit Miami. I have a condo there on the beach. It's nice. We could do a little shopping, a little clubbing, have a lot of sex, then come back home. That sounds good to you?" "Sounds great, where you been all of my life?" She said, smiling, looking over at him. This nigga didn't mind spending a lot of money while showing her the world at the same time. She wouldn't be surprised if he asked her to marry him. This shit was too good to be true, she thought but she would just keep taking it one day at time. "So Cali to Miami, you must do this all the time. New York to Vegas, Cali to Miami, Atlanta to Texas, your all over the place." "I try to be," he said, "It's the best way to do business. It's better to be bigger than the place you come from. So that's why I've fun all over the place, the world is my home. But I'm thinking we fly from here Friday morning, land there sometime in the evening, get some rest then arrive to the party." Double R was saying, but Toya wasn't paying attention. She was looking over his shoulder at T.J who walked in with a white girl in his arms. They both looked like they just stepped off of the runway. Her heartfelt like it just dropped to her stomach. She didn't know why, but T.J was looking good as hell. He pulled out the chair for his date then pushed it in when she set down. He went around to the other side of the table and set down when he looked up and seen Toya. His mouth fell open. "You hear what I'm saying?" Double R asked her, "Yeah I hear you," she lied, "You know that I really like you a lot and the short time we have spent together has really opened my eyes and I see what I want now and that's you and only you." This nigga better not, Toya thought, to marry me at least not yet. "I was just saying, I don't need no other women in my life but you. And I've been through enough to know what's right and what's wrong for me. And as of now, you're just perfect and I'm drawn to every inch of you. No woman has ever had this type of an effect on me. And you're probably thinking I'm just a lovey dovey tender dick ass dude. But I'm not. When I love something, I love hard, and when I love it's foreral. So when someone I love crosses me," he said, then slid his thumb across his throat, "Its over, that's why I don't trust no one, not even that succumb bag sitting behind me, with that white girl," Toya jump in her seat. Because she was surprised, she didn't know how in the hell he knew TJ was behind him with a white girl because he never turned around. He could tell what she was thinking, "This is where I sit at every time so I could watch my back and see who's behind me. There's a mirror on the wall behind you. I saw when they first came in. It's crazy how someone could be such a close friend to you then out of nowhere yall this close from killing each other. Sometimes people's energy doesn't match yours. I'm glad I got certain people out of my life. Because soon as I did I shot straight to the top and I left them niggas behind even though I had a lot of crabs trying to pull my back down, but I shook them off. And I'm still shaking them till this day. I wanna see you reach the top. The top of where you tryna go, and I'm gonna be right there by your side when you do make it to the top. That's what kind of guy I am. And if you're wondering or if you ever wondered, let me tell you this now. When you chose me, you can trust and believe you didn't choose wrong."

***

TJ couldn't believe his eyes as he sat down and saw Toya looking directly at him. While Double R was watching him through the mirror, he didn't understand why this bitch nigga wanted everything he touched. This restaurant was his spot, and he was the one that turned Double R on to it years ago, it was crazy how they always ran into each other. He hated this nigga with all of his heart. He turned to face his attention to the beautiful white girl that was in front of him. Her name was Amanda, and she was 22 yrs old from

South Carolina, he knew that she was gonna give him some pussy tonight. But he couldn't lie, Toya made his date look like trash the way she was looking. Toya was drop-dead gorgeous and now he was regretting leaving her at that restaurant that day. Maybe she would've stopped fucking with that nigga. But he knew Double R was really into her because he ain't never seen him with no bitch they way he was with her. He watched as they got up from the table and started heading for the exit. Double R had an urgent look on his face, and there was something on his mind. They walked out the door, Toya turned around and caught him staring at her, staring at her with complete lust in his eyes.

Chapter 44

Once they were inside the car, Double R sped away from the restaurant. He told her they had to leave early after he got a phone call. He told her that it was an urgent business he needed to handle. They did little talking in the car. "Is everything ok baby?" Toya asked him as he continued to speed "Yes, everything's good, I'm just in a hurry right now." He kept looking at his watch then started cursing when they were caught by the red light, "Shit," he said, then sped back off when the light turned green. "I was gonna drop you off home but your just gonna have to come with me and drop me off, then head back home yourself, ama meet you back there later." "Drop you off, are you sure?" She asked, "Yeah its cool, I'll be ok, I'll just meet you back at the crib later." She knew something was really bothering him and it had his full attention. They pulled up to a gated community, she watched as he put the code into the box then waited for the gate to open. He sped through and drove for a while then stopped in front of a newly built house. There were two cars parked out in the driveway that looked like some kind of jeep and a smaller Mercedes; he told her to wait there. Then got out and ran inside the house, he came out 5 minutes later with a bag over his shoulder. He ran to the Mercedes, opened the door, and threw the bag inside. Then he ran back over to where she was. "Listen, just follow me out of here then head straight home. Call me when you get there. I'll be there later tonight." She nodded her head then climbed over to the driver seat. He gave her a kiss then closed the door. He went back to the Mercedes and pulled off, Toya followed behind him until they made out of the community then she turned away, and he watched her until he could see the car no longer then he sped off. Getting on to the interstate, pressing his foot down hard on the gas pedal, he swerved in and out of traffic. The call he got back at the restaurant was a call he's been anticipating for the last two years. He had a hundred-thousand-dollar bounty out on someone that used to be his friend's head and now another one of his good friends was calling to collect that bounty. She told him to hurry up because he could be waking up any minute now. She had snuck something inside town two nights ago and they have been up in the hotel since then, her and the other girl. He was a very paranoid person. And wouldn't let them use their phones. But she drugged him and soon as he fell asleep, she called him. He pulled up to the hotel then called to let her know he was outside. He couldn't wait to get to this nigga; his palms were sweating. This was a nigga he showed mad love to. He put him in a position to win and to get rich. After all he did for him. This bitch nigga still fuelled him over in the end. He ran off with over a half a million dollars and 75 bricks. That wasn't even the fucked up part, he got jammed up a few months later and decided to tell the feds everything that he knew about him but the agent over the case was Coleman himself. If it wasn't for Coleman, he would be in the penitentiary right now. He saw the girls come out, they came over and got inside the car, he handed them the bag full of cash and told them to keep the car that he would pick it up later. They told him they took his gun and left the door propped open, and he was still asleep when they left out of the room. Double R got out of the car, and they drove off, he used the back door to get into the building then took the stairs two at a time up to the 4th floor. He walked over to the room, and just like they said, the door was propped open. He walked in and closed the door behind him. He was knocked out on the bed butt naked… caught him with his pants down. Double R thought as he walked over then nudged him with the gun, he didn't move. He was snoring loud. He put the gun lock on his waist, then used the sheets from the bed and hogged tied him. He picked a sock up from the floor then stuffed it into his mouth. He walked into the restroom. Picked him up from the bed, carried him into the restroom, and dropped him headfirst into the tub. He woke up immediately as the hot water burned the shit out of his skin. He tried yelling, but his mouth was gagged, he looked over to see Double R staring down at him. His eyes almost popped out of his head. Double R reached out then shoved his head under the water. He kept it there for over half a minute. He left him go; his head shot up then he slammed it back under. He let it go and stood up. "Nigga I treated you like family than you stab me in my back. You didn't just run off with my shit, you tried setting me up with the feds." He saw the shock on his face. Yeah I know what you did nigga. I know exactly what you told them. You must've thought if I was in jail then you could run the streets freely. But I could promise you that wasn't happening you sorry motherfuckah. I'm already sick of looking at you looking pathetic." He said, then pulled the suppressed nine-millimeter from his waist and shot him in the back of the head. He fell under the water, and the whole bathtub turned Red. He shot him twice more just for the hell of it, then walked out of the restroom and placed a call to his clean up crew. They were there within 30 minutes. He made another call as he walked out of the building the same way he came in. There was a car waiting for him. He got into the back seat and told the driver to drive. The driver asked where to, he said home. He wanted to get home to Queen as fast as he could. Because he didn't want to be nowhere else in the world but next to her. He was her king, and she was his queen and he know he wouldn't have it any other way but that way.

Chapter 45

One week later

"You don't have to pack all of them things, we could shop when we land," Double R told her as he watched her run in and out of the closet stuffing things into her bags. "I'm just packing a few things I know that I'm gonna need just give me five more minutes and I swear I'll be ready," Toya said. Double R shrugged his shoulder then set back down on the bed. He pulled out his phone and finished making a reservation. He got them a suite at the Ritz and rented a Rolls Royce Phantom. It would be waiting for them when they landed. She came back out of the closet then stuffed a few more things into her bag. She then zipped them up and started looking around, making sure she didn't forget anything. He grabbed the bags from the bed then walked out of the room, indicating it was time to go, she followed him out. They got into the Range Rover then drove off. It took them an hour to get to the airport. Atlanta was one of the busiest airports in the world. And it took them almost an hour to board the plane. They were escorted to firstclass. "This is so nice," Toya said as she set down. "Not as nice as you, you look gorgeous, have I told you that today yet?" he said as he reached over then squeezed her hand. “Nope you haven’t, I thought you didn’t notice.” “How can I not notice your beauty?” He said to her, then leaned over and kissed her on the lips. “Your so sweet Ryan you know that, right?” “Other people don’t think so.” “Well I don’t care what other people think because I know who you really are.” She said while caressing his chin. “And who’s that?” “My big sweet teddy bear.” She said, giving him another kiss as the plane took off down the runway. The flight took over six hours. Toya fell asleep two hours into the flight. She awoke when the plane landed. The Rolls Royce was waiting for them. It took them another 35 minutes to get to the Ritz Carlton hotel. They took the elevator up. “Please order some food, I’m starving,” Toya said as he entered the room. She went over and flopped down onto the bed, and her legs were slightly open. And he could see under her dress and between her legs, she was wearing a white thong. He was instantly turned on even after the long flight plus being jet logged. He didn’t want to do anything but lay down and get a little rest. But dam, he thought as he walked over, leaned down and parted her legs. She asked what he was doing but didn’t try stopping him. He put his nose onto the front of her panties and smelled them. “Damn things are fresh,” he said, “Ain’t that’s how it’s supposed to be?” She asked. He pulled her panties down then started eating her out. She couldn’t lie, his head was the bomb, she came instantly. He told her to bend over then he lifted her dress over her ass. He massaged both of her ass cheeks, then slid inside of her and starts to fuck her slow, then fast in heart until they both came. He fell onto the bed next to her. Neither one of them had any more energy. There was no way he was gonna be alone to order room service. He closed his eyes then fell asleep right after she did.

Chapter 46

"Baby it's only gonna be three days that's all I swear." Bezo said as he packed his things for his flight to Cali, Elisha was sitting on the bed asking why she couldn't come with him, "Because this isn't that type of trip. I need to handle some business." "When did business started taking 3 days Bryson?" He was planning on flying to Miami after he left Cali. Draco and Twan was gonna meet him down there. "You don't have to worry about anything, especially no other women, if that's what your worried about." "Well I'm definitely worried. Your leaving me for 3 days and all." "Well theres nothing to be worried about, I can promise you that." He said, then held up a red Ralph Lauren shirt up in one hand and a blue one in the other hand. "Which shirt do you think goes better with these shoes?" He asked her. "The blue one," she said. He chose the red one, "How you go ask me for my advice and when I give it to you. You don't take it." "I don't know, I thought the red one went better." He said, then leaned over and kissed her. He tried to lean back up but she pulled him back down and kissed him harder. She pulled him onto the bed. Coby was with Crystal and he knew she was horney, she began pulling at his belt. He undid his pants and let them fall to the floor. Then he climbs between her legs. She grabbed his dick and started rubbing it across her lips. Why did she stroke it gently? When she put him in, we was rock hard and she was soaking wet. He stretched out her walls as he slid all the way in. He wasted no time as he put her legs behind her head then started pounding away, falling all the way inside of her. She screamed and cum over and over again. She was soaking the bedspread. “Dam,” he said out loud as he kept pumping. She was still screaming. He felt himself about to cum. And she did too, because she pulled him closer to her then wrapped her legs around him. He exploded inside of her. She was shaking uncontrollably beneath him. He caught his breath, then pulled his pants back up. She was sound asleep. He grabbed his things, then left the house. He stopped by the stash house and grabbed another 10 bricks to drop off to Twan. He met him at the spot and told him he’d meet him in Miami and told him to be safe. He made it to the airport 30 minutes later. He parked the Benz in long time parking. He stretched out in his seat. He was flying first class. He popped a Xan as soon as the plane took off down the runway. He put his earbuds into his ears and pressed play on his mp3 players and closed his eyes, 10 minutes later, he was fast asleep.

Chapter 47

Draco walked inside of the house and told his goons to stay out front and keep their eyes open. Kiesha was in the kitchen, and his son was in the living room watching TV like always. "What up lil nigga." Draco said as he walked past him. "Why do you think you can just pop in and out of here whenever you feel like it. You can't be doing that, I might have company over here, and they might not like you just walking in here like that." Draco laughed because he knew she knew better than that. "You know I'll put a bullet in you then whoever in the hell your company may be. So don't even play with me like that." "I don't know why you trippin, you got bitches don't you. You told me we were not in a relationship. And not to jet that confused. All we got is a child together, and that's it but when your ass was all shot up. You wanna lay up all in a bitch shit and fuck all on me. Boy I ain't finna keep going for that shit," she said, looking at him with a serious look. "Bitch you gone go for whatever the fuck I want you to go for, stupid ass bitch the fuck you talking about?" "Who are you talking to?" She said, turning around walking in his direction. With quickness, he grabbed her around the neck then pushed her hard back against the refrigerator, "Bitch what the fuck wrong with you, you ever charge me like that again I'll break your fucken neck," he screamed while squeezing down hard on her neck. She was scratching at his hand, trying to get away from him, and she couldn't breathe. He let her go, and she started crying. "Now your fuck ass wanna cry, you's a dumb bitch. That's why nobody wants to be with your ass now." "So what?" She said through tears. He called his son in the kitchen. He came. "Son you know I love you, don't you?" He asked him. He nodded his head. "Well let me know if your mama got anybody else in this house when I'm gone. If she kisses anybody else or you hear stuff coming from her room that you ain't supposed to be seeing, let me know. All right?" "Ok," he said. Draco kissed him on the top of the head then let him go back in the living room. He stood up and walked over to Kiesha and pressed up against her. And tried kissing her but she told him to move. "So you go act like that?" He asked then tried squeezing her ass cheeks she slapped his hands away. "Yeah right," he said. Walking back towards the front door. When he walked out, his goons were standing right there. They followed him back to the car, and they pulled off for the next hour. They rode around and picked up cash and dropped off work. When he got to his last trap, which was in Nuccio. He saw they were throwing a body on the back of a truck. He got out and asked what in the hell was going on. They told him the guy had overdosed. "Overdose. This is the second overdose this week over here, where Mei at?" he asked. Mei was the one over the trap. They all said he was inside. Draco walked in then asked him, "What the hell was going on around here? Why in the hell everybody dying?" "Hell I don't know," Mei said, not looking Draco in the face. "What you mean you don't know? This shit ain't happening no were else but over here, so you must be fucking with the dope even after I told you not to." Mei didn't say nothing, he only stood there with his head down. "Come on man don't tell me you cutting my shit when I told you not to bra," "I was only tryna make a few more extra dollars and that shit moving them niggas was just weak they couldn't handle that shit," "What you cutting it with?" "Fetnol," "Fetnol?" "Yeah I had ran across some through my cousin." "How much of my shit did you cut?" "All of it," he said, "All of what?" "All what you dropped off to me, it's almost gone," Mei said. "Where is at?" Mei went to the back and came back out with it and handed him the bundle of heroin. Draco snatched it from him then looked at it. He could feel it wasn't the same. He took it and poured it out on the table. "Snort it," he said. "Ha?" Mei asked, looking at him, confused. "Nigga you heard what I said, snort it." "Man I ain't finna do that shit," "Nigga you gone do what I tell you to do. And don't make me say it again if I go shoot your bitch ass in the head," "Well you just go have to shoot me." Before he could say anything else, Draco snatched his gun from his waist, grabbed Mei by the neck, and shot him twice in the stomach. He let him go. He slid down the wall, then he shot him twice more, one in the head and one in the face. Everybody came running into the kitchen to see what was going on. Draco told them to clean that shit up. He looked around the room. Then pointed to a kid that didn't look no more than 16. He told him he was now in charge and not to fuck up because if he did, it would be his ass.

Chapter 48

The driver opened the back door, and Bezo slid from out the back seat. The driver shut the door behind him. The driveway was full of expensive cars and SUVs. He straightened the tie on his Giorgio Armani three-piece suit. His Cellini moon phase Rolex peeked from underneath his sleeve. He puffed his cigar as he was escorted inside the mansion. He was immediately approached by one of the party hosts carrying a tray full of sparkling wine. He took one, thanked him then looked around the room. He knew immediately this wasn't gonna be your ordinary party. There were different races of people here; they were talking, laughing and dancing with each other. There was an old white woman doing cocaine off of a younger Latino man's chest. He continued walking through the house. Until he got to the back door and walked out to the back yard, which was huge. There was a pool party going on and everyone was naked inside of it. There were bars and bartenders who were also half-naked. There were so many naked exotic women walking around. He could find cocaine all over the place. He stood there looking around smoking his cigar, which was a partaga's series D No. 4. It was a gift he got from Ricardo the last time he flew out here. Ricardo saw him and through up his hands. "Bezo my man you made it." He yelled out, then came walking over. He gave him a hug then stepped back to look him over. "I like the new style. It's sharp, you look and smell like money and I see you're enjoying those things," he said, pointing at the cigar. "Don't me I want." Bezo said as they started walking. Ricardo led him to the bar. Then told the bartender to give him whatever he wanted, "And this is a special guest, so treat him with extra respect." The girl nodded, then handed him a bottle of Rose with glasses. They walked over to a table where a white older guy that looked like Tommy Lee Jones was sniffing cocaine off the breast of a Hispanic woman. "Todd Guigger, he's a good friend of mine. Use to be a federal prosecutor. Now he's just an old homey little bastard, plus he's the shietiest bastard I know but in a good way. He's one of the reason's I've been able to survive out here this long. You have to have people like him in your corner when you have reached the level I have. If not then you have some rookie D.E.A agent running around sticking is nose in your business, then it's game over for you." Ricardo said then continued walking him around, introducing him to the party-goers. After a while, he told him he needed to go show some respect to the others they were just arriving. He told Bezo to have fun then left him standing next to the pool. He found a seat and set down. There were two Latina's kissing each other inside the pool right in front of him. He layed back in the chair and started sipping from the bottle. They started checking him out. He smiled at them, they giggled, then got out of the pool, then came and set down in the chair next to him, they asked if they could have some of his champagne. He handed it to them and they took it and started drinking from it. Some Spanish songs came over the speakers. They both jumped up from the chair and started dancing, gyrating their bodies, and slapping each other on the ass. They started kissing and touching. They set back down on the chair. He could tell they were both high. The darker of the two layed back and spread her legs. The other girl started eating her out. Damn this was crazy, he thought. Then called for another bottle, he sat there smoking his cigar and sipping champagne watching the show with a tall, dark-skinned gentleman, who was dressed nice and wearing a lot of diamonds in his jewelry. He was sparkling all over the place, "Hey Bezo, this is a good friend of mine. He's from Atlanta his names Double R." Bezo held out his hand Double R shook it. "I hear you from Florida, I'm heading down that way when I leave here," Double R said, "Me and my girl," he looked around then said she's somewhere around here, I guess she had to use the ladies. "All of these beautiful women." "Hey you can still have fun with your lady," Ricardo said. "That's only if she's down with the get down." "I don't know but I sure as hell wont mind finding out, gonna ask her if she wanna take one of these girls back with us." "Hey you'll never know unless you ask her. Plus, everyone loves beautiful women, even other women." He said while laughing and wiping at his nose. "I guess I'll just have to ask them," Double R said, "But I have to admit, you throw one hell of a party. All of your parties are one's for the book." "Well you know I try to do a good thing every now and then. There's people from all over the place here tonight. I even flew a few girls from Brazil for this special occasion and must tell you, women in Brazil are beautiful. So you both put Brazil on your to-do list, it's a great place in and out women in Brazil are beautiful. So you both put Brazil on your to-do list, it's a great place in and out all the I promise you will do," Double R said still looking around while drinking from his glass. Where the hell is queen, he thought. Two white girls walked by completely nude. Ricardo patted them both on their backs and told them to have fun. Then he caught up with both of the girls wrapping his arms around them. Bezo laughed. Ricardo was a weird dude, he thought. "What part of Florida you from," Double R asked him, "Tampa," "Oh Tampa, I know where that's at. I been through there a few times to handle some business. I use to do club promotions and I did a few promotions down there at a club called, The Underground . That place used to be jumping. I brought Future, 2 chainz, Gucci mane, and Young Jeezy down there to that club and made a lot of money too." "Oh yeah," Bezo asked. "Hell yeah," it's a lot of money in that business. You should check it out, plus it's a way to clean up some of your money. You should really consider it." He said then looked at his glass, it was empty. He looked around, still wondering where the back was towards the house. Bezo gulped the remainder champagne from the bottle, set it on the table then checked his phone. There were 3 missed calls from Elisha and one from Twan. He put the phone back in his pocket then grabbed one of the girls that were still kissing and eating each other out. He set her on his lap then began sucking on her rock hard nipples. Might as well have fun while I'm here, he thought as he got up then told the other girl to come here, she giggled then got up. He kissed both of them, then wrapped his arms around them and then they headed for the house. He was hoping he could find a room unoccupied so they could all get naked and explore each other.

***

Toya was upstairs hiding in the restroom. She was pacing back and forward, even looking out the window, debating if she should jump or not. Worse come to worse, she would, she wouldn't have no choice but to. She couldn't believe this shit not in a million years out of all the people in the world, how in the hell did she end up at the same party with Bezo. Way out here in California, dam my kick was so fucked up, she thought. She didn't want to believe it was him. But it was, she was certain of it. But he wasn't the same Bezo she knew a few months back, he was new and improved, he looked like a million-dollar nigga. Like a real boss. But what in the hell was he doing out here in California? Attending the same party, Ryan was invited to. How did they even know the same people? It didn't take her long to figure it out. Ricardo must be the plug, and he was throwing this party and inviting all of the key players, but how was Bezo a key player. She knew Rilo was rich but not as near as Rich as Ryan. She was sure Bezo had to have found Rilo Stash. But how much was he worth now was he pushing more dope than Rilo was pushing down there in Tampa? Did Bezo take over everything? It sure as hell looked like he did, and he was looking the part. She didn't know Ryan was gonna come looking for her. She looked down at the toilet and came up with a plan immediately. She knelt down over the toilet then shoved her finger down her throat, forcing herself to throw up. When he came in she was breathing hard clutching her stomach leaning over the toilet. "Dam baby what's wrong?" He knelt next to her. "I don't know, my stomach hurts and I feel dizzy, I'm ready to go back to the room, I just wanna lay down. "Ok baby let go, whatever you wanna do," he said, then lifted her up and carried her out of the restroom back down the stairs, she had her head down the entire time. He opened the back door and laid her down on the back seat. He turned on the car, turned up the A/C then told her to give him a minute, then he ran back inside. "What the fuck?" she said to herself as she seriously debated just jumping on the driver's seat and taking off, leaving him behind because she didn't know what the hell he was on. She lifts up and saw him running back out of the house. He jumped into the driver seat then pulled off. "You want me to stop by the store to get you something for your stomach?" He asked, looking in the back seat at her. "No I just wanna lay down and go to sleep. I'm so sorry for messing things up tonight but this came out of no were," "Don't worry about it baby, Ricardo understood. He's high as hell anyhow, probably wouldn't even remember he had a party when he wakes up. We can catch up on some fun when we get to Miami tomorrow," he said as they made it back to the Ritz. He valued the car. He helped her out o the car and all the way back to the room. He ran her a warm bubble bath. After stripping her out of her clothes, he carried her to the tub and set her on it. He lit a few candles then brought her a glass of champagne. "I hope this makes you feel better?" he said as he knelt down next to the tub, "Yes it does, I feel much better, thank you baby," she gave him a kiss. "And that party wasn't a party you take your girl to anyhow, that was a freak show everybody was doing drugs and having sex. And all the girls were but ass naked." Double R laughed. "Yeah Ricardo always throws parties like that. He's kind of a weird dude. But you would have loosened up and started liking it after you had a few drinks," "Yeah maybe if someone dropped something inside of it," they both laughed. He helped her out of the tub, dried her off, then carried her to the bed. He made love to her until she fell asleep. He rolled over and set there thinking to himself for a moment he was hoping that she was pregnant. And that was the reason her stomach was hurting. Because he did wanna have a baby with her, and he didn't mind spending the rest of his life with her. She was perfect, and she was the best thing that ever happened to him in his life. He was complete, and she completed him. He reached over, pulled her close, wrapped her in his arms, closed his eyes, and fell asleep.

Chapter 49

Bezo woke up, but the two women he went to bed with last night were still sound asleep. He rolled over and looked at the clock. It was one o'clock. He missed his flight. He thought as he rolled out of bed. He would just have to catch the next flight out. He checked his phone and it was dead. One of the girls' ass cheeks was hanging out from under the sheet. He woke her up. She bent over the edge of the bed and he fucked her real quick. When he was done, he got dressed then left the room. His driver was out front waiting for him. He told him to on the charger. He took a shower, ordered room service then booked the next flight out to Miami. He returned Elisha's phone call. She immediately wanted to know why he wasn't picking up his phone. He told her that the six-hour flight left him lagged, and soon as he got to his room, he fell asleep and now was just waking up. He knew she knew that was bullshit but she let it go. They talked for another 30 minutes on the phone. He ate his food. Then checked out of the room and was driven to the airport. L.A.X was packed but it didn't take him long to board his flight. He was flying first class again and was escorted to his seat. He popped a Xan and was hoping Twan and Draco would be down there when he arrived, but he knew it was a possibility they wouldn't be.

He put his earbuds in his ears and closed his eyes then dozed off before the plane was even airborne.

Chapter 50

Draco was pissed the fuck off with Twan. He waited until the last minute to tell him he wasn't going because he had too much business to handle. He tried to convince him to let one Gf the homies handle it for him. But he refused and said he was scared to fly and how that's the real reason he wasn't tryna go. Fuck em, Draco thought as he made it to the airport. An hour later, he was landing in Miami, he rented a red Lamborghini from the luxury car rental at the airport. He threw his bags inside. Then put the address for the Blue Foundation into its GPS system. He sped off, reaching speeds of 180 mph on the interstate. He slowed down when he got on Collins Ave, then he drops the top. He had over twenty thousand dollars on him. He was planning on having a hell've good time while they were down by landing. He wanted him to rent the same kind of car he had so they could stunt in traffic. He got to the Blue Fountain, grabbed his bags, and left the Lambo with the valet. It was 6 PM, he walked to the front desk, gave the hotel clerk his name then received his room key. He took the elevator up to his suite, which was on the 5th floor. When he stepped in, the only thing he could say was dam. The room was lavish, it was huge, he was paying $1,500 a night for this place. He walked around, checking everything else out. When he was finished, he set down on the couch in the living room. Dam I need some drugs, he thought. He was bad at himself for not having a plug down here in Dade County. He went back up from the couch and walked out of the door. He went back down the elevator and retrieved his car from the valet, he headed back down on Collins. He was dressed down in Versace and had all his jewelry on. He looked like a rapper as he got out of the car then walked into the Gucci store. He purchased another outfit with the shoes; everything came out to $3500. He paid for it in cash. When he walked out, two yellow bones were standing out on the sidewalk window shopping when they saw him. They started watching him as he walked to the Lamborghini. When he lifted the door, one of the girls yelled out and asked if he was a rapper. "Knaw I'm just a street nigga," he said, looking at them from over the car. They both laughed. "You ain't from around here is you," the taller one asked. "No but how you know that." "I don't know, your just different from the Niggas around here, your swags different you mind if we chill with you tonight?" She asked him to look them both over. They were both fine as hell, he told them if that's what they wanted to do. They said, "Hell yeah," then ran over and got into the car. The smaller of the two set in the lap of the other girl. Draco pulled off, "Yall know where to get some weed from?" He asked them, the girl on top pulled out a bag from her purse. It looked to be about an ounce, he knew it was granddaddy pulp. "Can you get your hands on some money and lean?" "Yeah I'll have to call my cousin. He'll meet me anywhere I need him to." Draco nodded his head then pulled back up to the hotel. "I ain't never been to the Blue Fountain girl," "Me either but I heard the rooms are real nice inside." Bezo was checking them out as they walked inside, neither one of them could be no older than 21. And both of them had phat ass on them. And the small shorts they were wearing were cutting up in their ass. He knew it was going to be a fun-night tonight. They walked into the room and they both were surprised how huge the room was. Bezo told her to call her cousin and tell him you want an ounce of molly and a pint of lean. She called him and told him what she wanted and where she was at. 15 minutes later, he called back and told her he was downstairs parked outside in the parking lot. She told Bezo she was gone and needed $500. He pulled out his bankroll and gave it to her. She came back up 10 minutes later with both the molly and the lean. She handed both of them to him. "So what yall just be down on Collins looking for niggas to chill with?" He asked them as he mixed the drink. "Hell naw, we got left on cousins by our shiesty ass cousin this our first time doing some shit like this," "Yeah right," he said as he licked the molly off of his palm. He asked them if they got high. They both said yes to the molly but no to the drink. He watched as she took a little less than he did. Then they all set down on the couch. He lit the blunt then asked them what they do for a living. "Oh we strip." "Oh yeah," "Yep at the club, Live and King of Diamonds," "That explains why you so damn rivc," he said as he passed them the blunt. He felt the molly doing its job as he sipped the lean from his cup. His phone was hooked up to the stereo. He pressed play and the music started playing. The system had surround sound and it sounded good. "Look I got $500 a piece for the both of you. But I'm going to need yall to take all that shit off and do whatever I want for y'all to do for the rest of the night." He pulled out his bankroll again then looked at both of them. They told him to give them the money he peeled off 10 $100 bills. They put it in their purses. And without another word, they both got butt ass naked.

Chapter 51

There was no way in hell Twan was going to Miami knowing that he would have Kiesha all to himself for at least two days without having to look over his shoulders. This was gone be his 3rd time fucking her and he was planning on fucking her the whole time that nigga was gone. She had to find someone to watch her son. Then he met her at her grandmother's house and picked her up. He was in a rental with dark tinted windows, so he wasn't worried about anyone knowing that it was him. She leaned over and gave him a kiss. After he pulled off, Dam she smells good, he thought as he looked over at her. She had on a small black dress. So her thighs were out. And he could see the paw prints going up them. She turned him all the way on. "What you are looking at?" She asked him. "I'm looking at your sexy ass," he said, then reached over and pulled the front of her dress down, she didn't have on a bra and her breast set up perfect. He tried to lean over to suck one of her nipples, but she pushed him out of the way and told him to pay attention to the road before he killed both of them. "Were we going at anyways?" She asked him. "I don't know probley get a room or something, you wanna grab something to eat first?" "Yes, I'm hungry let's go to the firehouse and get some subs." Twan nodded his head, then drove the short distance to the restaurant then backed up into the parking lot. Kiesha ordered their meals off of her phone. When she was finished, Twan told her to come over there on his side. "Come over there?" She asked, "Yeah just put one leg right here then the other one right there," he pointed. She did as he told her to. He leaned over and started eating her out. Her pussy was pierced as well, he pulled on the ring a little then started sucking on her clit. "Oh my God, yes Twan," she moaned as he continued to suck and lick on her. Once she came. She crawled over and undid his pants and pulled his dick out. She started jacking it until it was rock hard. She put it in her mouth and starting sucking and pulling on it, still jacking him off while it was in her mouth. When she knew that he was ready, she straddled him. Slid down on his dick, then took him on the ride of his life, he came within 5 minutes inside of her. She climbed back over to the passenger seat, then reached in the back and used a T-shirt to wipe off her pussy then his dick. She threw the shirt back into the back seat, then pulled his pants back up. "You think the foods ready?" He asked her. "Oh shit," she said then got out of the car and ran inside, he watched as her ass bounced up and down inside of her dress. Dam he said, squeezing his dick, it was back hard. He couldn't lie, he was starting to be real fucked up about her. But he needed to be careful because if he dind't, shit was gone be really ugly and he want no parts of Dracos fiery.

Chapter 52

Toya stood out on the balcony, looking out at the beach, sipping vodka and orange juice from her glass. She had on a Versace gown. There was nothing underneath it. They took the first flight out of Cali, which was 8′ o clock this morning. They landed a little after two, which was really five because of the three-hour time difference. They drove straight here to Ryans condo from the airport. He bought this place two years ago for 1.5 million dollars. After him and his friends came down here one summer and couldn't find nowhere to stay on the beach because everything was booked. He vowed to never go through that again and bought the condo cash money. He walked behind her, wrapped his arms around her and stuck his hand inside her gown while sucking on her neck. "Mmh," she moaned, leaning her head back. He started playing with her clit in a circular motion. "Yes that feels good baby." He didn't respond. He only continued to suck on her neck and rub down harder and faster on her clit. She didn't know what kind of drug he was on but he was very sexual and couldn't keep his hands off of her. He left for two hours when they first got there. When he came back, he was high as a kite. He leaned down and lifted the back of her gown. He spread her ass cheeks and slid his tongue inside of her. Her gown was now all the way open. Her head was tilted to the sky and her eyes were rolling in the back of her head. He licked her all around her ass the started sucking hard on her clit. She tried holding on to the glass, but she couldn't and it slipped out of her had and glided down to the earth. He stood up then slid in her from the back. She exploded immediately. He pounded her hard from the back as she gripped the railing. The excitement of them being eleven stories up and knowing that she could fall as he fucked her hard and fast made her cum over and over again, there was a sensation running through her body. She knew he must've slipped something in her drink or in her pussy when he was eating her out. She didn't know what it was. But she knew she was high and the high felt good. He was making animal sounds as he pounded her faster and harder. Once he came, he started howling like a dog. "Wow," was all she could say once he pulled out of her. They went back inside and made love on the bed then inside the shower. She told him to get out so she could take a shower. When she got out, he was buttoning up his Versace shirt which was a long sleeve he left two off the buttons open at the top. He had on 5 Cuban link chains. A Cuban link bracelet that was flooded with diamonds. Pink Rings on both of his pinkies and a presidential gold Rolex on his wrist, he put on his Versace sunglasses, put his cigar in his mouth then asked her how he looked, "You look like money baby," she said, he smiled off his icy white teeth. She finished lotioning her body then put on all of her makeup. She slid into her all-white Bottega Veneta dress and Giuseppe Zanotti hills. She sprayed herself with her Tom Ford Jasmin rouge perfume, grabbed her clutch then told him she was ready to go. They took time elevator down. There was a chauffeur waiting for them outside with the back door open. They both slid inside the Bentley. The chauffeur closed the door, got in and pulled off. Toya was looking around the car; she was astonished how big and beautiful it was. He reached over and squeezed her hand. She smiled then kissed him. "Tonight, I'm go show you how real niggas with real money ball. This right here is my second home. Atlanta that's the crib but Miami my second home. All the real niggas fuck with me down here. All of them from every side and all the strippers the regular bitches to," "Well them hoes better recognize tonight because they see who you with," "And who is that," he egged her on, "Queen," she said, "The mother fucken queen, I don't know what you talking about," they both laughed. They were both high and feeling themselves. They pulled up to Club Live, he told the driver to pull over to the side of the building. Then he pulled out his phone, placed a call, and let someone know that he was at the club. Five minutes later, two SUVs pulled up. The doors open and dark-skinned nigga's with big long dreds jumped; Toya knew that they were Zoe pound. He told her to let's get out. He went over and embraced them. Then they all walked into the club without getting searched. They walked straight to their booths then bottles of ace of spades were waiting for them with four beautiful strippers. Double R orders fifty thousand in one-dollar bills. Birdman was in the booth next to them. Double R nodded at him, and Birdman nodded back. He knew it wasn't gonna be any problems tonight because he was with one of the most respected group of people in the city. They began poppin bottles. Toya was already throwing money and dancing with the strippers. He grabbed a wad of ones in the air and watched as they floated down to the floor. They were partying for about an hour when a familiar song came over the speakers and everybody starting screaming. He looked down and saw Looney run on to the stage and started rapping his new single turn on the trap. He couldn't believe this shit, he looked at Toya who was tipsy, she was dancing with one of the strippers, singing along to this fuck nigga song. What the fuck was she doing? Why was she showing him love? He didn't understand. He could see Terry down in the booth next to the stage he was drinking from a bottling looking up at Looney with a huge smile on his face. I can knock his bitch ass off right now he wouldn't even know what hit him. Double R thought as he continued to look down at him. He watched Looney performed another song, the crowd went crazy the whole time. Dam, they was loving this nigga way down here. He didn't like that shit. He went back and set on the couch. Toya came over and started dancing in front of him, he pulled her down on his lap then kissed her on the cheek. "Come on baby let's throw some money. Don't let them get you mad." She said, grabbing him by the face kissing him back on the cheek, then stood back up and starting throwing singles down on the strippers below. Damn, was it that obvious how upset he got when he saw Looney and Terry. He hoped she didn't think he was hatin' because he wasn't. He was the one with the real money, he thought. He was the real millionaire. He was sure Terry had millions but not his type of millions them niggas was baken on a budget. And who did this bitch ass nigga Looney think he was pewee long way with all that fake ass jewelry on, all that shit couldn't be real. He stood back up from the couch, popped another bottle then walked were Toya was and wrapped his arms around her why she danced on him. Fuck them niggas, he wasn't go keep worrying about them he was gone enjoy the rest of his night, well at least, try to.

Chapter 53

After Looney finished performing, he left the stage then headed back to the booth were T.J and the rest of the crew was waiting for him. There was a table full of bottles and singles. This was his second show this week here in Florida, the other one was in Orlando where he and Jay Ratchet took the stage together. T.J had a few connections and knew a few good niggas down here in Miami. There were a few straight drop niggas here with them tonight. They were a well-respected group of niggas throughout the whole Dade County area. T.J checked in with them as soon as they got here. "Is that Double R up there with Toya?" Looney asked, T.J nodding his head in the direction of there booth. T.J looked up there and said, "Yeah that's them." He could see Double R looking down at them with a smile on his face and his arms wrapped around Toya, who was dancing and throwing money. He knew the niggas who he was in the booth with, they were Zoe's. He turned around, focusing his attention else were. But deep down inside he was boiling because he was feeling a certain way. Every time he saw that nigga he wanted to kill him. Especially when he saw him with Toya, that shit hurt, he admitted to himself. He let that bitch nigga come and sweep her right from underneath him. He couldn't lie, he was tired of that nigga. And that nigga ain't have no more chances to get outta line. If he did, he was pushing the line on him and it would be on all-out war back in the A. He walked back over to where the naked women were dancing inside the booth. He needed to stay focused. They had 3 more shows to do before they made it back home; one here at Club Rolex tomorrow night, another in Tampa and then in Tallahassee. Then they had more in the Looney and Ratchet, he was hoping things turned out the way he was thinking it would turn out. If it did, he was through with the dope game, it was more money in this shit here and he was finally getting through Looney's thick ass skull. All they had to do was keep believing and this was gone pop off. Looney passed him the blunt then went back over and started slapping the stripper on her ass. "So we taking a few of these bitches back with us tonight or what?" Jay Ratchet walked over and asked him. "You damn right what type of questions is that? He needs to take at least 5 of these bitches down here." T.J said, "You see that bitch right there?" T.J pointed at one of the strippers. "Yeah I see here," "She from the A, I used to fuck with her back in the day until she moved down here. I know when she see's me she go be ready to fuck on the spot," "Man I'm trying to hit that shit to, I'm trying to hit all these hoes tonight," T.J laughed because he knew he was dead serious. Looney was pouring champagne on to one of the strippers as the other one was licking it off. Ratchet ran over to where they were having the time of his life. The club was gonna be over in the next hour and T.J wanted to get out of there a little earlier. So he let his crew know they'll be moving within the next 30 minutes, he gathered up a few strippers. Then they were all led out by the straight drop niggas. They were parked out front in two black on black

G63 Mercedes trucks with dark tents. He saw Double R when the walked out, he was standing next to his Bentley Mausane, his shirt was all the way open and his gun was showing, he was surrounded by the Zoe's, "Yo whats up with fool, he good?" One of the straight drop niggas asked T.J "Yeah he good fuck em," T.J said then started getting into the driver seat. Double R called out his name, he paused then turned around. "What up," he said. "I'm tryna see why you niggas feel like this city big enough for all of us," he said, looking around at his crew, "What the fuck is that suppost to mean?" T.J asked, "Just what I said nigga, I'm already letting you niggas make it in the A. so why do yall think yall can party down here when I'm here. I come down here to get a break from you niggas. But I come here and still got to see yall, that ain't go work my nigga, I'm telling you now it ain't so." "What you want us to do because we obviously don't give a fuck about you or your vacation. Or how you feel we didn't even know you were down here. But if we did we still wouldn't give a fuck because you don't matter to any of us. So if you would excuse us, we got other shit to attend to besides you," T.J said then got into the truck. "Oh yeah," he said, peeking his head back out the door, "Make sure you take care of my leftovers," "What's that suppost to mean nigga?" Double R said, "You know exactly what that's suppost to mean and I'm done talking," he said then slammed the door and sped off. Everybody in the truck was touching. "Dam that nigga was hating," one of the strippers said. "That ain't nothing new," Looney responded as he pulled her tittie out and started sucking it. She giggled. When they were far away from the club and he knew they were good. He sent out a text and let the goons that were following them be good. The other G wagon was in front of them. With the rest of the crew and the other strippers, they stopped to grab something to eat. When they pulled back off, they were caught by the red light. Ratchet was over in the passenger's seat, devouring the wings he just got from Wing Stop. Looney and the girls were doing the same in the backseat. His plate was on his lap and he was gone wait until they got back to the room to eat. Everybody was focused on their food. And T.J was watching the lighting waiting for it to turn green that he didn't see the window roll down on the SUV next to them; a masked man hung out the window with a rifle in his hands and he pulled the trigger. It sounded like a bomb going off over and over again as slugs flew into the truck. T.J slammed his foot on the gas, Ratchest's food flew every were as his plate went flying in the air. The SUV sped alongside of them still firing inside of the truck. T.J tried swerving through traffic, but they kept coming and was keeping up with them. T.J swung a hard left and jumped the medium driving into the coming traffic, the back window was riddled with slugs, T.J kept his foot on the gas and kept driving. He looked through the rearview mirror and saw his guys firing from the other G wagon, the SUV that was firing at them turned on a side street and sped away. "Oh shit," Looney said. Both strippers were screaming at the top of their lungs. "Oh, shit he dead," Looney said, reaching for Ratchet, "Oh shit big bra he dead," he said again. TJ looked over at Ratchet for the first time. His head was blown off the whole top half. "Shit," he said then started driving faster, "dam," he slammed his fist on the steering wheel. "Please lord no," he said out loud. Looney was still saying, "Oh shit," the strippers were still screaming, telling them to just let them out. Looney told them to shut the fuck up. As they sped up to the hospital, T.J slammed on brakes and threw the truck into park. He ran over and snatched Ratchet out of the passenger's seat. And ran him into the hospital, Looney was behind him. The nurses saw him then ran over. They laid him on a stretcher then pushed him in the back through the double doors. T.J tried to follow but Looney grabbed him and told him they needed to go bra was dead, it wasn't shit they could do. They both turned around then ran out of the hospital. The strippers were still inside of the truck when they got back in and sped off. "That was it my nigga, that was the last straw, that nigga dead bra I promise that nigga dead," T.J yelled out as he swerved through traffic. "Man, I tried so hard but this nigga don't get it, niggas like him don't never get it until it's a bullet in their head. I don't understand at all my nigga, I don't get it," T.J explained.

"That nigga got to get his is all you got to understand right now T.J," said from the bloody passenger seat. When they made it back to the hotel, they all rode the elevator up to the room in silent as soon as they got in the room, Looney started packing while T.J started placing calls to his hitter's back in the A. He was gonna try to get Double R whacked why they were still down there, but he told all his people to make on all Double R spots and do what they were supposed to do. Anything and everything was done. The strippers were sitting on the bed in complete shock. A few moments later, the rest of his crew came barging in the room, T.J told them to drop the girls off wherever they wanted to go then hurry back. They did what they were told. Looney and T.J stayed back and finished packing. When T.J was finished, he looked at his reflection in the mirror, he was covered in Jay Ratchet's blood. Blood was all over his clothes, heads, and face. He couldn't believe this shit.

Looney was back on his phone, handing out instruction. When he hung up, he looked over at T.J who was just staring in the mirror at himself. Looney placed his hands on his head and took a deep breath. "Man what the fuck happened? Why would he do some shit like that? I already called Reecio, they moving on them Niggas right now back home. Ain't no way in hell we letting this go." T.J didn't respond but he set down on the bed. He had to let his mind wonder. He was trying to understand what the fuck was all this about. All he could think was Toya, he was feeling someway about Toya because it couldn't be anything else. Because for the last couple of years, he and Double R didn't have no run in, they didn't speak to each other or didn't cross paths. This didn't make any since, none at all. The shit he pulled out of the club confused the shit out of him because that wasn't him, that ain't how he got down. All he could think about is that Toya had that nigga head gone. So, when he said that he left over shit that sent him over the edge. That bitch nigga was in for a rude of wakening. He thought as he got up from the bed and told Looney to let's get up out of there. They rode the elevator back down and met the rest of the crew outside. They pulled into the G wagon. T.J didn't know what all was gonna come out of this after the smoke cleared but right now, at this moment, he really didn't even give a fuck...

Coming Soon… GABOS II

Made in the USA
Columbia, SC
20 May 2021

38264630R00159